Doriana turned off the TV and dropped the remote on the bed. Thinking about Logan teased her with questions. Why was Logan at the fire site with her dad? That story about his having fire experience didn't ring true. What were Logan and her father hiding?

Thankfully, the workweek had been short with the two-day holiday. She needed time away from Logan and all the longings, confusion and guilt he stirred in her.

She trusted Anita to keep her secret. Would her own guilt force the truth? Logan hadn't cared enough to stay around the first time. Would knowing about Josh keep him here now? Doriana got up from the bed and ran impatient fingers through her hair. She was obsessing way too much about Logan.

She walked toward the bathroom, pulling her sweater over her head. Too bad she couldn't peel away her problems as smoothly. The ring of the phone stopped her. Slipping her sweater back on, she hurried to answer it. Josh calling to say goodnight? She doubted it.

"Hello," she said into the receiver.

"Hello, sexy." At the crude, unfamiliar voice, she tightened her grip on the phone. Chills chased up her spine.

"Who is this?" Her voice shook.

"Oh, you don't know me. Not yet. But I sure know you. You're sexy as hell, especially in those tight black pants."

Doriana slammed down the phone. Her insides quivered and she ran trembling hands along the sides of her black pants. Had her caller guessed at what she wore? Or was he watching? She gulped air.

The phone rang again and she let out a small cry. She balled her hands, digging her nails into her palms. She would not pick up the phone. The answering machine clicked on.

"You can't get away from me that easy." The harsh voice, laced with menace, froze her. "I know you're alone." Almost seeing his leer, she shoved a shaking fist to her mouth.

"Let me in, bitch. I'll show a hot number like you what a real man is. Not like that pretty boy you've been hanging around with."

Logan's
Redemption

by

Cara Marsi

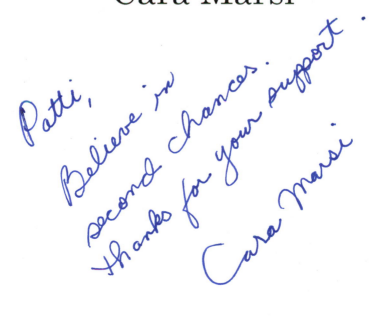

Patti,

Believe in
second chances.
thanks for your support.

Cara Marsi

Logan's Redemption

Cover Art by *Kim Mendoza*

The Wild Rose Press
PO Box 706
Adams Basin, NY 14410-0706
Visit us at www.thewildrosepress.com

Publishing History
First Crimson Rose Edition, 2007
Print ISBN 1-60154-101-5

Published in the United States of America

Dedication

To my good friends and critique partners Dottie Promiscuo and Gwen Schuler. I couldn't have done this without you. You're the best.

Thanks to Linda Eighmy and Sue Misey for your unwavering support.

CHAPTER ONE

Dan Callahan needed his help. Logan Tanner smiled as he scanned the plush office with its platoon of secretaries. Who would have imagined it all those years ago when he was sneaking dates with the great man's daughter?

Doriana. The Callahan princess. Vice President of Project Development. Probably an honorary title. He'd come all this way for a job. Seeing Doriana again had nothing to do with it. *Yeah, right.* He almost believed it.

The door to the inner sanctum opened and Dan Callahan, CEO of Callahan Construction, approached, hand outstretched. The pictures of the business mogul that accompanied the news articles Logan read didn't do the older man justice. Despite his average height, Callahan exuded a power and confidence no photo could capture.

Logan stood to shake the offered hand.

"Tanner," Callahan said in clipped tones. "Let's go into my office."

He led Logan into a spacious room dominated by a large mahogany desk and windows that looked out to the smog-filled Philadelphia skyline.

Callahan sat behind the massive desk and gestured Logan to the leather chair facing him. He pulled a thick envelope from a drawer and pushed it across the desk toward Logan. "The dossiers you wanted on my top officers," he said. "I'll have information on the rest of the corporate employees in a few days." He handed Logan a smaller envelope. "The keys to your hotel room and the

1

car I rented. I had the car parked at the hotel." His thin lips curled into a smile. "Do you know how hard it was to rent a junker? The hotel wasn't too thrilled about having it parked in their garage either."

Logan returned his smile. "If I'm supposed to be a temp worker, I can't ride around in a luxury car. "

Callahan nodded. "I understand. What else do you need?"

"I want the names and addresses of all the workers at your construction sites." Logan stuffed the envelopes in his briefcase.

Callahan scrubbed a hand across his chin. "I can get what you need on our supervisors and regular employees, but we hire a lot of day laborers."

"I know," Logan said. "I was one of those laborers once."

Callahan's blue eyes widened. "You worked for me? Maybe that's why you look so familiar."

"We never met before today," Logan said. "I worked for you for a short time about sixteen years ago when I was nineteen."

"Well you look damn familiar." Callahan shrugged. "Why did you leave my employ?"

"I joined the Army."

"Good reason," Callahan said. "You're from this area?"

"Born and raised, but Arizona is my home." And he wouldn't have come back at all except this assignment was too good to pass up. And there was Doriana.

Callahan steepled his fingers and studied Logan. "I'll get the information on my construction crews, but why do you want to check out my top people? They're loyal to me."

"I've been investigating corporate crime for a lot of years," Logan said. "You'd be amazed at who sabotages a company."

"Well, you're the expert." The older man ran a hand over his graying hair. "I didn't hire you any too soon either. We had some vandalism at one of our sites last night. It's escalating just as you said it might."

"Then I'd better get started." Logan stood. "Have you worked out a cover for me?"

Nodding, Callahan pushed back from the desk and

rounded it to face Logan. "I've arranged for you to be temporary assistant to one of our vice presidents. Her regular assistant starts pregnancy leave next week. Stop by her office now. She's expecting you."

Vice President? It couldn't be. What were the chances? "Does this VP know why I'm here?"

Callahan shook his head. "As you instructed, I'm the only one who knows."

"Good." Logan thrust out his hand. "I look forward to working with you, Mr. Callahan."

"Call me Dan. My receptionist will give you the suite number where you're to report."

"I'll be in touch."

Logan walked from the room and the receptionist in the outer office handed him a piece of crisp white paper. After thanking the woman, Logan stepped into the hall. He glanced down at the paper in his hand. His breath came out in a rush. Damn his rotten luck.

****

"The temp your father hired is here."

Biting back a groan, Doriana Callahan turned from her computer and faced her assistant.

Lisa closed the office door and leaned her very pregnant body against it. A huge grin split her pretty face.

Doriana arched an eyebrow. "You find it amusing that my father overstepped my authority and hired your replacement?"

Lisa made an unsuccessful attempt to look sympathetic. "I know you're upset with your dad, but he is CEO. So I guess he can do whatever he wants." Her gray eyes twinkled. "Your father should do more of the hiring around here."

"What are you talking about?" Doriana asked.

"You'll see. Should I send him in?"

"Him?"

"Yup," Lisa said. "Your dad hired a guy."

Doriana made a face. "I've always had a female assistant. What will I do with a guy?"

Lisa giggled. "Trust me. You'll figure out what to do with this one."

"This pregnancy is affecting your brain." Doriana

pushed away from the desk and stood. "He can't be any worse than the candidates the agency sent over." She shrugged into her suit jacket and lifted her heavy hair free of the collar. She needed a haircut, but where would she find the time?

Lisa's gaze swept her. "You're the only one around here who wears a business suit. We do have a casual dress policy. And you might want to loosen up a little, considering."

"Considering what?" Doriana asked.

Lisa gave her a sly smile. "When you see your new assistant, you'll know what I mean." She patted her protruding stomach. "This baby's not going to wait much longer. It's a good thing your dad found someone."

"I suppose I should be grateful for that." Doriana sighed. "Wait about five minutes before sending him in."

"You need to primp," Lisa said.

"What?"

Laughing, Lisa opened the door and squeezed out.

Rubbing her aching temples, Doriana sat down and swiveled her chair to face the large window that took up an entire wall. Smog blanketed the Philadelphia skyline, obscuring her view of Billy Penn atop City Hall. She missed old Billy's comforting presence, especially now.

She needed time to mentally prepare to meet the temp her father hired. She did her own hiring for her department, but her dad had insisted on this temp. Why? Didn't her father trust her after a decade with his company?

Her gaze drifted to the long table under the window. Family pictures rested on the marble top. Most were of Josh growing up. She smiled, remembering how Franco wanted to name his new nephew Noel because he was born on Christmas Eve.

She couldn't believe Josh would be sixteen next month. She bit her lip as an ache, sharp as a stonecutter's chisel, stabbed her. Nearly sixteen and out of control. When had Josh stopped being her sweet, lovable little boy and turned into the arrogant, rebellious almost-man who fought her every chance he got? A hellion who reminded her more of his father every day.

Thinking of Josh's father brought the old, familiar

pain. She'd never revealed the identity of her son's father to anyone. Seventeen, scared and humiliated, she couldn't admit that her baby's father had walked away without a word.

She'd moved on with her life and even had a few relationships, but she couldn't forget the boy who stole her heart and disappeared. She'd never had a chance to tell him she was pregnant. Would it have made a difference? The old doubts and questions tumbled through her mind, making her head throb.

Inhaling deep breaths, she counted to ten, as she'd learned in a stress management seminar. It didn't help. Nothing helped these days. The demands on her time gave her constant headaches. Her son needed her, but so did Dad and the company, especially with the recent setbacks.

The intercom on the desk shrilled. "Doriana," Lisa said from the outer office. "Jenson is having one of his hissy fits. He wants you to call him. You have that meeting in a half hour. And Mr. Tanner is waiting. Should I send him in?"

Doriana's hand froze over the reply button. Tanner? Long hours had her imagination working overtime.

"Doriana?" Lisa said.

Doriana shook herself back to reality. "Tell Jenson I'll call him. And I didn't forget about the meeting. Please send in Mr..., the temp."

Wearing her best professional smile, Doriana stared at her office door. *Of course it couldn't be him... It couldn't be him...* The refrain ran through her head like a mantra.

The door opened and her gaze connected with gold-flecked hazel eyes. Josh's eyes. No, Logan's eyes.

"Hello, Dorie." His voice, deeper than she remembered, held the rough edge that had so excited her as a teenager. He closed the door softly and leaned against it, a black-clad Adonis who, despite the years and the hurt, took her breath. Unmoving, he studied her.

Was he looking for the young girl he'd romanced, then abandoned? That girl died the night her son was born. Their son. Anger and bittersweet sorrow roiled Doriana's stomach. She brushed hair from her face with a shaky hand.

"You look good," he said.

So do you. She couldn't say the words. Pulling her gaze from his, she glanced toward the window. The pictures. Josh. Fear splashed over her like ice water from the Delaware River. One look at the pictures and Logan would know. She wasn't ready for this.

Resolve stiffened her spine. She would protect her secret and her son until she discovered why Logan was here. "Is this some sort of joke?" she asked, returning her attention to Logan. "What are you doing here?"

"Working for you, last I heard."

He strode slowly across the carpeted room with the predatory grace of a mountain lion. A hunter with a lithe, muscular body and sun streaks gilding his light brown hair. Had he come to snare her with past memories that were better left dead, to destroy her orderly life? To make her son, and her, dream of things that could never be?

"Not glad to see me, Dorie?"

Heat spread from her neck to her face. *Dorie.* Logan's pet name for her when they made love. "Don't call me that."

He stood in front of her desk and stared at her with hooded eyes. "All our memories aren't bad, are they, Dorie?"

His low, seductive voice burned her with enough electricity to power a high rise. She stared at his full lips. Her own lips tingled as she remembered the feel of his mouth on hers, remembered his wildness and her own answering needs.

Standing on legs that had the consistency of wet cement, she curled her hands into fists. She wouldn't let the past hurt her again. Nothing mattered now except protecting Josh. And protecting her heart. "I don't know how you talked my father into this, Logan, but it won't work."

He pressed his palms on her desk and leaned toward her. She held her ground, inhaling his scent of citrus and outdoors. Faint lines bracketed his mouth and eyes. A smattering of gray wove through his hair. His eyes held a steely glint that warned of dangers she knew too well. The guarded look on his face and the rigid set of his jaw hinted at emotions kept in tight rein. Had he finally learned to harness the recklessness that had driven her to him, that had made her betray her parents' trust?

"I'm working for you, Doriana," he said. "I'm here to stay."

Like you stayed the last time? An iron fist of apprehension and fear squeezed her heart. Did Logan know her secret? Josh had accepted that his father left before he was born. Lately he'd begun asking questions. She promised to tell him about his father when he turned eighteen. What would her troubled son do if he knew his father was in town?

She wouldn't concern herself with unnecessary fears. In six months, Lisa would be back and Logan would be gone. "Sit down," she said. "We'll talk." She sank slowly into her chair and picked up a sheaf of papers, studying them, buying time. She lifted her gaze to find Logan staring at her. Seated in the chair nearest her desk, he stretched his long legs in front of him. The coolness in his eyes slowly gave way to an awareness that made heat coil in her stomach despite her anxiety.

The wild boy she'd known had matured into a gorgeous hunk whose chiseled features were roughened by the power and air of mystery that clung to him. Clad in black pants that hugged his muscular legs, black leather jacket and deep brown sweater, he looked like a man who'd seen too much of the dark side of life. And was comfortable with it. Excitement quivered along her skin.

He broke the connection and glanced away. Did Logan harbor his own secrets? She followed his gaze to the window. And the pictures. She didn't want him asking questions about Josh. Not now. The guilt she'd carried all these years pricked her. "Logan, why are you really here?"

He folded his arms across his chest and met her gaze, a challenge in his eyes and the arrogant set of his body. "To work for you." He scanned the room. "You've done well for yourself." His lips tilted in a mocking smile. "But then your dad owns the company."

She bristled. "I've had to prove myself time and again. I've worked harder than you can imagine. But I don't owe you any explanations."

"You don't." He straightened and his harsh features relaxed. "Look, Doriana, we've got to work together. Let's make the best of it."

She breathed deeply in an all-out effort to relax. She'd endured a lot in the years since she'd last seen Logan. Surely she could handle working with him and seeing him every day.

"How did my dad come to hire you?" she asked.

He shifted in his chair and shrugged. "I was between jobs and your dad owed a mutual acquaintance a favor. So here I am."

"You're between jobs? What do you do for a living?"

He stiffened slightly. "I do this and that, whatever pleases me. I don't like to stay in one place for long."

"You don't have a permanent home?" Logan would leave again. She couldn't tell him about Josh. Her son needed a real father, not a temporary one.

Logan leaned closer. "You never expected me to amount to much, did you, Doriana?"

Hurt chased across his eyes, spiking her curiosity. Was he as hard as he seemed? And why had he come back now? Maybe he knew about Josh. Was he toying with her?

The intercom buzzed and she started. "Excuse me," she said, glad of the interruption. She pressed the talk button. "Yes, Lisa?"

"I'm sorry to bother you," Lisa's stressed voice said. "Jenson keeps calling and you have that meeting. Also the fax machine is acting up again."

"Hang in there, Lisa. I'll call Jenson right away and then see about that damn fax machine. I told Purchasing weeks ago that we needed a new one." Doriana replaced the phone and turned to Logan. "I run a busy office and I need someone who can keep up with the pace. Your lifestyle isn't my concern. Do you have the job skills I need? Did my father even check that out?"

Logan's full lips quirked in a grin. "Your father is head of a multinational company. Do you doubt he has the expertise to hire your assistant?"

Doriana's face heated. "I have faith in my father's expertise, but not yours."

Their gazes caught. Something burned in the depths of Logan's eyes that made Doriana's heart teeter against her chest like loose scaffolding bumping a building.

"I have all the skills you need," he said. "I can handle

anything you throw at me."

How about a fifteen-year-old with attitude? "We'll see about that," she said, angling her chin. She had to end this discussion now, with her professionalism intact. "Are you prepared to commit for six months? That's how long my assistant will be on leave." Folding her arms across her chest, she waited for his negative response. Of course he wouldn't agree to stick around that long. Commitment was never Logan's style.

"I'll be here as long as you need me," he said in a tight voice. Glancing away, he shifted in his seat.

She let her breath out, willing to concede defeat for now. She'd talk to her dad about hiring someone else. She stood and leveled her gaze at Logan.

He rose slowly, towering over her by at least a foot. His gaze trailed her face, stopping at her mouth. He didn't try to hide the desire in his eyes. Her knees jelled. Disturbed by her attraction to him, she dug her nails into her palms. This could not be happening. This would not happen.

"Doriana?" His voice caressed. She shivered, unable to look away from the seduction of his gold-flecked eyes. His knowing smile made her stiffen. He was well aware of his effect on her. The thought cooled her like a powerful fan on a steamy day.

"When do you want me to start?" he asked.

"Tomorrow morning. Eight o'clock." Thank God she sounded normal again. "Lisa will go over her projects and duties."

"Tomorrow then." He turned and strode from the room, moving with a confident sensuality that made her pulse trip.

A trickle of foreboding caused a chill deep in her soul. How would it feel to see Logan every day, a constant reminder of what they'd once shared...of the youthful dreams that had died the day he walked out of her life? To look into his eyes and see Josh, and feel the guilt? Should she have tried to find Logan all these years? Didn't he have a right to know about his son?

Folding her arms, she crossed the room to stare out the window. The fog had lifted and she could see the skyline clearly now. "Oh, Billy," she said to the famous statue. "What am I to do?"

As if the statue answered, she glanced down at the table and picked up one of Josh's pictures. She couldn't risk her son becoming attached to a father who would walk away again.

She gathered up the photos, leaving only one of Josh as a toddler. She couldn't empty her office of all Josh's pictures. If Logan saw the picture, he'd assume she was the mother of a small child. Thank God Josh inherited her black hair.

She would have to keep up the pretense for only a short while. She'd convince her dad that Logan had to go. Guilt reared up but she brushed it aside.

****

Logan retrieved the briefcase he'd left with Doriana's assistant and walked out to the hall. The elevator came quickly and he stepped in. His mind barely registered the other riders crowding in with him. What was he thinking, coming on to Doriana like that? He had a job to do. He knew better than to risk an important assignment like this.

His gut tightened. Doriana was more beautiful and exotic than he remembered. The severe cut of her business suit couldn't hide her lush body and her smoldering sensuality...a sensuality he'd awakened long ago. He gripped his briefcase, fighting his body's response to her. But he couldn't stop the memories flooding him. The feel of her thick black hair brushing his bare chest as they made love. Her laugh and the way she made him feel important. And then the awful night that tore him away and ended his dreams.

He needed air and space. The other occupants pushed against him. He should have taken the stairs. The elevator came to a final stop and Logan stepped out, moving swiftly to the revolving doors of the Callahan Building and out to the sidewalk. He lifted the collar of his jacket against the November chill as pedestrians jostled by him.

He'd be glad to get back to the sunshine and tranquility of Arizona. With luck he'd get this assignment over quickly and be home for Christmas. Home. His stomach twisted. A sparsely furnished house without even a goldfish for company. Maybe he'd go away for the holidays. Some place noisy where he wouldn't have to think. Where he could forget.

He hailed a cab to take him to his hotel. He settled into the seat, anxious to escape to the quiet of his room. Hopefully the luggage he'd shipped earlier had arrived. Leaning his head back, he closed his eyes. But he couldn't escape Doriana or his memories. Her scent of roses followed him. She'd always worn rose cologne. That was one thing about her that hadn't changed.

Her eyes were the same...large and golden brown, melted chocolate laced with warm caramel. At seventeen they had flashed with happiness and a sense of adventure.

The loneliness and vulnerability that shadowed her incredible eyes now had gotten to him in ways he didn't like and couldn't afford. What had happened to her in the years since he'd last seen her?

That wasn't his problem. Doriana was hands off. They were from different worlds. He'd learned that lesson a long time ago. And he was damaged goods. Another lesson he'd been reminded of time and again. The familiar hurt wrenched him.

The cab jerked to a stop in front of a luxury hotel. The uniformed doorman rushed to open the taxi door. Callahan had spared no expense on his hired gun, Logan thought as he entered the plush lobby. The smell of old money mingled with the perfume of the fresh flower arrangements scattered around the cavernous room.

He walked quickly to the bank of elevators. He needed solitude. He had to study the dossiers Callahan had given him, had to immerse himself in his work. This job would be rougher than he thought. He hadn't figured on seeing Doriana every day. He'd been fooling himself all these years. He still wanted her.

Cara Marsi

CHAPTER TWO

"Where's Franco?"

"We haven't seen him, Dan."

Dan Callahan rubbed his hand over his face. Frustration and worry deepened the lines around his mouth. Doriana wanted to comfort her father and assure him that all would be okay. But he didn't need her assurances. He needed her brother to show up on time for the weekly staff meeting.

The conference room door flew open and Franco, heir apparent, breezed in. His thick, curly brown hair, so like their father's, was slightly mussed, as if he just came from a tryst with his latest blonde.

Which he probably had, Doriana thought. She loved her brother, but he refused to take anything, or anyone, seriously. And the company would some day belong to him. Her loving but sexist father believed that only a male was capable of running the company he founded. Bitterness vined in her stomach, forming a tight knot.

"Sorry I'm late, Dad." Franco smiled with the easy charm that made everyone forgive his many transgressions.

"Try to be on time in the future," her dad said, smiling back.

Doriana resisted the urge to roll her eyes. Since the day Franco was born, when she was four, her parents indulged and spoiled him. Her son worshipped his Uncle Franco and emulated him. The familiar ache stabbed her. She wouldn't allow Josh to grow into Franco, a self-absorbed womanizer always looking for the next party.

12

Was Josh headed that way? She controlled every aspect of her life. Why couldn't she control her son?

Franco, seated across the table, winked at her. She narrowed her eyes and he laughed softly.

While her father shuffled the stack of papers on the table in front of him, Doriana's mind drifted to Logan. She'd tried to concentrate on work after he left her office today, but he consumed her thoughts. On some level she'd always known he'd return and had dreaded the day. Her fears for Josh welded with her own suppressed yearnings. If Josh knew about Logan would he dream of having a father in his life? Would the dream be shredded...as her hopes were splintered like a chunk of dead wood the day Logan walked away?

Despite his dark edge, Logan still carried the sadness that had touched her from the first time she saw him so long ago. As hard as she'd tried then, she'd been unable to erase the melancholy that clung to him. She had to be very careful now or she'd be hurt again. Or worse...Josh would be hurt. She squeezed the pencil she held. It broke in two. Her father peered at her from above his reading glasses. Face burning, she looked quickly away.

"Let's get started," her dad said. He laid his glasses on the table and looked around at the faces staring back at him. "We've had more bad news."

Tension snaked around the room. Doriana sat straighter, focusing on her father, the man she adored, the man she tried so hard to please.

Her dad waved a piece of paper in front of him. "We lost the Trenton bid. To Ackerly. They beat our price by eleven percent, just enough to get the job."

A collective groan went up from the other officers.

Bryce James, the sales director, licked his lips. Sweat beaded his forehead. "That's the third job we've lost in four months. What's going on?"

"That's what I want to know." Her father pounded the table. "And there's more." A muscle throbbed in his jaw. "We had vandalism last night at the Riverfront project. Someone managed to sneak past the guards and throw paint on the walls. It will be hell getting black paint off white lacquer." He scrunched the paper in his hand and threw it on the floor.

Gathering her courage, Doriana took a deep breath. "Dad, it has to be someone in the company who is leaking the bids. The figures are sealed."

"Come on, Doriana," Bryce James said. "That's ridiculous."

Her father gave him a withering look. Bryce sank into his seat. Doriana sensed the others in the room backing away, wanting to distance themselves from the coming wrath.

"No one in our company would be that disloyal." Her dad stared at her with eyes dark as storm clouds. "I refuse to believe that one of my employees would betray me. Their jobs depend on the company's success. I will not tolerate any more talk about sabotage, or whatever you call it."

She bit her lip, holding back her anger at her father, as she always did. Whispers and murmurs skirted the table.

"Dan's right," the chief financial officer said.

"It can't be any of us," one of the attorneys said.

Doriana looked at the others, pretending a confidence she didn't feel. "It's not coincidence that our last three bids have been undercut by our competitors just enough to get the jobs. And now the deliberate destruction of property. What's next? We can't continue to lose money like this. We should look into the possibility of corporate espionage."

Franco snickered. "Lighten up, Dorie. Corporate espionage? You've been watching too much TV. You need to get out more."

Anger at his attitude and his dig at her lack of social life stiffened her spine. And he'd called her Dorie ... Logan's name for her. She fisted her hand on the table. "Don't patronize me. I'm an officer in this corporation with as much right to speak as anyone."

"Cut it out, both of you," their father said in a tight voice. "This is a business meeting."

Doriana glared at Franco until he looked away.

Her dad's sharp gaze rounded the table, seeming to settle on each person in turn. Chairs squeaked and plastic hit wood as the meeting attendees squirmed in their seats and tapped their pens on the wooden table.

"What we have to do," her dad said with a firmness that demanded attention, "is a better job of putting together our bids. The sales department has gotten very lax and I will not tolerate it." He narrowed his eyes at Bryce James. James' face purpled.

Her father glanced down at the appointment book in front of him and back at the sweating sales director. "Clear your calendar tomorrow. I want to meet with you and your staff. I want an action plan as to how your department intends to correct this problem. We will not lose any more bids. And we need to review your security policies."

"I'll get with them as soon as this meeting is over," James said, running a finger under his shirt collar.

Doriana forced the tension from her muscles. She wanted to remind her dad that he'd taken drastic measures after the last setback, to no avail. But he turned a deaf ear to her advice. She knew she was right. Someone was sabotaging them. For what? Money? Love? Greed? Whatever the reason, it surpassed any loyalty he or she felt for the company. Could it be someone seated around this table? She shivered.

Right now, she needed to talk to her dad about Logan. If he wanted to keep Logan on the payroll, he'd have to find another place for him. But no way would he be her assistant.

When the meeting ended, she waited until the others filed out. Her father, seated at the table and gathering up papers, gave her a questioning look.

"Dad," she said, taking a deep breath. "I need to speak with you about the assistant you hired. He won't work out."

Her father fixed her with one of his strong glares. She stared back.

"He'll work just fine," he said. "I checked his credentials. He has the skills to do the job. He stays."

His firm voice brooked no argument. She dove in anyway. "What do you really know about this guy? He said you hired him as a favor to a mutual friend. What friend?"

Her father raised his eyebrows and looked at her over his glasses. "Is that what he said?"

"Did he lie?" She leaned across the table.

"Of course not." He began stuffing papers into manila folders, not looking at her.

"Dad, who is the mutual friend?"

"Someone you don't know," he said, busy with his papers.

"I know all your friends."

He took off his glasses and leveled his gaze at her. "Apparently you don't. Logan stays. End of discussion."

****

Doriana crossed her arms over her stomach and paced her bedroom. Ten o'clock. Where was Josh? He hadn't come home from school or gone to visit Mom or Nonna. None of his friends knew where he was. He didn't have his driver's license. Where could he be?

What a day. Logan shows up after sixteen years. Now this. Father and son. Cut from the same mold?

The sound of a revved-up car engine tore down the street, stopping in front of her house. A car door slammed, then running steps and a key unlocking the front door.

She hurried down the stairs to meet Josh in the entry hall. He looked at her with a sheepish grin that reminded her of the lovable child he'd been. His grin turned into the cocky smirk of the teenager he'd become.

"Where the hell were you?" Her voice shook.

He stared at her, his expression guarded.

She tapped her bare foot on the cold tile. "Answer me." Flaring her nostrils, she fought the urge to shake some sense into him and then hold him until all was right again.

"Chill out, Mom. I was with friends." His gold-flecked hazel eyes, Logan's eyes, mocked her.

"What friends?"

"You don't know them. God, I'm hungry." He dropped his backpack on the floor and loped away, heading for the kitchen.

"Joshua, stop right there."

He turned around. Impatience and arrogance blended together on his chiseled features. "Mom, I'm starving. Can I go eat?"

"Not until I get some answers," she said, walking up to him. "How dare you come in at ten o'clock with not even

16

a phone call to tell me where you were or who you were with. I tried calling, but you had your phone turned off." She sniffed and leaned closer. "Why do you smell like exhaust fumes?"

He backed away. "This is Philadelphia. It's a dirty city."

"Forget that," she said. "Who are these friends? Do they go to your school?"

"They go to public school." Challenge flashed in his eyes. "Do you have a problem with that?"

Anger boiled through her. "Don't pull that act on me. As long as your friends are decent I don't care what school they attend. But I do care that my fifteen-year-old is running around at night with people I don't know."

"I'll be sixteen next month and I'll have my license and a car."

She glared at him. "No car for you until you've earned the right."

He shrugged. "Grandpop said he'd buy me one."

She brushed fingers through her hair and fought tears of frustration and fatigue. "No car until I say it's okay."

"I'll get a car." He lifted a defiant chin. "Grandpop never listens to you."

His words slapped her with the old doubts and insecurities.

"I'm sorry, Mom," Josh said, looking contrite. "I shouldn't have said that."

She squared her shoulders. "You are grounded for one week."

"Aw, Mom. That's too harsh. I haven't done anything wrong. I was just hanging with some friends."

She shook her head and exhaled a deep breath. "You know the rules. You don't take off after school without letting me know where you are. It's been a long day. Tomorrow you'll tell me all about these new friends."

"God, Mom, relax."

"Any more backtalk and you're grounded for two weeks."

He groaned.

"Your dinner is in the refrigerator." She rubbed hands over her tired eyes and watched his retreating back. He looked more like his father every day. He had Logan's height, taller than the men in her family, and Logan's broad shoulders. Once Josh filled out, he would be the image of his father. His jet-black hair was the only legacy she'd passed on.

Her stomach churned with fear. Would Dad and Franco catch the resemblance between Logan and Josh? They had no reason to suspect. And men were usually clueless about those things. Mom and Nonna were a different matter, but they'd never meet Logan.

Heart heavy as a lump of clay, Doriana slowly climbed the stairs. She loved Josh so much. She'd done her best, bringing him up alone. Almost alone. Her family meant well, but they sometimes interfered too much.

Josh was becoming a man and he needed a father. Was it fair to keep Josh and Logan from each other? A knot twisted in her chest. Her son was troubled enough without disrupting his life with a temporary father. Her head pounded. She needed sleep. Tomorrow everything would look better.

****

She always had great legs and she knew it. In the week Logan had worked with Doriana she seemed to take pains to make herself as drab as possible, with her conservative suits and her long mane of hair clasped primly at her neck. But she wore her skirts short. He smiled at her small vanity as he followed her into her office.

When she reached her desk she picked up a folder and turned to him. He quickly settled his features into an indifferent mask.

"Here are the properties I told you about." Not looking at him, she handed him a folder and rounded the desk, putting the slab of oak between them.

Her body language spoke loud and clear. She was nervous around him. Why?

"Inside is a list of questions," she said, her voice cool and professional. "Call the agent for each property and get the information I need. I'll expect a report on my desk tomorrow." She sat down in the leather chair and began shuffling papers. He recognized a dismissal.

Once the snub would have made him defensive, a

holdover from his hardscrabble childhood. But not anymore. He ran a successful business and he was good at his work. Dan Callahan expected results for his money. But first he had a few issues to settle with Ms. Doriana Callahan. Logan set the folder on the desk and leaned forward until his face was inches from hers.

She jerked her head up. Surprise and another emotion he couldn't read flickered in her chocolate eyes...eyes that used to reduce him to slush. And still could, he realized as longing blitzed him. Releasing his breath, he forced his thoughts to a safer place.

She angled her chin. "Is there a problem with the assignment?" The huskiness in her voice gave lie to the rigid set of her body.

He lowered himself onto the chair in front of her desk and crossed his legs at the ankles, pretending casualness.

She arched an eyebrow and met his gaze with cool resolve. Picking up a gold pen, she waved a hand over her cluttered desk. "I'm very busy. Is there something on your mind?"

"Damn straight there is." He heard her sharp intake of breath and leaned forward. "You and I will be working together for the next six months." The lie clutched his gut. More like six weeks. He pushed the guilt away, hiding his feelings, the way he'd been trained.

"I'm well aware of that," she said in a tight voice.

Pride, anger and fear flitted over the exquisite planes of her face. The pride and anger he understood, but the fear...where did that come from?

"Look, Dorie," he said, running frustrated fingers through his hair. "I need this job. Your dad trusted me enough to hire me. I have no problem working with you, but you seem to have a huge one with me."

Her nostrils flared and her eyes narrowed. She looked like a cornered cat, ready to pounce. God, she was beautiful. His tenuous control slipped a notch. *Focus*, he commanded.

"You were forced on me," she said. "My father picked you. I'd rather do the work myself."

"You'd rather do the work yourself than look at me every day?" Logan kept a tight rein on the anger and hurt that twisted his gut. "Not very professional."

Her fingers wrapped tightly around the pen. "My professionalism has never been called into question."

Logan let his breath out and relaxed, willing calmness into his body. He needed this job. But he needed her acceptance too, if not her trust. "I'm not asking you to like me, but I am asking for a cordial business relationship. You may not have chosen me, but I'm here. That's a fact you can't change. So make the best of it and life will be easier for both of us."

Her brown eyes flashed. "I don't appreciate being lectured."

"And I don't appreciate being treated like backfill from one of your construction sites."

Pink tinged her smooth ivory cheeks. "I don't do that."

The phone on her desk rang, making her jump. She dropped her pen, but made no move to pick up the phone.

"You going to answer that?" he asked.

"It'll go to voicemail." She locked her gaze with his. "Of course, if my assistant were at his desk, where he belongs, he would answer that for me."

His laughter coaxed a smile from her.

"Hell, Dorie, it's good to see you smile. You don't do enough of that, at least not around me."

"Would you quit calling me that." Her soft voice belied the harsh words.

He sat straighter. "I'll stop calling you Dorie if you throw me a few smiles." He stared at the lush curve of her mouth. "I was always a sucker for your smile."

Her eyes widened.

He folded his arms across his chest and watched the play of emotions on her expressive face. Embarrassment, awareness and apprehension all took their turns until a cool mask slipped over her features.

"If we must work together," she said, "it will be strictly business. Is that understood?"

He gave a slight salute. "Aye, Chief. Whatever you say."

She blushed.

"But if you ever want to take it to another level, I'm game," he said, grinning.

She stiffened. "You have some nerve."

He stood. "Doriana, you're too easy. There's no challenge in teasing you. You never used to take everything so seriously. Lighten up."

At the startled look on her face, he laughed. The phone rang again. She reached for the receiver like a lifeline.

"Yes, Julie," she said into the phone. "Let me check my schedule." She opened her appointment book and scanned it. "I'm free. First floor conference room? See you then."

She replaced the receiver on the cradle and picked up the gold pen, rolling it between her fingers. Trying to calm her nerves? Logan wondered. She glanced away to stare out the large window that framed the Philadelphia skyline.

Logan studied her strong profile. Her elegant nose spoke of her Roman ancestry, passed down through her mother's family. Only her fair skin hinted at her Irish heritage. Her Old World beauty still reached out to him. He shifted uneasily.

"All right, Logan," she said, turning to him and drawing a deep breath. "I'm willing to work with you." Her lips tilted in a wry smile. "I don't have a choice as you pointed out. But there will be nothing personal between us and we will not mention the past."

"No problem." He picked up the folder he had set down earlier. "There's no reason to feel uncomfortable around each other. The past doesn't matter."

Her face paled. She glanced toward the table that sat under the window. He followed her gaze to the picture of her dark-haired toddler, the only photo on the long table.

"Nice looking kid," he said. Lisa had told him Doriana had a son but never married. She refused to divulge any more personal information about her boss.

Doriana sat very still, staring at the framed picture. Tension etched her mouth.

"Who's the father?" The question slipped from him.

Her face grew chalk white. "His father is not in his life." When she looked at him, sadness shadowed her eyes.

Logan tamped down the crazy urge to go to her and hold her until the hurt went away.

She lifted her chin. "Nor is the father part of my life.

And I would appreciate no further questions on the subject."

"Nothing personal between us." He tapped the folder in his hand. "I'll get right on this."

He felt her gaze boring into him as he walked away. Relief and anger burned through him. Relief that Doriana wasn't tied to the man who fathered her son. He refused to question why he felt so good about that. Anger at the man who deserted her clenched his stomach. What kind of guy walked out on his own kid? A guy just like his old man, and Logan bore the scars.

****

Doriana watched the door long after Logan closed it behind him. Turning slowly, she stared at Josh's picture. How long before Logan found out about Josh? She'd never been good at subterfuge. Nervousness had made her draw Logan's attention to the picture. If she continued to react like that, he'd guess she was hiding something.

By some miracle she'd managed to keep Logan a secret from her family all these years. Her humiliation that he'd walked out on her, coupled with fear that her father would hunt Logan down and hurt him, had kept her silent.

What if one of the employees let it slip that she was mother to a teenager? She had too many other worries. She couldn't waste time on something that might never happen. And from what she remembered about Logan, he stayed to himself. He wouldn't be fraternizing with his co-workers.

And Logan. What about him? She'd tried to ignore him all week, but her senses were on high alert every time he got near. His masculine power drew her, touching that part of her she'd suppressed all these years.

She'd never forgotten him. How could she? She had a son who was a constant reminder of him every day. Josh wasn't the only reason she'd never been able to forget Logan. No man had ever made her feel the way Logan did, made her want him so badly it hurt. Made her dream what could never be.

"No," she groaned. She threw her pen across the room.

CHAPTER THREE

Logan headed for the cafeteria. He'd rather eat alone, but employee cafeterias were hotbeds of gossip. And he needed all the information he could get to solve this case and get the hell out. The sooner he put distance between himself and Doriana, the better.

He hadn't counted on the torture of seeing her every day. He couldn't deny that he desired her, but he also wanted to crack the shell she'd built around herself. Where was the laughing, smiling young girl he'd once loved? Had he contributed to her aura of sadness?

He pressed the elevator button hard, as if he could pound away his thoughts. Doriana's life was not his concern. It never had been. He punched the button again, impatient now to be around others who would distract him from Doriana.

Long ago he'd allowed himself to dream of a good life, a life with her. But the world she'd inhabited only made the ugliness of his world more unbearable. Painful memories attacked him...the nights he'd lain awake scared his dad wouldn't come home, but more afraid that he would.

He banished the hurtful thoughts deep into his mind where they belonged. *Focus on the mission. Nothing else matters.*

****

Logan knew the minute Doriana entered the noisy cafeteria. Some sixth sense made him glance toward the doorway.

She stood there, proud and beautiful, staring at him.

23

What would he read in her eyes? Their gazes locked. Awareness sizzled between them like downed power lines. Straightening her shoulders, Doriana looked away and walked slowly toward the food line, her hips swaying gracefully as she moved. Other men gave her appraising looks. Did they see the sensuality she couldn't hide? Jealousy ripped through Logan.

"Logan, did you hear a word I said?"

He turned his attention to the voluptuous blonde sitting next to him. "Sorry, Candi, I was distracted."

Her bright red lips curled in a smirk and she looked around at the other women who shared their table. "We know what distracted him, don't we, girls?"

The others giggled.

Candi leaned closer. "Forget it, Logan. You don't stand a chance."

"What are you talking about?" he asked, pretending an indifference he didn't feel.

Candi folded her arms across her ample chest, a smug look on her face. "I'm talking about Ms. Ice Princess, the boss's daughter. She doesn't date co-workers. Thinks she's too good. I hear she doesn't date at all." The blonde ran her fingers down Logan's arm. "Doriana doesn't know how to please a man," she purred.

Logan shifted uncomfortably. Doriana had known how to please him all those years ago. Her wild passion stirred him as no other woman had before or since.

Doriana didn't date. A small seed of hope opened in him. He quickly squashed it. He didn't need complications in his life right now. He forced himself to relax and appear interested in Candi. He hated the playacting, but he needed Candi's friendship. Gossip had it that her boyfriend was fired from Callahan Construction. And as Assistant to the Sales Director, she had access to the bids. A possible motive and the best lead he had.

He smiled at Candi and the other young women surrounding him, his lunch companions the past week. "Doriana's not my type." The lie stuck in his throat. "She's my boss. I wouldn't want people to think I slept my way to the top."

The others laughed.

"Oh, Logan, you're so funny," said Karen, a petite

redhead from Accounting. She stared at him with wide, long-lashed eyes.

He returned her smile, flirting a little to keep up the pretense. She blushed.

Candi sidled closer to him. Staking out her claim?

He stood and glanced around the table. "Thanks for keeping me company, ladies, but I need to get back to work. Don't want the boss mad at me." Moans of protest followed him.

"I'll walk to the elevator with you," Candi said.

Logan kept a smile plastered on his face. Candi was dynamite. He trod a dangerous line with her. He wanted her trust and her confidence, but he'd never use her in any way that would hurt her. He'd figure out how to get what he needed without compromising his values.

****

For the next several days, Doriana endured the sights and sounds of a constant string of females visiting Logan. The teasing banter between him and the women grated on her. She'd even quit going to the cafeteria after the day she saw him surrounded by a group of adoring women.

"Hi, Logan, you'll have to stop working so hard. You'll make the rest of us look bad."

Candi Whiting's sultry voice drifted in from Logan's office, making Doriana want to growl. She lifted her gaze from the report she was reading. The blonde was perched on the edge of Logan's desk, long legs crossed. The miniskirt she wore barely covered enough to keep her decent.

The soft laughter from the other office roiled Doriana's stomach. Candi didn't seem Logan's type, but what did she really know about him? Was Logan the brassy blonde's latest conquest? If the rumors were true, the woman had bedded, and discarded, half the men, single and married, in the company.

If Logan chose to have an affair with Candi, that was his business. Before the thought could completely formulate, jealousy slashed Doriana like a razor knife.

Damn it. She was the boss. Logan worked for her. She told herself it had nothing to do with her feelings toward Candi,. She'd just had enough of these constant interruptions.

"Logan," she called. "Can you come in here."

"Sorry, Candi," she heard him say. "Duty calls."

The blonde's mouth formed a pout as she slid seductively off the desk. Hips swinging, she walked toward the door. Glancing back, she gave Doriana a sly grin.

Logan stepped into Doriana's office. "Yes?"

Her gaze, with a will of its own, slid slowly over him. His khakis hugged his impossibly long muscular legs and his black sweater stretched across his broad chest. No wonder half the women in the building acted like giggly teens around him.

"Doriana?" His mouth quirked in a grin he quickly suppressed.

She caught her lower lip between her teeth, disturbed by the awareness that swelled in her. Straightening, she gestured to a chair near her desk. "Please sit."

Logan sauntered toward her and settled into the chair. His gaze never left hers.

Doriana forced the tension from her muscles. "Your steady stream of visitors is very distracting. To me and to you. I hesitated saying anything, but it's getting out of hand."

Amusement flickered in his eyes. "I don't encourage them." He threw her a bone-melting smile that made heat curl in her stomach. "I admit I enjoy their attention." His mouth tilted in a teasing grin.

She stiffened, fighting her attraction to him. And her jealousy. "This is a place of business. Take you're, uh, flirting, somewhere else." She sounded like an old prude. What had gotten into her?

"I'll take care of the problem," he said.

He raked fingers through his thick wavy hair. Memories flooded her. Did his hair still have the same silky texture? She picked up her gold pen and wrapped her hand around it as if its cool smoothness could dampen her dangerous thoughts.

Their gazes caught. She swallowed, unable to look away.

"Is that all you wanted?" His glance slid to her

mouth.

She licked her lips. Desire leapt into his eyes. Could he see the same longings revealed in hers? She dropped the pen.

"Hey, Doriana!" She jerked at the sound of her brother's voice.

Franco swaggered into the office, followed by Janine, his blonde *dujour*, a model from New York.

Doriana threw them a genuine smile, thankful that their appearance relieved the sexual tension that hovered in the air whenever she was alone with Logan.

Franco slapped a folder on her desk and gave her his most charming smile.

"What do you want, Franco?" She braced herself, waiting for the favor he would try to cajole from her.

Instead, he turned to Logan and held out his hand. "Franco Callahan," he said. "Have we met before?"

Logan stood and shook the proffered hand. "I don't believe so. Logan Tanner. I'm filling in while Doriana's assistant is on leave."

Janine hooked her arm through Franco's and scanned Logan's body. "Assistant, huh? Lucky Doriana. I'm Janine."

Logan grinned at her. "Nice to meet you."

Janine fluttered her eyelashes. Did women still do that? Doriana thought.

Franco frowned at Janine then looked back at Logan. "Are you sure we haven't met before? You look damn familiar."

"What do you want, Franco?" Doriana repeated, more sharply than she'd intended. Her fear that Franco would see the resemblance between Logan and Josh plucked her already strung-out nerves.

"What makes you think I want something?" Franco asked. "Maybe I just had to see my beautiful big sister." He smiled with the suave charm of a crooked building inspector.

"Cut the insincere flattery," Doriana said.

Franco laughed and leaned over the desk. "The Tremont report is in here," he said, tapping the folder he'd laid on her desk. "Some of the numbers need rechecking. Dad wants it Monday, but Janine's in town for only a few days."

He straightened and snaked his arm around the model's waist, pulling her against him. He kissed her lightly on the lips. "We have some very interesting plans, don't we, baby?"

Janine giggled and bile rose in Doriana's throat. Doriana glanced at Logan. He stared at Franco with an expression of disgust. Logan turned to Doriana and smiled. Her heart swelled. Logan understood.

"Be a doll, sis," Franco said, pulling her attention. "Finish the report for me."

Confidence lit Franco's blue eyes. He always got what he wanted. Not this time. Doriana rounded the desk until she stood face-to-face with him.

"Maybe I have plans for the weekend," she said in a tight voice. "Do your own report."

His low laugh made her bristle.

"Get real," he said. "You with plans? You'll probably spend all weekend at work like you always do. As long as you're here, you might as well finish my report."

"Dad gave you the job, not me." She placed a hand on her hip and glared at him.

"Please, Doriana," Janine said in a little girl voice. "Franco and I are so much in love."

Until the next blonde comes along. Ashamed at her meanness, Doriana bit her lip.

"Doriana and I will do the report for you," Logan said.

Doriana swung around to stare at him. "What?"

Logan leveled his gaze at her. "Let your brother and his friend have their weekend. With the two of us working together, we'll get the report done."

"No," she said, shaking her head. What had gotten into Logan?

"Come on, Doriana," Franco said. "Logan's right. You and he will do a better job." He ran his hand down Janine's arm. "I couldn't concentrate with this tigress distracting me." The blonde nibbled on his earlobe. Doriana wanted to retch.

Franco turned to Logan. "Damn generous of you. Let me know if I can do anything for you." His mouth curved in a wolfish grin. "I can introduce you around. I know some of the hottest people in the city."

"And I have lots of model friends who would love a date with you," Janine purred.

"Thanks for the offer," Logan said. "I'll be working."

Janine stared wide-eyed at him. Doriana suppressed a laugh. Bet that was something the woman didn't hear often.

But things were getting out of hand. "This is my office, not a dating service," Doriana said. "Leave, Franco. I won't do your report."

"We can do it." The firmness in Logan's voice held her. "It's important to your dad, Doriana. And I know you want what's best for him and the company. Don't worry. We'll get it done. I'll work with you all weekend."

Apprehension mixed with excitement, making Doriana shiver. She and Logan together in a nearly empty building? She pressed her hand to her stomach. She couldn't do it.

"Thanks, both of you," Franco said before she had a chance to protest again. Arm in arm, he and Janine strode quickly from the room.

"Wait," Doriana shouted. Too late. The outer door clicked behind them.

She turned to Logan, her breathing labored. "Why did you do that? This is my office. I dictate what work I'll do. You had no right."

His hazel eyes shadowed. "I'm sorry, Doriana. I thought I was helping you and your company."

She crossed her arms. "I'll decide what's best for me and the company."

He ran a hand over his face. "Franco wouldn't have done that report and you know it. Your father would have given it to you Monday and you would have been up all night working on it. I didn't want to see that happen." His eyes softened.

The truth of his words made her throat thicken. She swallowed. "You don't know what you're talking about."

He moved closer. She felt his warm breath on her face and inhaled his faint citrus scent. Her insides quivered with need.

"You know it's the truth. Anyone can see how devoted you are to this company and your father." He stroked a gentle finger along her cheek. "Beautiful, smart, and loyal," he husked. "A sexy combination."

Heat pulled low in her stomach. His closeness and his touch made her ache for something more, something dangerous. Fear brought her back to reality and she stepped away from him. "Don't talk like that," she said in a voice that shook. "We're co-workers. You report to me, at least temporarily. I thought we agreed on a strictly business relationship."

He scanned her face. "Sorry. I forgot myself for a minute." He smiled, not looking contrite at all. "You are beautiful, you know."

"Stop it," she said. But she couldn't stop the fingers of pleasure that skittered up her spine. Trying to collect her wayward thoughts, she glanced at her watch. "I guess we're stuck with this report. Let's take a dinner break and meet back here in an hour and a half."

Feeling more in control, she looked up to find him staring at her with hooded eyes...eyes that seemed to know a reality she couldn't face. She dropped her gaze, fighting the longings she'd kept tightly wrapped all these years. Longings he released in her.

He moved closer and hooked his finger beneath her chin, tilting her face toward his. "Have dinner with me," he whispered. "We can discuss the report."

"No," she said, pulling free of his scorching touch. The part of her that could still think straight knew if she sat across a dinner table from Logan, the report would be the last thing on her mind. Working with him all weekend would test her enough. She needed a break to regroup her senses.

She glanced over at Josh's picture. "I have uh-babysitting arrangements to make."

Not a complete lie. Josh had been on his best behavior lately, but she couldn't trust him alone most of the weekend. She'd insist he stay at her parents'. He'd fight her, but he'd not risk another grounding.

"My offer for dinner is always open," Logan said.

Her chest tightened. Could she keep up this masquerade for six months? She had to.

She raised her chin. "Thanks for the invitation, but no dinner. Not now. Not ever."

"We'll see," he said. "I never give up, Doriana."

She grabbed her purse from the desk drawer. "See you in an hour and a half," she said, hurrying from the room. She pulled her cell phone from her handbag. She'd order a pizza for her and Josh. *Do not think about Logan. Think about the food.* But thoughts of Logan filled her and she knew she fought a losing battle.

****

Raking frustrated fingers through his hair, Logan watched Doriana leave. Damn, what was wrong with him? He had to stay away from her. They weren't right for each other. Had never been right for each other.

He strode to his office and pulled his jacket from the coat rack. A brisk walk in the chill November air would cool him. Shrugging into his jacket, he let out a low, bitter laugh.

He needed more than a walk. He needed Doriana. His body and soul burned for her. He'd tried to forget her. Other women had tried to break through the wall he'd built around his heart. None had come close. There was always Doriana. Just one more night with her, that was all he asked. One night to hold her and possess her and she'd be out of his system for good. He could go on with his life. He slammed the door, shutting out the lie, and headed down the hall.

CHAPTER FOUR

The key Callahan gave him fit easily into the lock. Logan turned it gently until he heard the click. He stepped into the office housing the sales department and closed the door softly behind him. Security lights illuminated the early-morning paleness. He stood still, allowing his eyes to adjust and getting the lay of the place.

A lucky break to have an excuse to be in the building on a Saturday. With Callahan's keys he could let himself in at any time, but he didn't want to arouse the suspicions of the guards who were on duty round the clock.

Working on the report with Doriana gave him reason to be in the building, but he wanted to help her because she'd end up with the job anyway. He wanted to make things easier for her. Why? Guilt? What happened between them was a long time ago. And he'd been forced to run. He pushed the thought aside for another time. He had a job to do.

He glanced at the digital clock on one of the desks. Six. He'd meet Doriana in her office in an hour.

Doriana had looked so tired when they finally quit work after midnight. He hoped she'd gotten more sleep than he had. He'd tossed and turned, his sleeplessness broken by dreams of Doriana. Hot, spicy dreams filled with a soul-baring yearning he couldn't shake, even awake.

When they'd first started work last night, tension cut around them like glass shards but once they delved into the project, the atmosphere lightened. He'd always felt good around Doriana. When they were teens she had a way of making him feel special. He drew a deep breath. Those memories belonged in the past. He knew better than to go there.

Logan moved farther into the room and forced himself to focus. His instincts and bits of evidence pointed to someone in Sales leaking the bids. Director Bryce James? That was almost too obvious. But he had to consider all possibilities.

Logan wanted to get a feel for the place, to see where everyone sat, visualize the culprit taking the sealed bids from the safe or hacking into the computer. His covert operations with the Special Forces had taught him to look for things easily missed by others, to pay attention to the slightest detail.

He circled the room, treading carefully, stopping at each desk and going through drawers and wastebaskets. Thankfully, the cleaning crew wouldn't come in until later today.

He found Candi's desk and sat in her chair. Framed pictures of her adorned every free space. Picking up one of the photos, he studied it. A beach picture, Candi wore a skimpy white bikini that exposed her lush charms. The skinny, dark-haired man in the picture with her had a sour expression on his face, as if life had dealt him a bowl of lemons.

Interesting. The man stood with his arm draped around a woman who left most men salivating and he looked angry. Logan needed to get the boyfriend's name from Candi or one of the other employees and check it against the list of fired workers. And he had to stay on good terms with Candi. A few subtle questions and she might give him the information he needed to crack this case.

He poked around her desk, pulling open drawers. A piece of paper stuck in the corner of one drawer caught his attention. He pulled it out and read it. Smiling, he carefully replaced the paper where he found it.

Logan let himself out of the quiet office. Mission successful. His search had yielded some surprising and useful information. Armed with his new knowledge, he felt more lighthearted than he'd had in weeks. Or did knowing that he'd see Doriana shortly have something to do with his mood?

****

Where was Logan? Doriana paced her office, clutching the Styrofoam coffee cup and taking small sips of the strong, hot brew. She needed lots of caffeine this morning. She and Logan had worked hard last night and they'd gotten a good portion of the report done. When they left past midnight, Logan looked as exhausted as she felt.

She glanced at her desk clock. A little past seven. The guards downstairs told her that Logan arrived at six. Where had he been for the past hour?

A frisson of foreboding crept up her spine. Did Logan have anything to do with the strange things happening around the company lately—the vandalism, the suspected theft of bids and the uneasy knowledge that someone was targeting them for reasons they couldn't fathom?

She didn't know anything about Logan's life. Where had he been all these years? And why had he shown up now? She gulped coffee too quickly, burning her tongue. The sharp pain distracted her from the questions that pounded her head like a construction worker wielding an oversized hammer.

Holding tightly to the warm cup as if it could absorb her fears, she walked to the window and gave a slight nod to the reassuring presence of old Billy surveying the city from his perch on City Hall. The pale sun peeking over the tangle of buildings seemed to mock her with its promise of a fresh day. After a restless night, she felt anything but fresh. Images of Logan had teased her with yearnings and unfulfilled promises she refused to acknowledge.

"Morning." The deep, masculine voice sent pleasure and sweet memories spiraling through her. She turned slowly to face Logan. He leaned against the doorframe, reminding her of the reckless young boy she had loved so much. Her heart took a flying leap against her chest and her anxieties and suspicions dissolved like the early-morning fog. Her gaze slid over him, devouring his beauty and sensuality.

Well-worn jeans, black sweater and black boots gave Logan a dangerous air. Her gaze traveled a return trip to

34

his face. The knowing look in his hazel eyes made her skin burn.

She pressed the coffee cup so tightly she was afraid the Styrofoam would crack. *Get a grip. Act like the professional you are. And remember Josh.*

"Where were you?" she said in a thin voice.

He held up a bright paper bag. "Donuts and coffee."

The guards hadn't mentioned that Logan had gone out. She pushed the disturbing thought aside.

Logan set the bag on the small worktable and began emptying the contents. "Sit," he said. "Nothing like jolts of sugar and caffeine to jump start the day."

She couldn't help smiling. He'd always known how to make her smile. "I already have coffee." She held up her cup.

"Live dangerously, Dorie. Have more coffee."

She shook her head. "Remember our bargain."

He grinned. She swore her toes curled.

"I forgot," he said. "You smile. I don't call you Dorie. Now sit."

Still smiling, she sat at the small table.

He placed a large container of coffee and a napkin holding a glazed donut in front of her.

"I never eat donuts," she said.

"Indulge," he said. "Develop some bad habits. You're too disciplined. Eat sweets. Drink too much coffee. Let loose once in a while."

Why did she have the feeling this wasn't about coffee and sweets?

"Oh, okay," she said, bristling that he had her figured out. Well, he didn't know everything about her. She sat down and took a bite of the donut.

He laughed, showing even white teeth. "See, that didn't hurt."

She glared at him while she chewed, not willing to let him know how much she enjoyed the pastry and his teasing. Despite all the hard work ahead of them, she felt strangely relaxed.

He sat across from her and pulled a cream-filled donut from the bag and bit down on it. A dollop of cream oozed out and clung to a corner of Logan's mouth. Doriana's hand froze around her coffee cup. She swallowed the urge to kiss the sweet concoction from his lips..

Logan licked the cream off with his tongue. She stared at him, still holding her coffee cup aloft. He caught her staring. His eyes darkened.

Face burning, she pulled her gaze away. "Let's get to work."

Hours later her head swam with numbers and her eyes hurt. She massaged the small of her back, trying to ease her tense muscles. "I need a break."

Logan laid down his pencil and rubbed his temples. "This is grueling work. Good thing we got through a lot last night."

Doriana rolled her eyes. "If we had weeks to finish like Franco, it wouldn't be so bad. But that's Franco for you. And next week he'll replace Janine with another blonde."

"Why do you put up with him?" Logan pushed his chair back and stretched his long legs in front of him. The denim fabric pulled across his thighs. Doriana's mouth went dry. Had Logan said something?

"What?" She swung her gaze back to his face.

"I asked why you put up with your brother."

She shrugged. "He's family. I don't have a choice."

He narrowed his eyes. "That doesn't give him the right to push you around."

She stiffened. "I don't let him push me around."

Logan leaned closer and touched his finger lightly under her chin. "You're his sister. He should appreciate and respect you, and be glad of his family."

Pain shadowed Logan's eyes. He had never talked about his family. He'd always been so proud, too proud. As a teen, she suspected he covered hurt with recklessness and bravado.

Doriana jerked free of Logan's touch. His problems didn't concern her. But his son did. And she would protect Josh at all costs. But was she right to keep them apart?

****

"I can't believe we're finished," Doriana said. The November darkness had fallen hours ago. But the report was done and stored in the computer.

"It's been a hell of a day," Logan said.

Doriana looked at him, sitting across the small table from her. Logan had been there for her last night and today. "Thanks. I couldn't have done this without you."

"No problem. I hope your father appreciates what you do for him."

"He does."

"You don't sound convinced." Logan studied her. "You give a lot to this company. I'm not sure the men in your family know what they've got in you."

She tightened her jaw. "They appreciate me. And it's really none of your business." The words slipped out.

Anger flickered in his eyes. "Sorry," he said, his voice harsh.

She relaxed her shoulders. She hadn't meant to be so nasty. "It's been a long day."

Logan stood. "Let's get out of here. We both need some fresh air. I'll buy you a cheesesteak."

"A cheesesteak? You must be kidding."

"I guess you're going to tell me you don't eat those any more either," he said.

She arched a brow. "I don't."

"What kind of Philadelphian are you? You used to love cheesesteaks."

She shrugged. "That was a long time ago."

His eyes warmed like molten gold. "I'll have to teach you to love them again while I'm here."

Excitement clenched Doriana's stomach. What else would he teach her?

She glanced away. "It's late. I need to get home. I haven't seen my son since yesterday."

****

At the mention of Doriana's son, jealousy, as unwelcome as a rattler on a desert hike, snaked through Logan. How could he resent a three-year-old? He loved kids. What he hated was the reminder that she'd been with another man, made love to that man and bore his child.

He was flirting with trouble, but right now he wanted to do anything he could to prolong his time with Doriana. The loneliness of his hotel room yawned like a bottomless pit.

"Have dinner with me," he said. "It won't take long.

It's not like we're going to some fancy restaurant. I haven't had a good old Philly cheesesteak since I left this town."

Her shoulders set in a rigid line. "I can't."

"Afraid to go out with me?" he asked. Or maybe she thought he wasn't good enough for her. He'd gotten over that hurt long ago and he wouldn't resurrect it now.

"I'm not afraid of anything," she said, lifting her chin.

He leaned over the table until his face was inches from hers. "Prove it. Let me buy you a cheesesteak." He smiled, trying to diffuse the tension between them. "I promise not to ravage you when the night's over, especially if we have grilled onions on our steaks."

Her lips quirked in a grin. Could he break through the defenses she put up and find the girl she'd once been?

"Donuts and cheesesteak. You're not good for me, Logan."

He laughed. "Is that a yes?"

"Your car or mine?" he asked a little later when they entered the deserted garage.

She looked over at his battered twenty-year-old Jeep and then at her dark red Jaguar.

"I think mine," she said.

The teasing response died in his throat. The hairs along his neck prickled with warning and his body kicked into fight mode. They weren't alone.

Logan put his hand on the small of Doriana's back, guiding her, but also protecting her if needed. He felt her stiffen, but didn't move his hand as he led her toward his wreck of a car. He had to be in control in case anything happened.

"We'll take mine," he said. "We're going to South Philly. We might have to park on the sidewalk. You wouldn't want to hurt that fancy car of yours, would you?" He forced a grin. "Are you embarrassed to ride in my junker?"

She looked up at him with those incredible chocolate eyes. He almost lost his footing. "I've ridden in worse," she said.

He gave her a wry smile. "I doubt that."

"Where did you get this thing?" she asked as she waited for him to unlock the passenger door.

"Borrowed from a friend." The lie formed a knot in his stomach. What would she say if she knew about the black Lamborghini parked in his garage in Tucson? But that didn't matter. He'd moved beyond trying to impress others a long time ago. And he had more immediate concerns.

Doriana slid into the passenger seat and Logan locked her door. He scanned the room as he walked around to the driver's side. Whoever was out there knew how to keep hidden.

"Stay there," he said. "I want to look around."

She frowned but stayed in the Jeep.

Logan did a quick circle of the nearly empty garage, looking into the few cars parked there. He opened the stairwell door. Nothing. Maybe one of the guards had come down for a forbidden smoke and hurried back upstairs when he saw them.

He couldn't shake the feeling that something more dangerous than a prohibited smoke was going down. Was this case just about corporate theft and vandalism? What was he missing?

Doriana rolled down the window. "Logan?"

He didn't want her suspicious. He unlocked the car door and slipped into the seat next to her.

"What was that about?" she asked.

"I thought I heard something," he said. "Probably one of the guards sneaking a smoke." He started the engine. "Let's go. I'm starving."

****

He stepped quickly back into the shadows, his heart thumping with fear and excitement. He'd almost been caught. Couldn't let that happen.

Hell, who would have thought someone would be around on a Saturday night? The guy suspected something. He'd have to be more careful next time. The old man's daughter was a real looker. Better than her pictures.

He'd have himself some fun and bring the old man to his knees.

****

Doriana shivered in the chill air and took another bite of her incredibly delicious and very messy mushroom cheesesteak, inhaling the succulent aroma of fried onions and ketchup mixed with the choking odor of exhaust fumes from the traffic on the narrow streets. She held onto the steaming hot sandwich, letting it warm her hands, as she glanced down the long counter at the other diners huddled against the cold night. Inside the small steak shop, the cooks labored over hot griddles. But the patrons ate outside regardless of the weather.

"We must all be crazy." She looked at Logan, standing next to her. "Only in Philadelphia would people eat outdoors in November. And in such a tasteful atmosphere."

And I'm crazy for being here with you. Why had she said yes to his invitation? Maybe the challenge he threw at her had something to do with it. If she wanted to prove that she was immune to Logan's charms, it wasn't working. Her body thrummed with life just being close to him.

Logan's smile lurched her pulse into high gear.

"We don't have anything like this in Arizona," he said. He bit into his sandwich, an ecstatic look on his face.

Doriana laughed.

He put his food onto his paper plate. "I made you laugh." The harsh overhead lighting caught the teasing sparkle in his eyes. "You should laugh more often."

Her face flushed and she looked away to study the oversized menu visible through the steam-filled windows. Warm memories nudged her. She and Logan had loved the cheesesteaks here. And she'd loved him so much then. Until the day he walked away, taking the joy with him. But he'd given her a precious gift—Josh.

"Doriana," Logan said.

She jerked her attention back to him.

"Where were you just now?" he asked. "You zoned out."

I was in the past, she wanted to say. *A most dangerous place.* "I'm tired," she said instead.

"You don't look tired now." He drew closer, his eyes darkening. "You look beautiful."

"Don't," she said, staring down at the Formica countertop. A thought left dangling a few minutes ago worked its way through her mind. She looked at him. "Arizona? Is that where you've been living?"

His jaw tightened for a second. He shrugged. "There, among other places. I don't stay anywhere too long."

Regret, like a sharp knife to the heart, stabbed her. He'd leave again. At least this time she wouldn't be seventeen, crazy in love with him, and pregnant with his child.

Needing to compose her thoughts, she bit down on her sandwich and stared at the other diners. She felt Logan watching her, but refused to look at him.

Horns blared all around them as cars wended their way through the congestion. Muted shouts came from inside the small row houses surrounding them. At the end of the counter two elderly men argued passionately in Italian.

Feeling in control again, she swung her attention to Logan.

A mistake.

They stared at each other. Away from the protective confines of her office with its computers and gadgets, she stood with Logan on a street that technology forgot. For a slice of time she was a teen again, sneaking dates with the wild kid from the rough part of town.

Her parents would have packed her off to a convent in Tibet if they could have seen her clinging to Logan's waist as they sped through the city on his sleek black motorcycle. She'd been so young and free spirited. What had happened to that girl?

"You're not eating," he said softly, breaking the spell.

"Yes, I am." She bit down on her cheesesteak.

They finished their food in silence. Around them the city hummed with noises. The wind blew litter along the gritty streets. She coughed as strong diesel fuel shot from the exhaust of an ancient Mercedes. All her senses were heightened. She hadn't felt this alive in years. Did being with Logan do that? Fear shot a bullet of caution through her. She could handle Logan. Couldn't she?

"The dirt blowing around and the fumes from the cars add something to the taste," she said, trying to lighten the mood.

He laughed softly.

"Logan, why did you come back here?" The question that had burned her since the day he walked into her

41

office slipped out.

Logan glanced away. His breath hovered in the cold air before dissolving. When he looked at her again, tension bracketed his mouth.

"I was between jobs. A friend offered his apartment and car for a few months while he was out of town."

"So you really are a transient," she said.

He gave a short harsh laugh. "Yes, sweetheart. Do you have a problem with that?"

"Why should I care?" She hated how flippant she sounded. But she couldn't let him know that a small part of her did care that his life took a wrong turn.

"Right, why should you care?" Bitterness and hurt laced Logan's voice.

Their friendly banter broken, Doriana concentrated on wrapping the remains of her sandwich. Her appetite had dissipated in the sadness that sliced her. Logan had walked out on her and left her to raise a son alone. Would things have been different for both of them if she'd had a chance to tell him about Josh all those years ago?

She sighed. There was no going back.

Determination to protect her own heart and her son's stiffened Doriana's spine. She made the right decision in not telling Josh and Logan about each other. Hadn't she?

"Thanks for dinner, Logan," she said later when they'd pulled into the company garage. The ride back had been quiet and tense. Too much hurt and too many memories rode with them.

"You're welcome," he said in a tight voice. He parked in the spot next to her Jaguar and cut the engine.

She unbuckled her seatbelt. She knew she should leave, but something held her. Something intangible that filled her with a bittersweet yearning for what might have been.

He turned to her, draping his arm over the back of the seat. "Doriana, understand that there are things about me I can't share with you. With anyone. My life is different from yours. It always has been. I've learned to survive."

"You don't owe me an explanation," she said.

He reached out to rub his knuckles under her chin. Excitement shivered up her spine.

"I'm not giving you one," he said. "Just don't judge me too harshly. Accept me for what I am."

The Jeep suddenly got very small. Logan's hot gaze seemed to weld her to the seat.

Memories rushed her. They were teens again, sitting in her Mustang, making out, doing things no well-brought-up girl should. Warmth pooled in her private parts. She welcomed the feeling. It had been so long.

"Doriana," he husked. He reached behind her to unclasp the large barrette holding her hair and tossed it into the back seat. Freed of its confinement, her hair fell over her shoulders.

He slid his fingers through her hair. His scorching gaze burned. "So beautiful," he whispered.

Then his lips were on hers, harsh and demanding. She held herself rigid at first, trying to resist his sensual pull. But she ached for him, for what she knew he could give her.

Lacing her arms around his neck, she surrendered to his touch. His lips softened against hers and he curved a hand around her nape, drawing her closer. Uttering tiny sounds, she parted her lips, welcoming the hot invasion of his tongue.

His sensual, practiced kiss burned her with needs that had gone unfulfilled for so long. How many other women had he kissed in the past years? She didn't care. Not now. Not with him sucking on her bottom lip like that.

Cradling the back of her head, Logan left her mouth to string a line of kisses along her jaw.

She twined fingers through his thick hair. The crisp waves sprang to life at her touch, just as she remembered.

He unbuttoned her coat and slid his hands to caress her back and the sides of her breasts. Her blood quickened. God, she wanted him.

The thought hit her like a block of ice thrown at her head. She jerked away. What was she doing? She wasn't sixteen. She was the mother of a teenager. How could she be in a car making out with a man she hardly knew anymore? Raging hormones, unused for so long, rendered her temporarily insane.

Logan looked at her with passion-filled eyes before a

harsh mask settled over him. He moved away. "Doriana, I'm sorry. I never meant that to happen."

"Neither did I," she said in a shaky voice. "It must have been the cheesesteaks." And too many memories.

"It's my fault," he said. "I know better." He hit his hand on the steering wheel. "Damn, how could I have lost control like that?"

"We both lost control," she said.

"No, you don't understand. I'm responsible."

She angled her chin, holding onto whatever pride she had left. "Let's forget it." She needed to go home and nurse her humiliation in private. She fumbled for the door handle.

"Stay there," he said. "I'll get it for you." He slid quickly out of the car and walked to her side, opening the door for her.

She headed toward her car with Logan close beside her. "I'm okay," she said when she reached her car.

"Get in and lock the doors." His features were tight and harsh as he scanned the room.

"What are you looking for?" she asked.

"Oh, hell, Doriana, get out of here. For your own sake." He reached out a hand, then dropped it.

She started to protest that he couldn't bark orders, but something in his eyes and his alert stance silenced her. She got into her car and locked the doors.

She backed out too fast, making her tires squeal on the cement. As she sped away, she risked a glance through her rear view mirror. Logan stood still, staring after her.

****

Logan watched until her car was out of sight. He wanted to throw something and curse to the heavens. What the hell was wrong with him? What if whoever was in the garage earlier still lurked? He had risked both of them by his carelessness. He wouldn't tolerate that kind of sloppiness in any of his people.

Damn! He hadn't been able to keep his hands off her. He wasn't a green nineteen-year-old. He knew the consequences. He had to stay away from her. He had a job to do, and he'd fallen down today. He couldn't bungle the assignment, but most of all he couldn't lose his integrity.

Sometimes it was all he had.

Doriana was off limits. As soon as this job was over he'd be gone. Back to the sunshine. And loneliness. The past was better left dead. For both of them. The memory of her full, sweet lips and her heated response tortured him on the long, cold ride home.

CHAPTER FIVE

The shrill ring woke Logan from a fitful sleep. Instantly alert, a habit learned from years in the military, he reached for his phone and flipped it open.

"Tanner, it's Callahan."

"What's happened?" Logan rubbed a hand over his eyes. The greenish light from the digital clock cast an eerie glow over the dark room and illuminated the time. Five o'clock. Monday morning? He'd gotten so little sleep over the weekend he wasn't sure what day it was.

"Our building was broken into sometime between Saturday night and this morning," Callahan said. "The guards found one of the rest rooms trashed."

Saturday night. A shiver shot up Logan's spine. He'd felt someone watching them in the garage. He should have done a more thorough search, but he was so intent on getting Doriana away from danger, he got sloppy. He could have put them both in jeopardy. That wouldn't happen again.

"Are you certain they broke in?" Logan asked. "Could they have used a key?"

"It was a break-in," Callahan said. Anger hardened his voice. "The culprit disabled the security cameras in the garage and forced open the side door. Damn guards. Probably sleeping. I had the agency fire them."

And will probably fire me too, Logan thought. Damn. He should have given this job to a subordinate. Being with Doriana skewered all his training and common sense.

Restless, Logan paced the large room, holding the cell

phone to his ear while Dan talked. Just like he couldn't keep the gray tendrils of dawn from forcing their way through the heavy curtains, he couldn't keep thoughts of Doriana from his mind. Or his heart.

"Those are my thoughts," Callahan said. "Any suggestions?"

Logan started. He had quit listening to Dan. He was really slipping. "I'll meet you at your office. We can discuss it better there."

****

Doriana heard about the break-in from the day guards when she arrived at work. An uneasy feeling stole over her as she rode the elevator to her office. Logan had been in the building Saturday at least an hour before her. He would have had plenty of time to trash a bathroom.

But why would he do something so juvenile? Was he trying to send a message? Was Logan involved in the thefts and vandalism?

When she got to her office Logan wasn't at his desk yet. The uneasiness stayed with her even as she brewed a pot of coffee and turned on her computer. She poured herself a cup of the strong brew, inhaling the nutty fragrance, and walked to the window to stare out at old Billy Penn.

"What reason would Logan have to sabotage us?" she asked Billy. "What's in it for him?"

Money. The thought chilled her. Did Logan need money? He was a transient. He told her as much. Is that how he made his living? Stealing? No, it couldn't be. Logan had too much integrity. He always did.

"Doriana."

She jumped at Logan's voice coming from the doorway. Coffee splattered on the floor.

"A little nervous this morning?" Despite his teasing words, his expression was grim. Why?

"You startled me," she said.

"Sorry." He walked slowly toward her.

His animal grace made her insides quiver with longing. She clutched her coffee mug as if it could protect her from her instant reaction to him every time he got near.

"This is yours," he said, holding out his hand.

The barrette he took out of her hair Saturday night rested in his calloused palm. The memory of their hot kiss in the car seared her. She reached out to take the ornament, careful not to touch him, and curled her fingers around the plastic, still warm from his touch. Her misgivings of a few minutes ago melted away at his closeness.

He looked tired. Her fingers itched to touch his faint stubble of golden beard and smooth over the lines of exhaustion around his mouth. Had he had as much trouble sleeping as she? Did dreams of the kiss they'd shared keep him awake?

She stared into his eyes. Knowing eyes. Sensual eyes. Excitement and the promise of danger skittered along her nerve endings. She straightened her spine. Could she trust Logan? Could she trust herself?

"About the other night," she said.

"No problem," he said.

"We just forget it, right?" She pressed the barrette into her palm.

He nodded. "Forgotten."

She let her breath out. "Stress and overwork. That's all."

He moved closer. She wanted to back off but held her ground.

His features tightened. "It was a hell of a lot more than stress and overwork and you know it."

He turned and strode quickly from her office. The click of the door closing mocked her with the truth of his words.

The barrette felt hot in her hand. She dropped it onto the soft carpet and walked to her desk. Holding her coffee mug, she sank into the leather chair and stared at the door. She ran her tongue over her lips, reliving the feel of Logan's hot mouth on hers. She'd wanted to kiss him and taste him again from the minute he'd walked back into her life.

Trying for calmness, she took small sips of coffee and glanced over at Josh's picture. She couldn't get involved with Logan again. She owed it to Josh. Heck, she owed it to herself. And what made her think she and Logan would get involved again? It was only one kiss. No big deal.

The lie didn't go down easy.

****

Logan sat on the corner of his desk and picked up a glass paperweight, holding it tight against the urge to fling it at the door. "Damn," he said to the empty room. What was wrong with him? Doriana was fire, a fire that threatened to destroy all he'd worked for. Why couldn't he leave her alone?

The truth hit him like a hard right to the jaw. Doriana had gotten under his skin a long time ago. An ice princess with a core hotter than the Arizona sun, she excited him like no other woman. But she was way out of his league. Daggers of regret twisted his gut.

He edged off the desk and plunked down the paperweight. It landed with a loud thud. A reminder that he wasted enough time on impossible dreams? He had a job to do. He powered his computer and sat down, scrubbing a hand over his tired eyes. His mind barely registered the images on the screen.

Doriana's kiss and the yearnings she stirred in him had kept him awake the last two nights. He'd used his insomnia to review the dossiers of Callahan's top managers. It had taken all his training to focus on the boring reports and not on his need for Doriana.

His study of the dossiers confirmed a feeling that had gnawed at him from the beginning. Something about the sales director, Bryce James, didn't ring true. A gaping hole in the man's report challenged Logan to find the truth. He trusted his instincts. Those instincts had saved his life and the lives of his men on countless covert operations for the Army.

He needed more on James' background. The man was Candi's boss. The pornographic note he found in Candi's desk was unsigned but he recognized James' handwriting. James was married. Did the man need money to support his family and his mistress?

Yesterday morning Logan had called his second in command in Arizona. Jo promised to get back to him with any information she found about James. Logan leaned back in his chair. He was on to something. He'd resolve this job soon and kick the dirt of Philadelphia off his shoes. Could he kick aside the memories of Doriana and the dreams that died that awful night so many years ago? He gripped the chair arms. Only two others knew about that night—his dad and Father Jessup. Shame and bitterness washed over Logan, but he forced the feelings away. He'd made his peace with God a long time ago. He turned to his computer. Better to concentrate on the numbing boredom of the Tremont report than pummel himself with what might have been.

****

Logan and Candi sat alone in the cafeteria. The blonde's cloying perfume overpowered the spicy aroma of Logan's chicken stir-fry.

He'd befriended Candi for the sake of the assignment, but he genuinely liked her. She wasn't his type, but beneath her brash, sexy exterior, he'd glimpsed sadness, a sadness he knew too well. He'd spent his younger years covering his hurts and fears with a macho bravado. The Army and maturity had knocked that out of him. What hurts did Candi cover with her blatant sexuality?

He suspected the brassy blonde held the key to the bid thefts, and maybe the vandalism. He had yet to establish that the theft and vandalism were connected. He'd caught looks between Candi and her boss, Bryce James. The looks solidified what he found in the note in her desk. He'd heard that Candi's boyfriend had done jail time. Did the boyfriend know about James? Candi was playing a treacherous game. A game she couldn't win.

"Logan, have you listened to a word I've said?" Candi's perturbed voice hammered through his thoughts.

"Sorry, Candi," he said, smiling. "I was too involved with my chicken stir-fry."

She snorted. "Food had nothing to do with your thoughts. You were mooning over Boss Lady."

"Why would you say that?" he asked with as much detachment as he could muster. He knew how to hide his emotions. He was really slipping if Candi had picked up his feelings about Doriana.

Candi leaned closer, touching his arm with one of her red-tipped talons. "I know you've got it bad for Boss Lady."

When he started to protest, she held up her hand.

"Don't worry, Logan. Your secret's safe with me." Tension tightened her pretty features. "I know other things, too." Tears glistened in her blue eyes. She dug into her oversized purse and pulled out a tissue, swiping at a tear tracking down her cheek.

"What's wrong?" Logan asked.

She looked down at the table. "I'm scared, Logan."

Logan sat straighter. Sympathy for Candi warred with his training. He couldn't become emotionally involved in a case.

"Tell me, Candi," he said, squeezing her hand.

"Hey, you two, quit hogging the table."

Logan looked up to find the redhead, Karen, holding a food-laden tray and staring down at them. Damn! He put on his best smile. "Sit down," he said, moving his chair so she could squeeze into the one next to him. He and Candi couldn't talk here. He had to see her somewhere other than work. She might furnish the clues he needed to solve this case. And he just might help Candi too.

****

Logan took the letters off the printer and headed for Doriana's office. She needed to sign off on them to make today's mail. The door to her office was slightly ajar. He started to push it open but Doriana's voice stopped him. She was talking to someone. But no phone call had come through. She must be on her cell. Guilt at eavesdropping nagged him and he started to move away.

"No, Josh," she said. "You can't come to the office."

Logan froze. Josh? A lover?

A heavy sigh from her. "Because you can't. I'll give you the money later. There's no reason for you to come all the way into the city."

Money? Blackmail? Logan shook his head at the outrageous idea. He'd been in the security business too long.

Doriana quieted. Logan figured the person on the other end must be doing a lot of talking. He knew he should step away, but curiosity and a twinge of jealousy held him.

"No," Doriana said more firmly. "You'll have to wait for the money. You are not to come to my office."

She was quiet again. The guy must really be pleading his case.

"No. And I mean it," she said at last. "We'll talk later. I love you."

The breath knocked out of Logan. Love? Doriana in love with another man? The thought wrenched Logan's gut.

Who was this Josh and why was she giving him money? Did she need money badly enough to steal from her father? Nothing he knew about Doriana remotely suggested she could be involved in anything sordid.

Gripping the unsigned letters, Logan stepped away from the door and fisted his hand at his side. If this Josh hurt Doriana in any way, the guy would answer to him.

****

Doriana exited the elevator into the quiet hallway. At seven in the evening, most employees had left for the day. If she hadn't forgotten the papers she needed for her meeting across town tomorrow morning, she'd be at the charity function now. God, she hated those dull parties, but she promised her dad she'd go. The sooner she arrived, the sooner she could leave.

A sound at the end of the hall drew her attention. Her dad and Logan stood close, talking in muted voices. They seemed chummy, too chummy. Her father kept his distance with his employees, other than his top managers. Why was he listening so intently to Logan?

Something was going on, something hidden just below the surface. She'd been unable to shake the feeling since the day Logan arrived.

She rushed into her office, driven by some instinct that told her not to let her dad and Logan know she saw them. She gathered up papers from her desk and stuffed them into her briefcase and snapped it shut. A quick glance at the clock told her she needed to hurry.

"You're far too beautiful for him."

She froze at the sound of Logan's voice and turned toward her office door.

Logan stood in the doorway, his arms folded across his broad chest. His gaze scanned her body slowly and deliberately, making her face flood with heat.

She squared her shoulders. She would not let his bold

52

sensuality intimidate her. "What do you mean?"

"I assume you're on your way to meet a guy," Logan said.

"You assume wrong, not that it's any of your business." She frowned. "What are you doing here so late?"

He moved into the room. "I wanted to get a head start on the Fisher proposal."

He stood close, too close. "You look sexy in that black dress." He gently brushed back a tendril of her hair and skimmed his thumb along her cheekbone. "But you look sexy in anything."

The huskiness of his voice and the roughness of his skin against her sensitized flesh sent pleasure jolting through her .

Anxious to escape the temptation Logan offered, Doriana pulled away and headed for the door. Her arm grazed his. The heat of his body seemed to reach out to her, warming her all over.

He grabbed her arm and pulled her back. "So beautiful," he whispered. He bent his head and kissed her lightly on the lips. Doriana held her body rigid, refusing to respond.

Logan's lips moved expertly over hers, drawing her despite her resolve. Unable to resist his erotic pull, she pressed closer and opened her mouth to him. His soft moans made feminine pride surge in her.

Footsteps and voices raised in conversation penetrated Doriana's brain. The sound of a vacuum cleaner cut the quiet and destroyed the sensual web Logan wove with his lips and tongue.

She pushed away from him. They stared at each other, their breathing ragged.

Doriana rubbed her mouth, as if she could rub away the memory of Logan's hot kiss. She turned and strode swiftly from the office. She knew Logan was watching her. She ran her tongue over her lips, tasting him. It would be a very long night.

CHAPTER SIX

Logan leaned over Doriana and studied her computer screen. The fresh scent of roses wafted from her glossy black hair. He itched to lift the heavy fall of hair and kiss the back of her neck. Was her skin there as soft as he remembered? Pressing his palm on the desk, he leaned closer. She stiffened and he knew she felt the heat that pulsed between them.

"Do you see what I mean?" she asked, her voice a little breathless. "These figures are all wrong."

Logan smiled. Despite their hot kisses earlier in the week, Doriana had tried to keep her distance with cool professionalism, but whenever she spoke to him her voice held a husky tone and she averted her gaze from his.

Reaching across her, he traced his finger over the lines on the screen. His hand lightly brushed the silky strands of her hair and he heard her sharp intake of breath. Her mind wasn't on the chart any more than his.

"You're right," he said, trying for coolness. "There's something wrong. Another Franco screw-up?"

She nodded, still not looking at him. "We'll have to re-do all the figures."

"I can come in tomorrow," he said.

The next day was Saturday. Was he the only worker in the country who dreaded the weekend? No Doriana to look at and talk to, and flirt with. Lonely hotel rooms got old quickly, especially when his dreams were peppered with visions of a chocolate-eyed beauty who had never really belonged to him, and never would.

She turned until their faces were inches apart.

54

Desire softened her eyes to velvet, making his pulse quicken. Her gaze scanned his face, resting on his mouth, and she licked her lips.

Logan reached out and lifted strands of her hair, letting the silky smoothness slide through his fingers. "Doriana."

Her lips parted for him and he leaned closer.

"Am I interrupting something?"

The throaty female voice jerked them apart.

Logan straightened and followed Doriana's gaze to the stunning brunette, dressed in black, who stood framed in the doorway, arms folded across her chest and her brown eyes sparkling with mischief.

"Anita." Doriana's voice shook.

Anita's gaze traveled over Logan's body. "He's certainly an improvement over Lisa," she said.

Doriana picked up a pencil from her desk and twirled it between her fingers. Her nervous habit made Logan smile. Did she do that only when he was around? What was bothering her? That Anita walked in or that they'd been about to kiss?

"Anita, what brings you to Center City?" Doriana asked.

The brunette strolled into the room, her hand outstretched to Logan. "I'm Anita Santisi, Doriana's cousin."

Logan took her hand and smiled. "Logan Tanner. Temporary assistant."

"Temporary? Pity." She glanced at Doriana. "He's a keeper."

Doriana gave Anita a quelling look. Logan grinned.

Dimpling, the brunette continued to hold his hand. "Have we met before? You look familiar, but if I'd met a gorgeous hunk like you I'd remember."

Laughing, Logan pulled his hand free. "We've never met."

Frowning, Anita studied him.

"What brings you here, Anita?" Doriana asked in a tight voice. "Don't you have a client with a hair emergency somewhere?"

"Meow," Anita said, laughing.

Logan rubbed a hand over his mouth to cover his

grin. Was Doriana jealous? He hoped so.

The phone rang. Doriana lunged for it as if she welcomed the intrusion.

"Yes," she said into the phone. Her face paled and she handed the receiver to Logan. "It's for you."

The short rings told him the call was internal. Dan wanting an update? Logan picked up the receiver. "Logan here."

"Logan, it's me." He stiffened when he heard Candi's breathy voice.

"Yes?"

"Can you talk?"

"I'll call you back." He replaced the receiver. "I've got some work to do in my office, Doriana. Can we talk about the chart later?"

She nodded, pink staining her cheeks.

He left the room, leaving the door slightly open.

"What a hunk," he heard Anita say. "I'll bet that was a woman calling him."

"You bet right," Doriana said.

"Why, Miss Doriana, I do believe you're jealous," Anita said in a fake Southern accent.

"Close that door, Anita. Right now."

Before closing the door, Anita winked at Logan where he stood just outside. He grinned back at her.

Was Doriana jealous of other women? He shrugged off the thought.

He picked up his phone and punched in Candi's extension. He hadn't had a chance to talk to her alone since Monday. "What's up?" he said when she answered.

"I need to talk to you." She sounded rushed. "Away from work."

"Are you okay, Candi?"

"No. Yes, I'm fine. I need to see you. I know a little coffee shop at the Italian Market. Can we meet there tomorrow morning?"

Logan got directions to the coffee shop and hung up the phone. Would Candi give him information that would help break this case? So far there had been no further thefts or vandalism. He wanted to catch the culprit before he struck again. Jo was Fed-Exing the information on Bryce James. Maybe he'd resolve this case and head home to Arizona sooner than he thought.

Home. Hot. Sunny. Lonely. Would his life be even lonelier now that he'd found Doriana again? Logan rounded his desk and signed onto his computer. He tried to concentrate on work, but thoughts intruded. He didn't belong in Doriana's world and he'd better remember that.

****

Doriana averted her gaze from her cousin. "I do not care what women Logan sees. He's a temp doing Lisa's job till her leave is over. Then he'll be gone."

At the thought of Logan's going, regret washed over Doriana. Despite her attempts at a professional attitude with him, Logan brought a vividness into her life that had been missing.

"Sure looked like there was something going on between you two when I walked in." Anita sat in the chair opposite Doriana's desk and stretched out her legs, encased in the latest stiletto boots.

"There's nothing going on," Doriana said. "Logan's not my type and he flits from job to job. Not very stable." *And not good father material*, she thought, glancing over at Josh's picture. Josh's three-year-old face smiled back at her, all trust and innocence. Where had that little boy gone?

"Don't be embarrassed, Doriana," Anita said, drawing her attention. "If you're having a little fling with hunky Mr. Temp, no one will think anything of it. It's been three years since Karl, jerk that he was. My God, woman, how can you stand being without a man that long?"

Doriana stood and pressed her palms on her desk. "That's enough, Anita. There is nothing between Logan and me. He works for me. And I have a fifteen-year-old to consider."

"You've always put Josh first," Anita said. "You're a good mother. But you need to do something for yourself."

"How would it look if I jumped into bed with every man I met?" Doriana asked.

"Settle down." Laughing, Anita leaned closer. "It wouldn't hurt to let loose once in a while. You can be discreet. Kids nowadays are pretty smart. Josh would understand if you have a boyfriend."

"I've never let a man stay overnight at my house with

Josh there, and I'm not about to start." Doriana cut the air with her hands and sat down. "Enough about my love life, or lack thereof. What are you doing here? The most sought-after hair stylist in Philadelphia must have clients clamoring for her time."

"Thanks, I think," Anita said with a wry grin. "I scheduled a free afternoon to pamper myself for a change. I figured I'd stop by to see what time you want to meet at the Italian Market tomorrow morning. You know Nonna will only use meat from Vito's for her wedding soup."

"The wedding soup," Doriana said, massaging her temple. "I may have to cancel. I'm swamped with work."

Anita narrowed her eyes. "You're not getting out of it, Cuz. Nonna looks forward to this every year. She gets to spend time with her two favorite grandkids. You can't disappoint her."

Doriana shook her head. "You know all the right buttons to push, Anita." She released a deep sigh. "Okay, I'll meet you at the Market at nine."

"Great," Anita said, standing. "And Sunday I'll take you to my shop and cut your hair. You need a new style. Something hot that will make Mr. Eye Candy out there sit up and take notice."

"Stop that, Anita. I don't care what Logan thinks."

"Yeah, sure," Anita said. "You were never a good liar."

"Subject closed," Doriana said.

"Okay, then, get a haircut to make you feel better. It'll be my Christmas gift to you, so you can't refuse." Anita smiled. "Do you know how many of my clients would sell their souls for a free haircut from me?"

"I know," Doriana said. "I can't get an appointment with you."

Laughing, Anita turned toward the door. "I've got to run. See you tomorrow."

****

The morning dampness seeped into her bones and Doriana shivered as she waited for Anita at the entrance to the Italian Market. Despite all the work waiting in her office, Doriana determined to put aside business and personal problems today. She wanted to enjoy the annual wedding soup day with Anita and Nonna and Mom. Josh had promised to stop by later, offering to be their official taste tester.

Doriana smiled. She and Josh had been getting along well lately. She loved him so much. Regardless of the hurt Logan inflicted on her by leaving all those years ago, he'd given her Josh. And Josh was so like Logan. They had the same expressions and mannerisms. They even walked alike.

What had possessed her to kiss Logan in her office Monday evening? She'd not been able to focus on anything else during the charity dinner. All she could think about was the feel of Logan's lips on hers, the touch of his hands and his heated skin.

Every night since, she'd tossed and turned, unable to sleep, her body and mind filled with yearnings that Logan had awakened in her. She'd tried to keep her distance from Logan the rest of the week, fighting her attraction to him, but she faced a losing battle.

"Sorry I'm late." Anita approached, dressed in her usual black, clutching two paper cups of coffee. "This will warm you up," she said, thrusting one of the cups at Doriana.

"Thanks," Doriana said. "I needed this. Let's get going. It's cold standing here."

They threaded their way through the crowd, walking past vendors and shops selling everything from fish kept cool on layers of ice to delectable looking cannolis. With smiles and small waves at the shop owners who sent good-natured whistles their way, the two women headed for the meat market at the other end of the street.

"Those cannolis are calling my name." Anita pointed to the cream-filled delicacies in the window of a pastry shop.

"Let's get some for Nonna," Doriana said. "You know how much she loves them."

"Great idea," Anita said.

They started to cross to the pastry shop when Anita grabbed Doriana's arm, stopping her. Doriana frowned. "What?"

"Isn't that your hunky temp over there?" Anita inclined her head toward the coffee shop next to the bakery.

Doriana followed Anita's gaze. Logan and Candi were seated by the window inside the small shop. Logan was brushing back the long strands of Candi's blonde hair and caressing her cheek.

Doriana's heart plummeted like a wrecking ball loosened from its chains. Shock cemented her to the spot.

As if he knew she watched, Logan turned his head and his gaze locked with Doriana's. The loud shouts of the boisterous crowd and the honking of car horns faded as she and Logan stared at each other. Electricity arced between them across the crowded street.

Someone jostled Doriana, breaking the connection.

"Let's get to the meat shop." She grabbed Anita's arm and dragged her away.

"What about the cannolis?" Anita asked

****

Candi jerked away from Logan and let her hair fall into place, covering her jaw again. She glanced out the window and back to him. "Who would have thought Boss Lady shops the Italian Market? She looked upset. She's got a thing for you."

"There's nothing between me and Doriana," Logan said. Was Doriana upset to see him with Candi? Of course not. Doriana didn't care about him. He'd be a fool to believe she did.

The waitress came with their coffee. Logan used the time fixing his drink to get his twisted emotions under control. Regardless of how Doriana felt about him, he didn't want her to believe he was the kind of guy who dated any woman who threw herself at him. Maybe he hadn't had Doriana's respect all those years ago, but he'd have it now.

First he had a job to do. He turned his attention back to Candi. "Forget Doriana. Tell me about that bruise on your jaw, the one you tried to hide with your hair. Who did it to you?"

Candi stirred her coffee, looking down at her cup.

Logan had seen enough bruises to know the one on Candi's jaw was about a day old and put there by someone's fist. Anger roiled him. He'd been on the receiving end of his father's fist more times than he cared to count.

60

Candi looked at him and tears welled in her eyes. "I walked into a door."

"I've heard that one before," he said. "Who is the bastard who did that to you?"

"No one," she whispered.

"Candi, tell me the truth."

She sipped coffee, avoiding his gaze and looking around the room crowded with breakfast patrons. Sighing, she put her cup down and looked into Logan's eyes. "He really loves me, Logan. He doesn't mean to hurt me. He needs me. He says he'll stop, but lately he's gotten worse. But it's not his fault. Life hasn't been good to him."

"Damn it, Candi," he said, banging his fist on the Formica table. Several other diners turned to stare. "Quit enabling him. It's not love when a man uses his fists on someone smaller and less powerful. There are groups to help. I'll put you in touch with some of them."

A mask came over her features and he knew he was losing her. He leaned over the table and took her chin between his fingers. "Candi, listen to me. Whoever the bastard is, he won't change. And you can't change him. I know. You need to get out of this relationship now. Before he kills you."

Fear flickered in her eyes. He'd been harsh, but he needed to be, for her sake.

Logan gave her an encouraging smile. Despite her brashness and overt sexuality, he liked Candi and felt sorry for her. "You don't deserve this kind of treatment. No one does."

She blinked and pulled free of him to grab her coffee cup. She drank quickly and set the mug on the table with a thud.

Logan signaled the waitress for more coffee. When the waitress had refilled both their cups, Candi turned to Logan.

Sadness shadowed her blue eyes. "I haven't been straight with him, Logan. I've done things. He needs me. And I've betrayed him."

Laughter at the next table drew Logan's attention. He looked over, using the distraction to gather his thoughts. He needed to convince Candi to leave the bastard, but he knew he faced an uphill battle.

He turned back to her. "His abuse is a betrayal. He won't stop, Candi. Let me help."

She shook her head. "He'll kill me for sure if I leave him or call the police." Desperation laced her voice. "You're a nice guy, Logan. But I'm not really a good person."

Candi's voice had hardened. Logan knew she was already making excuses in her own mind for staying with the jerk, whoever he was. Probably the mean-looking guy in the picture on her desk. In his line of work he'd seen other women in this predicament. Circumstances in their lives rendered them powerless to stop the cycle of abuse. Sometimes only death stopped it.

As a child he couldn't fight his old man. Then he became a man himself. He'd run away that awful night, afraid of his own strength and what he'd done to his father.

Candi needed him now. He wanted any information she had that might help the investigation, but he wanted to help her more. "Candi, it will never get better. You need to get out now before something worse happens. I'll do whatever I can for you."

She chewed her bottom lip. "I'll think about it, Logan."

He leaned back in his chair and sipped coffee, watching her. He'd lost her for now, but he wouldn't give up. The smells of bacon, eggs and melted cheese made his stomach rumble, reminding him that he hadn't eaten. But he had more important things to worry about.

Candi looked down at the diamond bracelet she wore, nervously turning it on her wrist.

"Nice bracelet," he said. The thing must have cost a fortune. Where would Candi get money for a chunk of jewelry like that?

"Thanks," she said. "A little early Christmas present to myself."

"You treat yourself well," he said, lifting an eyebrow.

"I worked hard for this," she said in a defensive tone.

Logan let out a frustrated breath. "Why did you want to meet, Candi, if you don't want my help with your abusive relationship?"

She winced but leaned closer. "I haven't known you

long, Logan, but I can't share this with the few friends I have at work."

"Share what, Candi?" Logan kept his face and voice free of emotion, wanting her confidence.

"I know about those things at work, the stealing, and the vandalism. I'm scared."

Logan sat very still, giving Candi time.

She tugged on her bottom lip, not looking at him. "Dan Callahan gave me a job when no one else would."

"Tell me, Candi," he said slowly. "Tell me what you know and we can figure out what to do."

She studied the diamond bracelet, rubbing the stones, lost in thought. Lights from the overhead lamps struck the facets of the gems, as if winking at him. This assignment was becoming more complicated by the minute.

"I can't." She stood. "I don't know anything. Sorry to take your time." Grabbing her purse from the back of her chair, she turned to leave.

Logan stood and reached out to touch her arm. "Don't go, Candi. Talk to me."

She shook her head and strode quickly from the coffee shop.

Logan resisted the impulse to thump on the table in frustration. He signaled to the waitress for their checks instead. He'd have to go slow with Candi and gain her trust.

****

A lone figure, face averted, pressed against the side of the building next door when Candi hurried by.

The slut. Cheating on him with Pretty Boy. The guy had the Callahan bitch. Now he wanted his woman. Greedy bastard. He'd show him. When he got done with the women, no one would want either of them.

****

"Such beautiful girls, and neither one married. What am I to do with you?" Nonna gave Doriana's cheek a playful pinch before doing the same to Anita.

"Oh, Nonna, marriage isn't everything," Doriana said, laughing. "Don't worry about me and Anita. We'll be okay."

Doriana looked down at their tiny grandmother,

standing next to her at the large wooden table in Nonna's pristine white kitchen. Love swelled in Doriana's heart for Nonna and for her own mother, Lena, busy at the other end of the table making the special bread that would go into the Italian wedding soup. Doriana smiled at Anita as they rolled ground beef and veal into the miniature meatballs that were an essential part of the flavorful soup.

An operatic aria sung by Luciano Pavarotti, Nonna's favorite, floated through the house. Aromatic chicken broth, flavored with pungent rosemary and sweet basil wafted over the women as they worked. Doriana took a deep breath. Opera and love. Nothing ever changed at Nonna's little rowhouse in South Philadelphia. Surrounded by the women who meant so much to her helped take away some of the pain of seeing Logan with Candi at the Italian Market earlier.

But the picture of him brushing back Candi's hair invaded Doriana's thoughts. She didn't want to care that Logan dated Candi. But he was the father of her son. He didn't know about Josh. Guilt rushed at her. Was she doing the right thing, keeping Josh and Logan apart?

"Nonna, you tell us to get married," Anita said. "But you raised five kids alone after Grandpop died. You didn't need a man."

Nonna sat next to Lena and lifted a head of escarole out of a bowl. She shifted her gaze from Anita to Doriana. Concern shone from her coal-black eyes. "I loved all my children and they were good kids, but I was lonely. You need a man to share your life."

"I've given up on both my kids ever marrying," Lena said with a dramatic sigh. "Franco's not the marrying kind, not with the type of women he dates." She rolled her eyes.

"And Doriana, darling," she said, "you are too much of a workaholic. Just like your father. You'll never find a man if you don't relax and have some fun."

"Exactly what I tell her, Aunt Lena," Anita said.

"Come on, please," Doriana said. "Let it go. I'm perfectly content with my life. I have Josh. I have my work. I don't need a man." But did she need a man? Was Logan that man? She shook away the thought...where had that come from?

Anita let out a soft laugh. "Don't believe Doriana. You should see the hunk she has working for her. Madone. He's gorgeous."

"Who's gorgeous?" Josh walked into the room, flashing a smile for all the women. Logan's smile. Doriana's pulse tripped.

"You're gorgeous," Lena said. "Come here and give your grandmother a kiss."

Laughing, Josh gave Lena and Nonna pecks on the cheek. "So you were talking about me?"

"You sound more like your Uncle Franco every day," Anita said. "And I don't mean that as a compliment." She glanced at Lena. "Sorry, Aunt Lena." She looked back at Josh. "We were talking about your mom's new assistant,"

Josh opened the refrigerator and took out a carton of orange juice. He opened it and raised the carton, ready to drink.

"Josh Callahan, you use a glass," Doriana said. "You know better."

With a shrug, he opened a cabinet and drew out a glass. He filled the glass with juice and took a long swallow. "Who's this new assistant, Mom?" he asked, putting the glass down on the tile counter.

Doriana's face heated. "It's not a big deal. Logan is taking Lisa's place until her leave is over."

Josh leaned against the counter and reached for a cookie from Nonna's ever-filled pastry jar. He bit into a cookie. "The guy's hot?" Crumbs fell from his mouth.

"Don't talk with your mouth full," Doriana said.

"Is he the reason you won't let me come to your office?" Mischief lit Josh's hazel eyes.

Anita stopped in the act of rolling a tiny meatball. She looked from Doriana to Josh and back again. "You won't let your son come to your office? There *is* something between you and Logan. I knew it."

"Anita, stop that right now," Doriana said. "If my hands weren't covered in raw meat, I'd throttle you."

Anita laughed. "Perhaps you protest too much."

Lena stopped mixing eggs and flour and looked at Doriana. "Tell us about this man, Doriana. He sounds interesting."

Lena wiped her forehead with the back of her hand, leaving a white streak of flour across her smooth skin. Doriana smiled. Her mom still retained the dark beauty that made Dan Callahan propose marriage within one week of meeting her. Sadness vined around Doriana's heart. Would she ever find the happiness her parents found with each other?

She shrugged the thought aside. "There's nothing to tell about Logan." She ignored the little pang of guilt at the lie. "Dad hired him. I don't know much about him, but Dad seems high on him." She couldn't keep the slight edge of resentment out of her voice.

Lena arched a brow. "So your father is interfering with your work? He always has to be in control."

Doriana leveled her gaze at her mom. "But he doesn't control my department."

Laughing, Lena went back to mixing flour and eggs. "So much alike, you two."

"Anita, you tell us about this young man," Nonna said. "He's handsome?"

"Yeah, Anita, tell us," Josh said. "Mom will just try to change the subject." Josh walked over to Doriana and gave her a quick hug. "Don't be ashamed if you like this guy, Mom. You need a life."

"Listen to your son," Anita said, waving a meat-crusted hand.

Doriana slanted Anita a quelling look. Anita laughed.

"Well, Anita, tell us." Lena stopped mixing and rested with her elbows on the table.

"I only met him for a few minutes, but he seemed nice," Anita said. "And he's scorching hot." She smiled as her gaze circled the table. "He's tall, great body. Looks like he keeps in shape. Wavy light brown hair. And absolutely awesome hazel eyes. A definite hunk."

Anita frowned and looked at Josh. "Josh, you have the same hazel eyes as Logan, down to the gold flecks."

Doriana's breath stopped. She focused on rolling a perfect tiny meatball. She knew Anita was staring at her.

"Maybe we should invite him for Thanksgiving dinner," Nonna said.

Doriana dropped the meatball. It fell off the table and rolled under the counter. Josh retrieved it and threw it into the sink.

"No," Doriana said. "We will not invite him for Thanksgiving. He's my employee. Thanksgiving is for family."

"Doriana," Lena said, staring at her wide-eyed. "Do you hear yourself? Our table is open to anyone."

"I'm sorry, Mom. I've been under a lot of stress lately. Can we just drop the subject?"

Lena and Anita exchanged looks.

Several times during the day, Doriana caught Anita staring at Josh and then back at her, a question in her eyes. Shivers of dread raced along Doriana's spine. Josh looked too much like Logan. She had to keep the other women in her family away from Logan.

When dusk settled, they all sat down to a meal of fresh wedding soup and crusty Italian bread. Doriana looked around the dining room table at her family and knew that they would stand by her no matter what she did in life.

Hadn't they all rallied around her when she was seventeen and pregnant? They'd never passed judgment on her and they never would. But if they guessed Logan was Josh's father, the women would try to push her and Logan together. Her dad would want to pummel Logan, or worse.

And Josh. What about him? Would he resent her for keeping him from his father?

A horn blast outside startled her from her thoughts. Josh jumped up from the table.

"I've got to go," he said.

Doriana put down her spoon and narrowed her eyes at her son. "Go where, Josh? You haven't finished eating and you didn't tell me you had plans tonight."

He shrugged. "It's not a big deal, Mom. I'm just going to the movies with some friends."

"What friends? Who are they? And why don't they come to the door?"

"Oh, Mom, no one comes to the door anymore. See you all later." He blew kisses to the women before striding out of the room.

"Josh, come back here." Doriana jumped up, hitting the table and sending soup sloshing over the side of her bowl. The lace tablecloth caught on the buckle of her belt, holding her.

"Let him go, Doriana," Lena said. "He's a good boy."

"Mom, he knows the rules and he's testing me." Doriana freed herself from the lace and raced out of the room. She made it to the front door in time to see Josh get into an older model car. Engine rumbling, the car shot away. Doriana closed the door and leaned against it. Just when things seemed so good between them. Anger and fear twisted in her like the lace that had held her hostage. Something was going on with Josh. Something secretive. A cold chill of dread made her shiver.

CHAPTER SEVEN

"Are you going to tell me?" Anita set the can of hairspray on the counter and met Doriana's gaze in the mirror.

Putting on an indifferent face, Doriana fluffed her hair with her fingers and studied herself. "I like the layers. Very edgy. I can see why you're one of the top hair stylists in Philadelphia."

"Stop that." Anita sat in the stool next to Doriana and swiveled Doriana's chair to face her. The expression in her brown eyes dared Doriana to look away. "You've had sixteen years to hide the truth," Anita said. "I will not let you out of that chair until you come clean."

Doriana forced her gaze from Anita's. She shivered despite the late afternoon sunshine slanting through the large windows of Anita's hair salon. They had the shop to themselves on a Sunday afternoon. She stared outside to where pedestrians hurried by on the city sidewalk.

"Look at me, Doriana."

Doriana slid her gaze to her cousin. She might as well admit defeat. Anita wouldn't give up. Tenacity was a Santisi family trait.

"What do you want me to say, Anita?"

Anita put her hand over Doriana's where it rested on the chair arm. "I want the truth from your lips." Anita squeezed Doriana's hand and smiled her encouragement.

Tears pricked Doriana's eyes. "Is it that obvious?"

Anita nodded. "My God, Josh has Logan's eyes. He even walks like Logan. Did you really think I wouldn't guess?"

69

Doriana tried to smile. "I'd hoped you wouldn't." Tears streaked her face.

"Let it all out, sweetie," Anita said, handing Doriana a tissue.

"Windows," Doriana managed to say, waving a hand toward the windows. Anita walked across the room and dropped the shades, shutting them off from any curious bystanders.

Ten minutes later Doriana wiped her tears and blew her nose.

Anita leaned against the counter and smiled down at her. "Something tells me you've needed to do that for a long time."

Doriana gulped deep breaths. "I did."

"You know I'm always here for you," Anita said. "What are families for?" She arched a brow. "I was pretty hurt all those years ago when you wouldn't tell me who Josh's father was."

Doriana swiped at some lingering tears. "I'm sorry, Anita. I couldn't tell anyone. I was so humiliated that Logan walked out on me. And I was afraid of what Daddy would do to him."

"Uncle Dan is a force I wouldn't want to cross." Anita patted Doriana's hand. "Why did Logan leave?"

Doriana bit down on her lip. "I don't know."

Anita frowned. "Then ask him."

"I'm afraid of the answer," Doriana said, taking a calming breath. "I don't know what to do. Logan appears after sixteen years from God knows where. Does he know about Josh? What does he want?"

Anita chuckled. "I can guess what he wants. I saw the way he looked at you the other day."

"Logan doesn't want me. If he did, he wouldn't have left me." Anger and hurt, like a knife plunged into her stomach, threatened her tenuous control. "And he was with Candi yesterday at the Italian Market."

She threw her tissue toward the wastebasket. It landed on the floor. A metaphor for her life right now?

Anita waved a hand. "I wouldn't worry about him and that woman. It's you he wants."

"Cut that out," Doriana said. She couldn't allow herself to believe Logan wanted her. She couldn't open her heart to hurt again.

"You need to tell him about Josh," Anita said.

"I can't."

"Why not?"

Doriana took a deep breath. The cloying odors of hairspray and shampoo made her sneeze. Anita handed her another tissue.

"Logan doesn't have a permanent job or home." Doriana crushed the tissue in her hand. "He left me once. If he leaves again, Josh will be hurt. I can't take that chance."

"Maybe you're selling Logan short," Anita said.

Doriana glanced away from Anita's knowing gaze. She scanned the upscale salon, done in soothing shades of blue and green. The colors did nothing to calm her nerves. The stylists' stations stood empty, waiting for tomorrow. *Like her,* Doriana thought, *waiting, but afraid of what tomorrow would bring.*

Cans of hairspray and styling products stood like silent sentinels over clips and brushes. Anita was like a sentinel, wanting only to protect and help her. She looked at Anita. "I know you care and I love you for it. Let me work this out for myself. I'll tell Mom and Dad when I feel it's right."

"Okay." Anita studied her.

"It'll be fine," Doriana said, brushing her new bangs away from her face.

Anita reached over and arranged the bangs back into place. "Don't mess with the hair. You look beautiful. Logan will go nuts when he sees the sexy new you."

"Stop that," Doriana said. She threw the tissue away. This time it landed in the wastebasket. Maybe things would work out after all.

Anita folded her arms across her chest and locked gazes with Doriana. "How did you meet Logan?"

"I don't want to talk about him," Doriana said.

"You owe me," Anita said with a smile. "After all, you wouldn't tell me about him when we were teens."

Doriana shook her head. "You never give up, do you? There's not much to tell. I was sixteen and Logan eighteen. I missed my school bus one afternoon and went to one of Dad's construction sites. I thought the foreman would drive me home."

"And Logan was there."

Doriana nodded. "He worked as a laborer." She took a deep breath, letting her mind travel back through time. "He was magnificent. Dressed in black with attitude to spare. When he looked at me, my toes curled."

Anita sighed. "The princess and the bad boy."

Doriana gave her a pointed look. "Logan drove me home on his motorcycle. Despite his dangerous looks, I trusted him."

"A motorcycle." Anita laughed. "Sweet. I love it."

"That's enough, Anita."

"Does anyone ever get over first love?"

"I did," Doriana said.

Anita's gaze bore into hers. "No, you didn't. You still love Logan."

"I can't," Doriana said, standing. "I just can't." Her fingers fumbled on the ties of the plastic cape she wore. She finally loosened it and let it slide off her to the floor. Why couldn't her problems slide away as easily?

She grabbed her purse from the counter. "Thanks for the haircut, Anita. I have to go."

"Running away from the truth?" Anita asked, her soft laugh following Doriana from the shop.

****

The loud ringing jolted Doriana. Heart pounding, she sat up in bed and groped for the phone. The digital numbers on the bedside clock glared at her. Only trouble called at two o'clock on a Monday morning. Dread racketed to fear and she reached for the phone with a trembling hand.

"Hello," she croaked.

"Ms. Callahan?" The female voice sounded professional. Doriana's pulse hammered.

"Yes."

"Ms. Callahan, this is Becky Palmer, Olde City Security."

Doriana jumped out of bed. "What's wrong? Who's hurt?"

"No one's injured as far as we know," Becky Palmer said. "There's been a fire at your riverfront site. You're on the list to call in an emergency."

Doriana's shoulders sagged. As long as no one in her family was hurt, she could handle this.

"Thank you," she said. "I'll go right away. Did you call Mr. Callahan?"

"Yes, Ma-am. He's on his way there now."

****

Doriana parked her Jaguar next to her father's Cadillac and cut her engine. Police cars and fire trucks ringed the construction site. She got out of her car and closed the door, shivering in the early morning cold. She'd grabbed the first wrap she found in her closet, a light jacket.

The acrid odor of burning wood made her choke. Holding a hand over her mouth, Doriana picked her way through gravel to where her father stood talking to several men. One of the men turned as she approached.

Logan? Why was he here? Apprehension sliced a path up her spine.

Her father, standing next to Logan, turned also. "Doriana, you didn't have to come here. It's late." He glanced quickly at Logan, but not before Doriana caught the sheepish expression on her dad's face. What was going on?

"Why are you here, Logan?" she asked.

"Logan's had some experience with fires," her dad said.

Logan's eyes challenged her to question her dad.

"What happened?" she asked.

"Looks like someone set a pile of lumber on fire." Dan glanced at the middle-aged man in a fire department uniform standing next to him. "Thanks to the quick work of Captain Smith and his people, no real harm was done."

"Ma-am," Captain Smith said, touching the rim of his cap.

Doriana nodded and looked toward the smoldering pile.

"When do you think it was set, Captain Smith?" she asked.

"About midnight," the captain said. "Luckily it was a slow burner."

A heavy feeling of foreboding struck Doriana like a chunk of wood hitting her chest. Josh had come home at one o'clock, way past his curfew for a school night. He had no explanation for the dirt smudges on his face. Could it have been soot? Why would she even think that? Josh would never do anything to hurt his grandfather. But where had he been?

"Doriana? Did you hear me?" Her dad's voice pierced her thoughts.

She jerked her attention to him. "Sorry, Dad. What were you saying?"

"Why don't you go home? Logan and I can handle this."

"This is my company too," she said.

"Mr. Callahan, Captain Smith, we need your attention over here." One of the firefighters standing by the pile of charred wood signaled for the two men to join him.

Her father and the captain walked away, leaving Doriana alone with Logan. She hugged herself against the cold. She refused to look at Logan.

"Here, put this on," he said, slipping his leather jacket off and settling it on her shoulders.

She pulled the buttery soft leather close, inhaling Logan's masculine scent laced with citrus. Memories of wrapping herself in Logan's black leather jacket all those years ago rushed at her. The leather in that old jacket wasn't nearly as soft as this one, but its roughness against her skin always reminded her of Logan, hard but soft around the edges.

"Dorie, it will be okay," he said, touching her chin with his finger and tilting her face toward his.

Doriana looked into his eyes, shadowed in the pale moonlight. Need overwhelmed her. She was so tired. Tired of dealing with her son and the long hours at work. She longed for someone to share her burden.

She stiffened and pulled away. She could handle Josh. She always had. But could she handle her growing feelings for Logan?

Logan put his hands on her shoulders. The heat of his touch seared her through the heavy leather. It would be so easy to walk into his arms and let him take care of her. She couldn't.

His gaze studied her. "Stop trying to carry the weight

of the world, Doriana. Your dad and I will take care of this. Let someone else worry for a change."

Had he read her mind? Logan always had a way of seeing into her soul.

She wanted to insist it was her company and her responsibility, but her bone-weary body wouldn't listen. Her fight with Josh a few hours ago had drained her and the new fear that Josh might have something to do with the fire gnawed at her. She couldn't think straight anymore.

She slid the jacket off and handed it to Logan. "Thanks. I'll see you at the office in a few hours."

****

"Did you manage to get any sleep?"

Doriana looked up from her desk to where Logan stood framed in the doorway.

"A little," she said. She picked up a pencil and rolled it between her fingers. The soft wood soothed her ragged nerves.

Logan pushed away from the door and headed toward her. The lines of exhaustion around his mouth and eyes and the faint stubble of golden beard couldn't diminish his glorious masculinity. Her heart did a crazy flip.

He perched on the edge of her desk and reached out a hand, taking the pencil from her and setting it down.

She bristled at his breach of professional etiquette, but his nearness and the heat in his hazel eyes mesmerized.

"I like the new haircut." He smoothed strands from her face. "You look tired."

"I'll manage," she said. "I always do."

"I know."

He shifted, his gaze never leaving hers. "Doriana, about the other morning. At the Italian Market."

The memory of Logan brushing back Candi's hair, touching Candi the same way he touched her, hit Doriana like a blast of wintry air off the Delaware River.

"You don't have to explain," she said.

Logan leaned closer. She inhaled his unique scent of citrus and outdoors. She grabbed the pencil again to keep from stroking her fingers along the chiseled lines of his face.

"I want to tell you," he said. "Candi is a friend, a friend who's in trouble. That's all."

Could she believe him? Did she want to believe him? When they were teens, Logan never lied to her. He never hurt her until the day he left. She looked away from him, breaking the connection. She needed distance from him and time to sort out her feelings.

"What's this?" Logan asked. He stood and picked up one of the papers from her desk.

"Nothing," she said. "Just some doodling." She tried to grab the paper from him, but he waved it away.

Logan scanned the drawing. "This is more than doodling. This house is beautiful. You designed it?"

She nodded. She held her hand out and he gave her the drawing. She stuffed it in a drawer.

Logan watched her for long seconds, making her fidget. " I remember you wanted to be an architect," he said. "What happened?"

Another dream that died the night he walked away. "Life got in the way."

"Life?" He arched an eyebrow.

A baby and no husband. "Dad needed me at the firm." *And my son needed me at home.*

Logan leaned closer and traced her lips with his finger. She knew she should pull away but her traitorous body wouldn't move.

"The feisty girl I knew wouldn't have let anyone stop her from doing what she wanted," he whispered.

"That girl died a long time ago, Logan."

"I wonder," he said softly.

Heat burned her face. Had that girl really died? Being with Logan again triggered old hopes and bittersweet yearnings about what might have been.

The phone rang, breaking the mood. Doriana grabbed for the phone, feeling she'd just been thrown a rescue rope against her own damning thoughts.

****

"Dan, what can you tell me about Bryce James?" Logan tapped his fingers on the FedEx package that rested on the small table where he and Callahan sat.

Pale afternoon sunshine slanted through the windows in Dan's penthouse office, reflecting the confusion in Callahan's blue eyes.

"Why are you asking about Bryce?" Dan shifted his weight in the chair.

Logan leveled his gaze at the older man. "Because you left out something very important in his dossier."

Dan stiffened. "Bryce James has been with me for twenty-five years. He had a little trouble a while back. He took care of it. What are you saying?"

Logan slipped some papers from the envelope in front of him and scanned them. "Let's see. A gambling addiction so severe he checked into a treatment center." Logan looked at Dan. "Gambling debts to the mob. Did you pay off his debts?"

"What if I did?" Looking defiant, Dan fisted his hands on the table. "Bryce is a friend. He paid back every cent. He hasn't gambled in years. I'd know if he was at it again."

Logan leaned closer. "How can you be sure? And what about the mob? Could he still have ties with them?"

Anger flashed from Callahan's eyes. "I'm sure he's not gambling or involved with the mob."

Logan took another sheet of paper from the envelope and handed it to Dan.

Dan's face flushed as he perused the paper. "What's this?"

"Could be why Mr. James needs a little extra cash," Logan said.

Dan slid the paper back to Logan. "Those are just copies of receipts. They mean nothing."

"His name is on the receipts," Logan said. "Do you pay him enough for diamond bracelets and top hotel rooms?"

"Where did you get these?" Dan asked.

"I'm in the security business," Logan said. "There's not much information I can't get. And I think we can be very sure that James isn't spending this money on his wife."

Dan's features tightened. "Who is she? The home wrecker? You must have her name."

"I can't share that information yet." Logan didn't want to implicate Candi if she had no part in the thefts. If he found she was involved, he would have no choice but to tell Dan.

"You're implying that Bryce is selling the bids?" Callahan asked.

Logan nodded.

Callahan shook his head. "Even if he is selling the bids, which we have yet to prove, he's not the type to vandalize anything."

"I've wrestled with that too," Logan said. "The vandalism may be coming from a different source." He sat back and watched disbelief, then anger, slash across Dan's face.

"You mean there may be two people out to get me?"

"It's possible," Logan said. "Maybe someone you fired has it in for you. I'm still sorting through the lists of fired employees and doing a background check on each one. The vandalism worries me more than the thefts. That fire early this morning means our friend has taken things up a notch."

"Find the son-of-a-bitch who set that fire," Callahan said, standing. "And I won't make a move on Bryce without proof."

"We'll get the proof," Logan said. "I've got some ideas we can go over."

"I've already restricted access to the bids to just a few key employees." Dan looked at his watch. "I have a meeting in a few minutes. Let's get together tomorrow."

Logan stood and gathered his papers into the envelope. "If I can get away. I don't want Doriana suspicious. It was a close call this morning at the fire site. I think I put her off, but she's a smart lady." Guilt formed a ball in his stomach. He hated lying to Doriana. But the assignment demanded secrecy.

"My daughter is smart," Dan said. He threw Logan a wry look. "She's lots smarter than Franco."

"She works hard for you," Logan said.

"I know she does," Callahan said. "She works too hard. The job and her son. They're her life."

What about this Josh guy? Logan wanted to ask. Did Doriana have a secret life no one could guess? How deeply did she love this guy? Doriana's love life wasn't his concern. So why did twin fists of hurt and jealously punch him in the gut at the thought of her with another man?

CHAPTER EIGHT

Doriana pulled off her boots and flopped onto the bed. She'd eaten too much, but it was Thanksgiving.

Mom and Nonna had served up their usual outstanding fare, Italian dishes—eggplant parmesan, ravioli and wedding soup—along with turkey and all the trimmings. And enough pies and pastries, or *dolce*, as Nonna called dessert, to feed a small country. She had enough food in her to last until the New Year.

Doriana grabbed the remote and turned the TV to a mindless sitcom, then spiked up the volume. With Josh spending the night at her parents, the house was way too quiet.

Thank God for her parents, even though they meddled at times. They understood that she and Josh needed space from each other. She couldn't tell her parents of her nagging fear that Josh was involved with the fire at the construction site. He still refused to tell her where he'd been until one o'clock this past Monday morning.

She picked up the remote again and flipped through the stations, barely noticing what flashed on the screen. Josh was more uncontrollable every day. Was he becoming like Logan as a teen, wild and rebellious?

Doriana turned off the TV and dropped the remote on the bed. Thinking about Logan teased her with questions. Why was Logan at the fire site with her dad? That story about his having fire experience didn't ring true. What were Logan and her father hiding?

Thankfully, the workweek had been short with the

two-day holiday. She needed time away from Logan and all the longings, confusion and guilt he stirred in her.

She trusted Anita to keep her secret. Would her own guilt force the truth? Logan hadn't cared enough to stay around the first time. Would knowing about Josh keep him here now? Doriana got up from the bed and ran impatient fingers through her hair. She was obsessing way too much about Logan.

She walked toward the bathroom, pulling her sweater over her head. Too bad she couldn't peel away her problems as smoothly. The ring of the phone stopped her. Slipping her sweater back on, she hurried to answer it. Josh calling to say goodnight? She doubted it.

"Hello," she said into the receiver.

"Hello, sexy." At the crude, unfamiliar voice, she tightened her grip on the phone. Chills chased up her spine.

"Who is this?" Her voice shook.

"Oh, you don't know me. Not yet. But I sure know you. You're sexy as hell, especially in those tight black pants."

Doriana slammed down the phone. Her insides quivered and she ran trembling hands along the sides of her black pants. Had her caller guessed at what she wore? Or was he watching? She gulped air.

The phone rang again and she let out a small cry. She balled her hands, digging her nails into her palms. She would not pick up the phone. The answering machine clicked on.

"You can't get away from me that easy." The harsh voice, laced with menace, froze her. "I know you're alone." Almost seeing his leer, she shoved a shaking fist to her mouth.

"Let me in, bitch. I'll show a hot number like you what a real man is. Not like that pretty boy you've been hanging around with."

His loud cackle shot knifepoints of fear through her and she stifled a scream. The phone clicked off.

The silence of the empty house closed around her. She glanced toward the windows. Could he see her through the sheer curtains? Trembling, she sank onto the bed and clutched the chenille spread as if she could hide herself in its folds. She couldn't stay here, but she dared not leave. He could be waiting outside. She hadn't set the security alarm. She reached for the phone. Her dad would know what to do.

With her hand on the receiver, she froze. Her dad had looked tired all day. He'd been under a lot of stress. Remembering his doctor's advice to take it easy, she knew she couldn't put more strain on him.

The cops? Would the police even get involved? And if they did, they'd come eventually and look around, then leave. And she'd still be alone.

Logan. He would help. She had his cell phone number somewhere. She ran to her purse where it lay on the floor and rummaged through it with nervous fingers until she found the slip of paper with Logan's number.

Taking calming breaths she punched in the number. *Please answer, Logan, please.*

Her spirits sank with each unanswered ring. Was he with Candi? Or another woman? Hurt mingled with her fear.

"Tanner here."

Relief spiked through her at the sound of his voice.

"Logan?" A sob escaped her.

"Doriana? What's wrong?"

The concern in his voice made tears spill out. Despite the tension between them, Logan would protect her. "Someone called," she said, swiping at tears. "Outside. He knows where I live. He could hurt my son." Anger, swift and hard, tightened her stomach. "That bastard will not touch my son."

"No one will hurt your or your son, Doriana. Did you recognize his voice?"

"No, but he's watching me, the son-of-a-bitch . He said awful things. How dare he do this to me."

"I'm coming right over. Give me your address."

Doriana chewed her lip as she paced her living room, waiting for Logan. The wool of her Oriental carpets rubbed against her bare feet. She welcomed the slight pain as a respite from the numbing fear that clenched her stomach.

She'd set the alarm. If anyone activated it, the security company would be alerted. But by the time help arrived it might be too late. "Stop it," she whispered to the empty room. The heater kicked on and she started. She had to calm down. Logan would be here soon.

She looked at the brass clock over the mantle. How far away was Logan? She had no idea where he lived.

Her gaze slid to the side table next to the sofa. Pictures of a smiling teen-age Josh adorned the teak surface. Doriana ran around the room, gathering up all the pictures of Josh, except for a few baby ones. She threw them into the desk drawer and pushed it shut.

The doorbell rang. She jumped.

She walked cautiously toward the door. "Who's there?"

"Logan."

She disarmed her security system, threw open the door and pulled Logan in, locking the door behind him. "Logan." She flung herself into his arms.

He gathered her close. "It's okay, sweetheart. You're safe."

He kissed the top of her head and held her against his strong chest. Her trembling started anew and he pulled her closer.

"Tell me what happened," he said.

The steady beat of Logan's heart gradually soothed her.

"Phone call. Horrible and vile." Her voice sounded muffled against his chest.

"And you have no clue who he is?" The dead calm of Logan's voice sent a chill through Doriana.

Shaking her head, she pulled away to look up at him. "He knows what I'm wearing."

Logan stiffened. "The bastard. Don't worry, Dorie, he won't hurt you. I'll make sure of that."

The glittering anger in Logan's eyes left no doubt. She shuddered. "I know you will, but what can we do?"

"I don't think the police will get involved unless there's been a definite threat," Logan said. "Maybe the phone company can put a tracer. It's too late to call them tonight."

"I don't want to be alone, Logan."

He pulled her to him again. "I won't leave you, Doriana. I'll stay as long as you need me."

Like you stayed all those years ago when I needed you? The thought shot through her mind. She forced it away.

"He's on the machine," she said, pointing to the phone with a shaking finger. "The scum who called."

"I'll listen in a minute," Logan said, "but first I want to check every door and window. Where's your son? Is he okay?"

"My son?" She pulled away. "He's at my parents."

"Good," Logan said.

A pinprick of guilt stabbed her. She hadn't lied. Josh was at her parents.

"Where's your basement?" Logan asked.

"Off the kitchen."

"Stay here. I'll go through each room."

She nodded.

"Everything's locked tight," Logan said, entering the living room minutes later after checking the house.

Too nervous to sit, Doriana stood next to the couch, hugging herself against her fear.

Logan's gaze pierced hers. "No one will hurt you while I'm here, Doriana."

"Please stay with me until the morning, Logan."

He was at her side in two steps. Reaching out, he rubbed his thumb over her cheekbone. "I won't leave you."

His eyes told the truth of his words. He wouldn't abandon her, not tonight. Bittersweet sorrow tightened her chest. A long time ago he'd pledged his heart forever. He hadn't kept that promise. She released a sigh, determined to forget about the past for now.

He studied her. She read concern in his eyes, but something else, something smoky and dark. The heat of arousal pulled low in her belly and she dropped her gaze. She couldn't allow hope into her heart. She'd learned that lesson a long time ago.

"Get some rest, Doriana," he said. "I'll listen to the phone message then settle down on the couch. You're safe now."

"I'm not sleepy," she said. "Would you like some tea?"

He nodded. "Okay."

"I'll be in the kitchen while you replay the message," she said, hurrying out of the room. "I can't hear that vileness again."

****

Logan hit the play button on the answering machine. The evil spewing from the mouth of the scum who threatened Doriana made white-hot anger boil through him.

Who was 'pretty boy'? Josh? Was the slime ball on the phone stalking Doriana? Rage pounded through him. He'd tear the city apart until he caught the jerk.

He found Doriana leaning against the kitchen sink, her head down and her body rigid. He put his arms around her waist and pulled her against him. She slowly relaxed and he held her closer, liking the way her head fit under his chin.

He inhaled her cologne, expensive and spicy, not the usual rose scent she wore to work. Had she been with the Josh guy earlier? Had she worn it for him? He closed his eyes against the sudden pain that gnawed his insides. That didn't matter. She'd called him, not Josh. She needed him and he wouldn't let her down.

She felt so good, as if she belonged in his arms. For a few minutes he allowed himself to imagine that she was his again. He straightened. He had a job to do. He would protect her and keep her safe.

"I listened," he said, still holding her against him. "Sick bastard. He blocked his number from your phone's ID system. Maybe the phone company can find the number. We'll call them in the morning. Stupid jerk recorded his voice. Maybe the phone company can use that."

He pulled her closer. "No one will hurt you, Doriana. I promise."

"I know, Logan."

She turned in his arms to look up at him. The trust in her eyes threatened his control. It would be so easy to give in to his baser instincts, to kiss her full lips until she begged for more.

"How about that tea," he said.

She smiled through the tears that glistened in her eyes. "And some pumpkin pie."

"With whipped cream?" he asked, smiling.

"I've got whipped cream," she said.

84

"Then we're all set."

****

Doriana, sitting across from Logan at the center counter in her kitchen, smiled at his unabashed enjoyment of the dessert. Cinnamon and nutmeg and ginger tea laced with honey melded with the soft sounds of jazz playing on the radio. She could almost forget the ugliness of the past few hours. Could almost tell Logan about Josh.

"My mom made the pie," she blurted. She couldn't tell him about Josh.

"Can you cook like this?" he asked.

She laughed. "Not at all. I didn't inherit the cooking gene from Nonna or Mom."

"You've got whipped cream, though." His crooked grin warmed her more than the mug of tea she cradled.

"Logan, thanks for coming over. Things are strained between us sometimes, but you were there for me when I needed you."

He gave her that lopsided grin again. Her pulse did a little dance.

"All in a day's work," he said. "You are my boss after all."

She laughed. Logan could always make her laugh. "I think this goes above and beyond your job description."

His intense look made her glance quickly away to stare at the clock on the wall behind him. Was it really only midnight?

"Doriana?"

She turned to him.

"Did you love him?"

Her chest constricted. "Love who?"

"Your son's father."

"Why do you ask that?"

He shrugged. "I wanted to know. But it's none of my business."

"I loved him very much," she said.

"What happened to him?"

Tell him. Tell him, her conscience urged. "He left, Logan, I..."

"He's a fool," Logan said.

"What?"

85

Cara Marsi

"The guy who left you." His jaw clenched.

"He's no fool," she said.

"How can you defend him after what he's done?" Anger sparked from Logan's eyes.

Doriana half rose in her seat. "You don't know..."

"Forget it," Logan said. "I shouldn't have asked."

She blew her breath out and settled back. "Okay." Guilt curled around her heart. She should tell him. She couldn't. She had to think about it.

"Great pie," he said, smiling.

Despite his smile, anger lingered in his eyes. "Nothing like home-baked pumpkin pie on Thanksgiving," he said, pushing his empty plate away.

She studied him. Thick lashes framed golden-green eyes. She'd always loved Logan's eyes.

"If you keep staring at me like that, I may forget I'm a nice guy."

Her face heated. She cut a chunk of pie and put it in her mouth. She chewed slowly, wishing she could digest her wayward thoughts away.

"What are you thinking?" he asked.

She swallowed her pie. "Where did you have Thanksgiving dinner?" The question slipped out.

"I ate with the guys at the shelter."

She choked and took a quick sip of tea.

"You live in a shelter?"

He smiled. "No, Doriana, I'm not that hard on my luck. I helped serve meals at the shelter. I do it every Thanksgiving and Christmas. It's what people without families do." Sadness flicked in his eyes for a few seconds.

Fighting her guilt, she reached out to put her hand over his big one on the counter. Should she have invited him to her parents? She couldn't. Too much was at stake.

"That's a very generous thing to do," she said.

He pulled his hand away. "Don't give me more credit than I deserve."

"You have no one?" she asked. "You never talked about your family. Before, I mean." She chewed her lip, wishing she could bite back the words. She hadn't wanted to bring up the past, their past.

He stiffened and a muscle worked in his jaw. "My mom died when I was thirteen. I don't know if my dad is

86

dead or alive, and frankly I don't care."

The bitterness in his voice and the loneliness that washed over his features squeezed her heart with pity. She knew he didn't want her pity.

"Oh, Logan, no matter what he did he's still your father."

"Don't go there, Doriana."

She studied the golden tea in her cup. The clock on the wall ticked loudly, but time seemed to stop. Releasing her breath, she looked into his eyes. "You left me."

Surprise widened his eyes before he quickly recovered and the cool mask slipped on again. "I had to go."

"Why?" Now that she'd opened the cage to the ugly monster between them, she couldn't put it back.

Tension held him rigid. "It was a long time ago."

She knew by the stubborn line of his jaw that he wouldn't say more. Her shoulders sagged.

"Go to bed, Doriana."

"I'm not sleepy."

"You're probably more tired than you realize." He stood. "Go on up. I'll clean the kitchen. You've had a rough day."

She pushed herself off the chair. "You'll stay the night?"

"I'll stay as long as you need me."

She looked deeply into his eyes before turning from the room. How long did she need him? Just for tonight? There was a time when she couldn't imagine life without him.

****

Doriana brushed her teeth, fluffed her hair and bit down on her lips to give them color. "What are you doing?" she asked her reflection. Trying to make herself attractive? She was going to bed. Alone. Logan would sleep on the couch. And that's where he'd stay.

She padded to the bedroom and opened a dresser drawer. Her fingers brushed over a silk nightgown, a sexy extravagance that she'd never worn. "No you don't," she whispered.

She pulled out a high-necked cotton gown and slammed the drawer shut, locking away the silk and her own dangerous desires. Doriana slipped the nightgown on and buttoned the neckline. Too bad she couldn't button the restless yearning that fired her senses. Her body and soul cried out for the warmth of Logan's arms and the passion of his kisses.

"Stop it, Doriana." Fear and insecurity had weakened her. That's all it was. Logan walked out on her once and he didn't care enough now to tell her why. She'd made a life for herself and Josh without him. She didn't need Logan. So why did she feel this aching loneliness?

She yanked her bedcovers down and climbed into bed. She would not think about Logan. She would not dream about him. Doriana reached over to turn off the bedside lamp. Josh, framed in his latest school picture, smiled back at her. His eyes and smile, so like Logan's, seemed to mock her. She opened the night table drawer and slid the picture in.

She lay in the darkened room, listening to the house sounds. Did her house always creak like this? Did Logan lie awake on the sofa and think of her? They had a son, but they'd never spent the night together. Now she and Logan slept a floor apart, breathing the same air, hearing the same sounds. So close and yet they might as well be an ocean away.

She punched her pillow as if the act might purge her thoughts. A faint sliver of moonlight glimmered through the sheer curtains to reflect on the ceiling. Did the moonlight skim Logan too?

The shatter of glass brought her upright. Logan.

She threw back the covers and leapt out of bed. The staccato of her heart kept beat with her feet as she raced down the stairs. A break-in? The alarm hadn't gone off.

The pillow and blanket she'd given Logan were folded on the couch, but no Logan. A string of soft curses came from the kitchen. She hurried toward the sound and froze when she reached the doorway.

Logan, clad only in jeans, swept away broken glass with a broom.

She couldn't quite stifle her laugh.

"Damn," he said and turned toward her, dropping the broom. He let out an exasperated sigh. "Sorry about the mess, Doriana. I broke a glass."

"Don't worry about it," she said with a shrug.

They stared at each other. His masculine beauty held her. Her gaze scanned his muscular chest, covered with a light matting of golden hairs that narrowed to a vee before disappearing into the waistband of his jeans. Her throat went dry. "You're very tan," she said in a whisper.

She clutched at the neck of her nightgown as his hot gaze traveled her body. She glanced down, The bright kitchen light made the thin cotton of her gown transparent as silk. Her face burned and she knew she blushed.

"Go to bed, Doriana."

The roughness of his voice hit her raw emotions, releasing the tension of the past weeks and the numbing fear earlier tonight. A sob escaped her. Her knees watered and her body sagged. Logan grabbed her before she could sink to the floor.

She clung to him, digging her nails into the firm skin of his shoulders. Tears spilled from her eyes.

He brushed a tender kiss on her forehead. "It's okay, Doriana. It's been a tough night."

She gripped his shoulders and pressed her face against him. The rough hairs on his chest brushed her sensitized skin, filling her with an aching awareness. She inhaled his male scent, woodsy like the leaves rustling outside.

"Doriana, sweetheart," he said. "I know you're upset, but I think you've scarred my shoulders with your nails."

She jumped back, swiping at tears. Hysterical laughter bubbled out of her. Logan's hands spanned her waist.

"I didn't mean to hurt you," she said, finding her voice.

"It's okay, Dorie. You didn't hurt me."

At the catch in his voice she locked her gaze with his. He stared at her with eyes darkened by desire. She reached out to skim a finger along the fullness of his lips.

He groaned and gently pushed her away. "Leave, Doriana, before we do something we'll both regret in the morning."

He was right. But why did she feel so...cheated?

His gaze softened and he brushed his thumb over her

cheekbone. "I know you're scared. I'll stay with you until you fall asleep. Okay?"

She nodded.

Logan followed her up the stairs, so close his body heat warmed her. No one would harm her while Logan was in the house. But who would protect her heart?

She got into bed and gathered the covers close under her chin. Protection against Logan? Or herself?

Logan sat on the edge of the bed. The pale moonlight caressed his chiseled features and sculpted chest. He looked like a statue, a golden Adonis. But Logan was flesh and blood. Her pulse kicked up.

Doriana turned her back to Logan and to the longing he stirred in her, a longing that only he could satisfy.

"I'm here for you, Dorie," he whispered. He rubbed her shoulder, his touch heating her through the bedclothes.

A feeling of peace, laced with sadness, stole over Doriana. What would her life have been like if she and Logan had married all those years ago? Would he ever tell her why he left? Would it be reason enough to forgive him?

****

Bright sunlight teased Doriana's eyes open. She let out a contented sigh and snuggled against the warm body nestled next to hers. She hadn't felt this peaceful in years. Warm body?

She stiffened and turned slowly to face a sleeping Logan. Despite the chenille spread separating them, his heat reached out to her. She should wake him, should insist he leave immediately. But she just wanted to lie there and drink in his beauty.

Golden eyelashes curved against his high cheekbones. His tousled hair begged for her touch. Unable to resist, she smoothed hair back from his face. He looked soft and young, with traces of the boy she'd loved. What in his life had put the hard edges to his features? Where had he been all these years? And had he thought about her at all?

"Logan." The word sighed through the room.

He opened his eyes slowly. "Morning," he said, his voice thick and rich. Awareness dawned in his sleep-filled eyes and he rolled off the bed to stand in front of her in all his masculine glory. Sunlight bronzed the gold of his skin. She forgot to breathe.

"God, Doriana, I'm sorry." He scrubbed a hand over his face. "I didn't mean to stay in your bed, but I nodded off."

She sat up and shivered in the sudden chill as the covers slipped off. "I'm glad you were here." She couldn't tell him she'd had the best night's sleep in a long time.

His gaze skimmed her and he blew a breath out. "You're determined to test my willpower, aren't you?"

"What?" She glanced down. She had felt warm during the night, and half-asleep, she had unbuttoned her nightgown. The tops of her breasts were exposed now and her nipples pebbled under Logan's hot gaze.

She licked her lips. A small groan escaped him.

Their gazes locked. The years seemed to peel away like the layers of bedclothes. They were young and reckless and so in love. Did their bodies recognize what they weren't ready to acknowledge? Hope and desire heated a sensuous path through her.

"Logan," she said in a soft voice. Her body wanted the man he'd become, but her soul yearned for the boy she'd loved.

"What if I asked you to make love to me," she said.

Desire, pain, and fear flitted across his face. "I couldn't," he said in a tortured voice. "We can't."

Humiliation washed over her and she looked quickly away.

He eased on the bed and took her hands in his. She burned where he touched her.

"Look at me, Dorie."

She turned to him.

He touched her face with gentle fingers. Was she just imagining that his hand shook? "I want you. But there are things about me you don't know. Things I can't share."

Hurt and anger formed a knot in her stomach. Would he ever trust her enough? She pulled free. "Go. Leave me alone."

"I wish I could leave you alone." He skimmed a calloused finger over her lips.

"I think it would be best if you leave now," she said.

He flinched as if she'd hit him. Pain shadowed his eyes. He stood. "I'll call the phone company from downstairs. They probably can't do anything yet but I want to put them on notice."

"Ill get dressed and be downstairs in a few minutes," she said.

He studied her. "I don't like leaving you alone over the weekend. I can stay with you."

She clenched her hand around the sheets. "No."

He held up his hand, stopping her protest. "No strings attached. You can bring your son home. I'll make sure you're both safe."

Panic seized her. "You can't. I can't." She drew a calming breath. "I'll go to my parents for the weekend."

He gave her a long look. "Okay. I'll meet you downstairs." He turned and left the room. His footsteps on the stairs seemed to rebuke her with his rejection.

Was she a fool for Logan all over again?

****

Logan slammed the door to his rattletrap Jeep and thrust the key in the ignition. How had he allowed things to get out of control? He'd compromised his integrity. She'd asked him for protection. And he'd hurt her.

He started the car and eased out of the driveway, resisting the urge to drive like the wild boy he used to be. He wasn't a teenager any more. And he wanted Doriana the way a man wants a woman, passionately, completely, all-consuming. She didn't want him, not really. She'd only reached out today because of her own fear and vulnerability. He'd done the right thing, walking away. He felt like hell.

CHAPTER NINE

Doriana smiled a greeting at the other riders and eased into the crowded elevator. She punched the number for her floor, then punched it again when the elevator doors didn't close quickly enough. She glanced at her watch. A half hour late. She was almost never late for work.

Each stop of the elevator increased her agitation. After the long holiday weekend where sleep eluded her most nights, she'd been unable to wake herself this morning. Or maybe it was dread at facing Logan that made her wish that Monday wouldn't come. She hadn't seen him since Friday morning when she'd humiliated herself by asking him to make love to her. And he'd turned her down. Doriana stiffened her shoulders. She'd act like Friday never happened. *Yeah, right*, a small voice taunted.

The elevator doors opened to her floor and she stepped out. Taking a deep breath, she headed for her office. Gratitude tempered her apprehension. Logan came to her aid when she needed him. He'd called her cell phone every day since Friday to be sure she was okay. A twinge of guilt pulled her. He thought she spent the weekend at her parents.

When she entered her office Logan looked up from his computer. Relief flashed in his eyes and he came around the desk. "Are you all right, Doriana? I was just about to phone you."

The concern in his voice sharpened her guilt. "I'm fine. Overslept. Holiday weekend."

"And a rough one at that," he said softly.

Her face heated. Was he thinking about Friday morning? But she read only friendly sympathy in his eyes. Apparently her clumsy attempt to get him into her bed meant nothing to him. She should feel relieved. Instead she felt rejected.

"Everything okay?" he asked. "No more phone calls?"

She shifted her briefcase to her other hand, wishing she could shift her thoughts as easily from the picture of Logan in her bed and her overwhelming need for his touch and warmth. She'd thrown herself at him because she felt scared and vulnerable. That was all. And he'd recognized her insecurities. She was glad for his restraint. Someday she'd actually believe that.

Doriana shook off her thoughts and threw him a smile. "No more calls. Logan, I really appreciate your coming over Thursday night, especially on a holiday."

"It was nothing," he said. "I wasn't doing anything." His eyes darkened. "Even if I were busy, I would have helped you. I'd never let anyone hurt you, Dorie."

The caress in his voice and his pet name for her squeezed her heart with regret for what might have been. *But you hurt me all those years ago, Logan.* The painful words came unbidden to her mind.

"Are you sure you're all right?" he asked.

She notched her chin. "I'm fine. Just thinking about all the work ahead of me. I guess I'd better get busy." She brushed past him to her office.

****

Logan released a breath and rounded his desk to sit in his chair. Why did he have the feeling that he'd somehow hurt her now? If she only knew the effort it cost not to take her into his arms and hold her until the wall she'd built around her feelings dissolved.

Maybe he'd let her down all those years ago, but he'd had no choice. She'd had her whole future ahead of her, a future that couldn't include him. Doriana deserved better than a guy with too much scarred baggage, a guy who carried the mean streets of Philadelphia in his soul. He wouldn't disappoint her again. He'd protect her and keep his hands off her at the same time. Whatever they once shared died the night he left Philadelphia. A small voice he couldn't silence mocked him with the lie of his words. Logan punched the computer keys, not caring what he typed. He should have given this job to one of his subordinates.

****

"How about lunch?"

At Logan's softly spoken words, Doriana looked up from her computer. "Lunch?"

He lounged against the doorframe. Despite his casual stance, he looked like a dangerous animal, coiled and ready to spring. Was she his prey? She swallowed.

"You need to eat." His lopsided grin made heat curl in her stomach. "Let's go."

"Go? Together?" Her throat tightened. After Friday she couldn't trust herself with him. "I can't. I'm swamped."

"Lighten up, Doriana. The world won't end just because you didn't stay at your desk for an hour." He walked into the room to stand in front of her. "You've been under a lot of stress. You need to relax. I thought we were friends."

She shifted uncomfortably. "Not exactly friends."

"Then what are we?" he said, moving closer.

"Co-workers."

Arching an eyebrow, he straightened. "Reminding me that you're the boss?"

The challenge in his eyes made her bristle. "I'm not some snooty elitist."

"Prove it." He planted his palms firmly on the wood surface of her desk. Sunlight glinted on his days-old growth of beard and the firm set of his jaw. She grabbed a pencil and twisted her fingers around it, resisting the urge to touch his face.

"I don't want to spar with you, Doriana. I just want to take you to lunch."

She met his unwavering gaze. She'd prove to herself that she could handle her emotions where Logan was concerned. He'd be gone in a few months anyway. The thought darkened her mood like the sudden clouds that scudded over the sky and obscured the weak sunlight.

"It's my turn to pay," she said, standing. "You paid for the cheesesteaks."

95

"You're on," he said, throwing her a devastating smile that weakened her knees like steel girders set in sand.

The little deli was crowded but they'd managed to find a small table squeezed into a corner at the back. Doriana looked down at the thick sandwich in front of her. The spicy odor of warm pastrami and hot mustard churned her stomach in delicious anticipation. What had possessed her to order such a thing? She hadn't eaten pastrami since high school. She raised her gaze to find Logan staring at her, an amused light in his eyes.

"What?" she said.

"You going to eat all that?" Laughter tinged his voice. "How do you manage to keep so slim? You wolfed down your cheesesteak the other night."

"I only eat like this when I'm around you."

His mouth quirked in a knowing grin. "Why is that?"

"Shut up and eat your turkey sandwich," she said.

His unaffected laugh made her laugh too. How long since she'd laughed like a kid? Being with Logan stripped away the years, making her feel young and carefree again. She picked up her over-stuffed sandwich and took a bite, as if she could chew away her traitorous thoughts.

Logan watched her. She stopped chewing, lost in the intensity of his eyes. Could he read her mind? Did he know the effect his nearness had on her? Of course he did. Hadn't she practically begged him to make love to her the other morning? Face burning, she tore her gaze away.

A prickling at the back of her neck made her look toward the door. A man, slender and dark-haired, with a sharp nose and whip-thin body, watched her. His pale blue eyes impaled hers. She shuddered.

"What's wrong?" Logan followed her gaze to the door. "Who is he?"

"I don't know." Her voice shook slightly.

"Mean-looking dude," Logan said. "He looks familiar. I don't like the way he's staring at you." He pushed up from his seat.

Doriana placed her hand on his arm, stopping him. "Let it go, Logan. Maybe he thinks I'm someone else."

With a smirk in her direction, the man slunk away.

Doriana picked up her glass of iced tea and took a

sip, hoping the cool liquid would calm her. And cleanse her. Why did a man she'd never seen before make her feel so dirty?

Anger lit Logan's eyes. "After what happened to you over the weekend, I don't like strange men looking at you. There was something weird about him."

She shrugged, trying for a composure she didn't feel. "It was probably nothing, Logan. I'm perfectly safe." But was she? A small shiver worked its way up her spine.

"Hell, I don't like any man looking at you, Dorie."

The possessive tone of his voice almost made her drop the glass she held. "What?"

"Forget it," he said, his voice tight. He picked up his sandwich but his gaze held hers. "Until we find the scum who called you, I don't want you going out alone."

"Are you telling me what to do?" she asked. "I can take care of myself."

He slapped his sandwich onto the plate and leaned closer. "I know you can take care of yourself, but that phone call Thursday night wasn't anything to dismiss lightly. Take precautions."

"Okay," she said. "I'll get Josh to go with me."

The breath whooshed out of her lungs. What had possessed her to say Josh's name?

Logan tensed. "Do whatever you need to stay safe."

They finished their lunch in silence. The crowd at the deli thinned. Doriana glanced at the clock on the wall. The hour had gone by quickly, too quickly. She paid the bill and asked to have half her sandwich wrapped up.

"Thanks for lunch," Logan said.

"You're welcome."

"Admit this was better than sitting at your desk." He gave her a teasing grin.

"It was," she said, laughing. The tension between them disappeared with the lunchtime crowd.

"I love to hear you laugh," he said softly. "Doriana, why didn't you ever marry?"

She froze. "That's really none of your business, Logan." She leaned closer. Two could play this game. "Why didn't you ever marry?"

His eyes glinted. He folded his arms across his chest and smiled. "How do you know I've never married? Or that I'm not married now?"

Chills, as if someone had dropped a cup of ice down her back, raced through Doriana. "Married?" The word came out a croak. She cleared her throat. "You can't be married."

Logan arched a brow. "Why not? You think no decent woman would marry me because I don't have a regular job?"

"Of course not."

The waitress brought the bag with her sandwich. Clutching the bag, Doriana stood. She needed to get out. Now. She'd let Logan kiss her. Wanted him to do more. And he might be married. She'd never thought. She'd just assumed.

Logan grabbed her hand. "Sit."

The deli's few other patrons glanced over at them. Only her fear of attracting more attention kept her from running. She sat slowly down.

Logan smiled. Damn his smile that could melt her bones a mile away.

He reached out to skim his finger over her lips. "Does it bother you that I might be married?"

"I couldn't care less."

"Liar," he said. "But don't worry. I'm not married. Never been married. I was just teasing you, Doriana. You've always been so easy to tease. I couldn't resist."

Relief flooded her. She squashed the urge to smile. But she wouldn't let him off too easily. "I knew you were teasing," she said, standing. Head high, she walked away.

Laughing softly, Logan followed her out of the deli.

****

"Damn it, Tanner. You're supposed to be one of the best in the business. And I'm paying you a truckload of money. I want results."

Logan sat at the small conference table and watched Dan Callahan pace the spacious room like a caged lion, impatience and frustration on his rugged features.

"You know I'm the best in the business," Logan said as calmly as he could. He knew enough about Callahan to know the man was as much bluster as action. "I've been on this assignment less than a month. I've made progress. Things would have gone a little easier if you'd been up front with me."

Callahan whirled to face him. "What do you mean by that?"

"James's gambling problem," Logan said.

Dan waved his hand. "Oh, that. I'd forgotten all about it. Bryce is rehabilitated. All that happened a long time ago. No need to bring it up again."

Some of the air had gone out of Callahan's bravado. He sat on the wide windowsill and faced Logan. Behind him the muted Philadelphia skyline jutted through the gray sky, a shrouded contrast to the pale sunlight earlier in the day when he and Doriana had lunch at the small deli. Logan brushed away the image of Doriana. He had trouble enough with her father.

Logan tamped down his annoyance with the older man. "You can't decide what's important and not important, Callahan. Leave that to me."

"You accuse Bryce of stealing from me," Callahan said. "He wouldn't do that."

"You can't tell what people will do if pushed," Logan said. "I've pretty much ruled out the others who have access to the bids. But I'll delve into their backgrounds a little more." His gaze held Callahan's. "Bryce James might have an incentive for needing money. Gambling debts or maybe a woman."

Sadness passed over Dan's features. "You're sure he has a mistress?"

"Positive." Logan leaned forward. "But something bothers me about this whole thing. James is almost too convenient."

"I agree," Callahan said. "Bryce's betrayal would hurt more than anyone's, other than Doriana or Franco."

"We need to set a trap," Logan said. "We catch James or prove his innocence. You never know what a trap might snare."

"What do you have in mind?" Callahan asked.

"Do you have any jobs coming up for bid?"

Callahan nodded. "The Devlin project."

"How about two bids," Logan said. "A fake bid Bryce knows and the real bid that only you know. If the fake bid is leaked, we've got our man."

Dan rubbed a hand over his face. He looked haggard.

Pity for the older man settled over Logan. Callahan carried a lot of responsibility on his broad shoulders.

"It won't be easy," Callahan said. "Three other people besides Bryce and me are privy to the bids."

Logan nodded and glanced at the clock. "See what you can do. I'd better get back. Doriana thinks you wanted to see me about the fire at the site. I don't want her suspicious." Logan stood and began gathering papers. A thought that had been gnawing at the back of his mind made him stop.

"Callahan, did you start this business alone or with a partner?"

Dan slid off the windowsill with a questioning look. "Why do you ask?"

"I read as much as I could on your background before I started this assignment. One obscure article mentioned a partner. I'd forgotten until now."

Dan shrugged. "I started with someone, but he didn't have the heart for it. A little lazy. I bought him out long before the company took off."

"What happened to him?" Logan asked.

"Sad story," Callahan said, shaking his head. "Turned to alcohol. He's dead. Died broke."

Memories wrenched Logan. He knew what alcohol could do to a man, to a family. Was his own father broke and living on the streets? Was he dead? He didn't want to care, but a small part of him did. He shoved aside the painful memories.

"What was your partner's name?" he asked.

Callahan frowned. "Chuck Rove."

"Does he have family in the area?"

"Wife and son. Lived in Delaware County last I heard."

Logan stuffed papers into his briefcase. "I'll run a check on Rove's family. Seems like a long shot, but you never know."

Logan slipped into his office and put his briefcase under the desk. Doriana's door was partially open. He tapped lightly on it before opening it all the way and stepping into her office.

She looked up. Did he imagine the awareness in those deep chocolate eyes before a professional mask settled over her fine-boned features? Sadness for what might have been threatened his composure. He straightened and plastered a smile on his face. He'd been dwelling too damn much on the past lately.

"Just wanted you to know I'm back."

She nodded. "That took a little longer than I thought."

"You know your father. He likes to talk."

She arched one beautiful black brow. "Apparently he likes talking to you."

"Am I interrupting anything?"

The deep voice, laced with humor, came from behind Logan. He turned quickly.

Franco stood in the doorway, his arm around the waist of a curvaceous blonde who towered over him by six inches. The woman's green gaze raked Logan, like a cobra looking at dinner. Where did Franco get these women?

He heard Doriana's breath hitch. "What do you want, Franco? Can't you see we're busy?"

Franco lips quirked in a leer. Logan held himself rigid, hands balled at his sides. He'd sure like a go at wiping that smirk off Franco's face.

"Busy?" Franco said. "Is that what you call it?"

Doriana stood up and walked to the front of her desk. "If you came here to foist another job on me, forget it."

Franco made an attempt to look offended. "Doriana, you'll give Linda a bad image of me."

"Linda?" Doriana glanced at Franco's latest piece of arm candy. How did she keep track of Franco's women? Logan wondered.

Franco walked into the office, his arm still around Linda. "Doriana, Logan, this is Linda." Franco squeezed Linda's waist.

"Nice to meet you both," Linda said in a sultry voice. She stared at Logan and ignored Doriana.

"What do you want, Franco?" Doriana asked.

"I don't want anything, sis. I came to thank you for helping with the Tremont report."

Doriana coughed. "You want to thank me?"

"Sure." Franco threw her a charming smile that made Logan want to gag.

She rolled her eyes. "Spare me, Franco."

Franco reached into his jacket pocket and pulled out two tickets and handed them to Doriana. "For the Flyers game tonight. Luxury suite. You've got to share it with a couple of contractors, but they're good guys."

He rubbed his hand down the blonde's arm. "You and I have other plans, don't we, baby?"

Linda giggled. Doriana and Logan exchanged looks.

"I've got a lot of work to do," Doriana said.

"Screw the work," Franco said. "Take Josh. He'll love it."

"Josh can't make it."

Did Logan imagine that Doriana's hands holding the tickets shook?

Franco shrugged. "Those are good tickets. Hate to see them wasted." He looked over at Logan. "Take Logan. He helped you with the report. But don't tell Josh you took someone else to see the Flyers."

"We'll work out something," she said. "I'm busy now." She grabbed papers from her desk, ignoring Franco.

"Enjoy the game," Franco said.

Consumed by jealousy at the mention of Josh's name, Logan barely noticed the sound of the office door closing.

"Take the tickets, Logan," Doriana said.

He turned to her. She looked pale and scared. Scared of what? Her face had drained of color when Franco mentioned Josh. What hold did this Josh guy have on her? Pride stiffened Logan's spine. To hell with Josh, whoever he was. "I'll only take them if we go to the game together."

She jerked her head up. "Together? We can't. My son. Can't leave him."

"We'll take him with us," Logan said. "Kids love hockey."

Her face got even paler.

Logan moved closer and touched her chin with his fingers, tilting her face toward his. "Don't trust yourself alone with me?"

"Don't be ridiculous," she said, pulling free.

"Then get a sitter and come to the game with me. You deserve a night out."

They stared at each other. The apprehension in her eyes softened to an awareness that made his groin tighten. "I guess one hockey game can't hurt," she said.

CHAPTER TEN

"Go, Flyers!" Doriana screamed. She jumped up. Her knees hit the table in front of her, tipping the bucket of popcorn and spilling kernels onto the floor. Beer from the glass she held sloshed down her jeans. Beside her, Logan was also on his feet, shouting for the Flyers to score.

The Flyers' puck slid into the other team's net. Logan grabbed Doriana in a crushing hug. More beer splashed.

"My drink," Doriana said, laughing.

"Can't have you wasting good beer," Logan said. He took the glass from her and placed it on the table. The luxury suite at the Wachovia Center had plush seats, tables, a bar and even a hostess to serve them.

Doriana, held in the circle of Logan's arms, smiled up at him. She hadn't had this much fun since...the last time she was with Logan.

"Logan, you're..." She looked into his eyes and the words dried in her throat.

"I'm what?"

"Too much," she whispered.

"Really?" His sexy grin could melt the ice on the rink. "Is this too much?" He bent his head and captured her lips in a kiss that promised much, much more.

He tasted like beer and popcorn and magical nights. She wanted to devour him. The cheering of the crowd and the loud music faded in the passion of Logan's kiss.

"We are at a hockey game, you two."

The laughter and good-natured jibes from the others in the suite cooled Doriana's ardor like chunks of ice hitting her. She pulled out of Logan's arms.

103

Smoothing her hands down the sides of her jeans, Doriana turned to the three middle-aged men who stood at the bar smiling at them. Lost in Logan's feel and taste, she'd momentarily forgotten the others who shared the luxury box with them.

The trio, contractors she knew slightly from business dealings, had started out merely cheerful a few hours ago and were now very drunk. She and Logan had become fast friends with the men in a short time. What was happening to her? Drinking and joking with business associates. Kissing Logan in front of them.

Her professionalism vaporized like steam whenever she was with Logan. She should feel embarrassed, but she just felt ...free.

"I guess I got caught up in the moment," she said to the smiling men.

Logan leaned closer to whisper in her ear. "You can get caught up like that any time."

"Stop it," she whispered back. He laughed.

The game over, Doriana and Logan threaded their way through the crowd to the parking lot. Doriana sighed. The Flyers win had capped off a perfect evening. And it was perfect. She couldn't deny that. For a few hours tonight she'd been able to forget all her problems and pretend she was young and carefree and desperately in love with Logan. In love with Logan. Could it happen again? A knot of fear constricted her chest. She couldn't open her heart to that kind of pain a second time.

When Logan pulled his Jeep in front of her house much later, regret wound its way through Doriana's heart. Back to the real world with its problems and fears.

"Doriana, are you okay? You're so quiet." Logan's voice, husky and thick, filled her with a longing that threatened to melt her right into his arms.

She forced a smile and reached for the door handle. "I'm fine. Just tired. I really had a good time tonight, Logan. But I'd better go. We've got a heavy workload tomorrow." She needed to get out of the car before she did something stupid, like kiss him.

"I'll walk you to your door," Logan said.

"I'll be okay," she said.

"I will walk you to your door. I want you safely in the

house."

Apprehension traveled up her spine. What if Josh opened the door?

She hopped out of the Jeep and hurried up the stairs, Logan close behind. She pushed her key into the lock. *Please, God, let Josh be asleep.*

"I'll see you at work," she said with a quick glance at Logan. She unlocked the door with a shaking hand.

"Doriana." Logan turned her towards him and took her face between his calloused hands.

Her whole body thrummed with awareness. Unable to stop herself, she reached out to touch his high cheekbones. She'd always adored his face, the curves, valleys and ruggedness that gave him a dangerous air. The danger was still there and more potent than ever.

He bent toward her. She lifted her face, on fire for his kiss.

The blast of heavy metal music from inside her house yanked her back to reality. Josh! She pulled away from Logan, losing her balance. He held onto her arms, steadying her.

"I have to go," she said.

"Your babysitter has a great sense of timing," he said with a wry grin. "And won't she wake your son?"

"Babysitter?" She frowned. "Babysitter. My son. I have to go." She was babbling. She pushed open the door a crack, praying Josh wasn't on the other side.

"Doriana." Regret tinged Logan's voice.

"Good night." She slid through the door and locked it behind her. Trembling, she braced herself against it.

Another jolt of ear-splitting music propelled her up the stairs to Josh's room.

Josh threw her a dark look and flicked off the offending music. "I knew that would get you in the house," he said in an accusatory tone.

Standing with his arms folded across his chest and his legs apart, he looked so much like his father. Doriana swallowed around the lump in her throat.

"Was it necessary to wake the neighbors?" she asked.

"You were ready to trade spit with some guy." He wrinkled his nose. "You reek of beer."

Doriana bristled. "That is no way to talk to your

mother. I'm a grown woman. I don't need your permission to go out." *Not even with your father.* She put a hand on her hip. "Didn't you tell me at Nonna's the other day that I should date."

Defiance lashed his features. "This is different. You wanted to kiss him. Who's the guy, Mom?"

He's your father. A small voice dared her to say the words. She couldn't. Not yet. She'd always known she'd have to tell Josh about his father someday. She hadn't expected that day to come pounding at her door so soon.

Drawing a harsh breath, she walked into the room and leaned against the dresser. She ran her finger over the dust on the smooth surface, stalling for time.

"You really need to clean this room, Josh."

"Don't change the subject, Mom."

She shrugged, trying to diffuse the tension that lay heavy over the room like painters' cloth.

"Logan is just a co-worker," she said. *Liar, lia*r, her conscience prodded. She ignored it.

"I don't like him," Josh said in a voice filled with indignation and hurt.

"You don't even know him, Josh." She kept her voice calm and smooth, hoping Josh wouldn't guess at the turmoil clenching her stomach.

Some of the belligerence left Josh's face. He ran fingers through his wavy hair in a gesture she'd seen his father do countless times. Her heart squeezed.

"He looked dangerous," Josh said. "And you like him."

Hurt and fear washed across Josh's face, making him look like a little lost boy. Doriana ran to him and hugged him. He stood stiffly in her arms at first. Then he relaxed and wrapped his arms around her.

What would Josh say if he knew the truth about Logan? Would he want Logan in his life? Could she share Josh after all these years?

She looked up at him. "Josh, you know I love you more than anyone in this world. You'll always be first with me, no matter what happens."

He gave her a searching look. "What's going to happen?"

Doriana stroked a finger down his high cheekbone.

"It's late, sweetheart and we're both tired. Go to bed."

"Something's going on, Mom. Why won't you tell me?"

"You're growing up too fast, Josh." *And you're way too perceptive for your age.* She patted his cheek. "Now go to bed."

What tangled webs we weave. The words mocked her as she headed down the hall to her bedroom. Tangled webs indeed. Her head hurt. She had a confused son. And she feared she was falling in love with his father all over again. God help her.

The phone rang just as she entered her room. Logan? She raced to answer it.

"Out with him again, weren't you, bitch?"

Riveted by fear, Doriana gripped the receiver.

"What did I tell you about that pretty *boy?*" The malicious words slithered over the phone lines. "He can't give you what I can. A woman like you needs a real man."

She slammed down the phone.

"Mom, who was that?" Josh called.

"Wrong number." She hoped Josh didn't notice that her voice shook. She stuffed her fist into her mouth to stop her scream. The scum knew she'd been out. What if he tried to break in while Josh was alone?

****

"That's it," Logan said. "I'm moving in with you. Tonight."

Doriana felt the blood draining from her face. "You can't." She shouldn't have told Logan about the call last night. She shivered despite the sunlight streaming into her office window.

Logan gripped her upper arms. "The hell I can't. You've got a pervert stalking you. You live alone with a small child. You need protection."

"That's not your job," she said.

"I'm making it my job." His eyes were hard as marbles and just as unyielding.

"No, no," she shook her head and tried to free herself from his grasp, but he held her firmly.

"Then take your son and stay with your parents until the scum is apprehended."

"I can't," she said.

"Why not?"

"Their new house is smaller than the old one. My grandmother's staying with them while her house is being painted. There's no room for me." Doriana squared her shoulders. "And no one is chasing me from my home."

"Then think about your son," he said.

"I will protect my son."

Logan gripped her arms tighter. "The guy calling you is unhinged and dangerous. You can't be alone." He narrowed his eyes. "You didn't stay with your parents Thanksgiving weekend like you promised, did you?"

She shook her head.

"You lied to me." He sounded so much like Josh last night, accusing and hurt at the same time.

"When I promised I'd go to my parents I'd forgotten about Nonna's staying there."

"You didn't tell your father about the calls, did you?"

She shook her head.

"Damn it, Doriana, this is serious."

"What's serious?" Her father's voice boomed from the doorway.

Logan released his grip on her. They turned to stare at her father.

Frowning, Dan shifted his gaze between the two. "What's going on?"

"What are you doing here?" Doriana asked. She needed a dead bolt for her office door with all the family that kept popping in at the worst times.

Her father focused his piercing blue eyes on her. "Devlin's in the lobby. I'm on my way to meet him. You need to get up to the conference room right away with the report."

Doriana glanced at her watch and back at her father. "He's early. Why didn't you just have Nancy call me?"

"She's busy copying notes for the meeting. I figured I'd walk to your office and then the lobby. I need more exercise."

"I'll be right up," Doriana said.

Dan looked at Logan. "I want you at the meeting too, Tanner. To take the minutes."

Doriana didn't miss the pointed look between the men. Somehow she would discover what they were keeping from her.

"After the meeting, you'll tell me whatever it was you two were discussing when I walked in." Her dad tossed the words over his shoulder as he left.

The meeting droned on well past lunch. John Devlin, an important potential client, liked to expound on his many business successes. Doriana's head ached from stress and hunger. But she smiled at all the right times and laughed at Devlin's jokes along with the rest of Callahan's senior management.

Devlin's corporation owned several major casinos in Las Vegas. He wanted to build a new casino in Atlantic City. Callahan Construction wanted the job badly. They couldn't afford to lose the bid.

While Nancy, her dad's executive secretary, served sandwiches, Doriana allowed herself to relax. She settled back in her chair and glanced over to where Logan sat making notes into his laptop. He looked up and their gazes locked. Awareness throbbed between them before his eyes took on a hooded look.

Logan wanted to move in with her. Her pulse quickened. What would it be like to spend every day and night with Logan? Was she crazy? What about Josh?

With the meeting over at last, Doriana tried to slip out the door with the others.

"Doriana, stay," her father ordered. "You too, Tanner."

Feeling like a teen caught playing hooky, she sat down.

"Do you have something to tell me?" Dan asked as soon as the others had gone. "You two were having a pretty heated discussion in your office a while ago." His gaze searched Logan's before locking on her. "Was it work? Or maybe it's none of my business."

Doriana wanted to sink into the floor. Now her father was picking up vibes between her and Logan. She shifted in her seat. She felt Logan's stare but didn't dare look at him. Letting out a sigh, she clasped her hands together on the table. Her father wouldn't let her leave the room until she told him.

"I've had some calls, Dad. I didn't want to worry you. I know you've been under a lot of stress. The phone company's been alerted and Logan's helping. It's not a big deal."

A vein throbbed in Dan's neck. "What kind of calls?"

"Someone's been watching me." She placed her hand over her dad's where it rested on the polished wood table. "It's okay, Dad. Really. We have everything under control, don't we, Logan?" She looked at Logan for confirmation.

Logan nodded at Dan. "Things are in motion. We'll get this scum."

"Some stranger's watching you? He knows where you live?" Dan's face reddened.

"Dad, your blood pressure," Doriana said, patting his hand.

"The hell with my blood pressure." Dan's raised voice brought his secretary to the door. He waved her away. Pulling his hand from Doriana's, he turned to Logan. "Someone tell me what kind of calls."

"He's made sexual suggestions," Logan said.

"And no one thought to tell me?" Dan's face got redder.

"Dad, please," she said.

"Don't 'please,' me, Doriana." The vein in her dad's neck stood out more. "My daughter is being stalked by some pervert and no one tells me? What if he breaks in? My grandson could be in danger too."

"I've got things under control, Dan," Logan said.

Dan gave Logan a hard look. "Did you call the police?"

Logan shook his head. "The police won't touch it unless the caller makes a direct threat."

"I know the police commissioner," Dan said. "He owes me. I'll give him a call. But we need to do something now to protect my daughter and grandson."

Logan gave Doriana a look. "I'm moving into her place tonight."

Doriana stood up. "And I told him no. I can take care of myself. I'm careful and I always put the security alarm on, even when I'm home."

Her father stared at her. She knew that expression. He was mulling over the idea. Dread washed over her.

"Doriana, I don't want to tell you what to do," Dan said.

She rolled her eyes and sat slowly down. "That's a

new one. You're always trying to tell me what to do."

He chuckled. "And you're always fighting me." His features turned serious. "Logan's right. You can't be alone. Either Logan moves into your house or you stay with your mother and me."

Doriana's secrets, past and present, were rapidly colliding. She wouldn't give up yet.

"Nonna's staying with you," she said. "I'll go to a hotel."

"Your grandmother can go to a hotel," her father said.

The rope of her deceit tightened. "I won't send Nonna to a hotel."

"Then it's settled," her father said. "Logan moves in with you and Josh for a while."

"Josh?" Logan said.

She turned to him. He sat very still, tension in every line of his body. Only the muscle working in his jaw hinted at strong emotions held in check.

She swallowed. "Josh is my son."

"Your son." The harshness in his voice could cut through cement. "I thought..."

The roaring in Doriana's ears got louder as her world crashed around her. Her father only wanted to protect her and Josh. But she felt like a mouse cornered by one of the construction site cats.

Both men stared at her, waiting. Head high, she picked up her papers and left the room without a word. No way would Logan move in with her. It wouldn't happen. The heaviness in her chest told her otherwise.

"Logan, stay," her father said. "I want to look over your notes."

Doriana walked slowly towards the elevator. Her throat felt thick. How could she tell Josh he was going to meet his father tonight? She couldn't.

What if Josh grew attached to Logan? Logan would leave. She could handle the hurt, but could her son?

****

The rushing noise in Logan's head muffled Callahan's words. Josh. Doriana's son. She'd argued with her son on the phone, not a lover. He asked for money. Was on his way into town. Not a small child.

"Tanner, have you heard anything I've said?"

Callahan's sharp voice snapped Logan from his thoughts.

"Sorry, Dan. What were you saying?"

Callahan gave him a wry look. "You'll move in with Doriana?"

Logan nodded. "I can better protect her and her son if I'm there all the time."

"I agree." Callahan smiled. "It will also save a bundle on your hotel expenses. Not that I care about that. The safety of my daughter and grandson is paramount."

"They'll be safe with me, Dan. It's all part of my job."

Callahan studied Logan. "My daughter is a beautiful woman. I trust you to maintain a professional relationship."

Little too late for that. "Doriana is beautiful. But I know my place."

Dan nodded. "Now back to Devlin."

Callahan sat at the conference table and tented his fingers in front of his face, lost in thought. Sighing, he pressed his palms on the table and looked at Logan.

"I want that casino job. It means a lot to the future strength of this company. I won't take a chance on one of my competitors getting the bid."

Logan pulled out his laptop and turned it on to the meeting notes. He scanned the screen. "It won't be easy. We'll have to figure out a way to give James another bid without his being the wiser. You'll have to get the real bid to Devlin."

"You're right about it not being easy." Dan's features tightened. "I hope you're wrong about Bryce."

"I hope I am, for your sake," Logan said softly.

"Let's brainstorm right now," Callahan said. "I've got an hour before my next meeting."

Logan glanced at the clock. He would have to use all of his powers of concentration to focus on working with Callahan when his mind screamed Doriana. He had to get answers to the questions that gnawed him.

Thankfully the hour flew by. Logan put his laptop back in its case and headed out of the conference room. "Callahan, can I ask a question?" he said, turning back.

"Shoot," Callahan said.

"How old is Doriana's son?" Logan stood very still, afraid of the answer, but somehow knowing what it was.

Callahan threw him a surprised look. "Josh will be sixteen Christmas Eve."

The breath knocked out of Logan.

"Tanner, are you okay?" Callahan scowled at him.

"I'm fine." Logan exited the office quickly.

Once out in the carpeted hallway, Logan leaned against the wall for support. His mind spun and his heart thumped wildly against his chest. He swallowed, trying for control.

He'd been under fire, afraid for his life, more times than he could count. But nothing had prepared him for this. He did the math in his head. It all added up. Why hadn't she told him?

He was good enough to father her child but not to raise him. The old hurts and insecurities hit him like a knockout punch.

He had a son. He was a father. Straightening, he walked toward the stairs. Time for a showdown with Doriana.

CHAPTER ELEVEN

"Stay in the lobby, Josh. I'll be right down."

Doriana's voice hit Logan like a fireball, fueling the anger and hurt he'd carried from Callahan's meeting. He dropped his briefcase on the floor by his desk and marched into her office.

He grabbed the cell phone out of her hand, ignoring her startled cry.

"Josh," he said into the phone. He kept his voice dead calm, not wanting to take his fury out on the boy. "This is Logan Tanner, your mother's assistant. Come up to the office. I'd like to meet you." He snapped the phone shut and tossed it onto her desk.

"What are you doing?" Doriana shrieked.

Logan gripped her upper arms, pulling her close until only inches separated them. White-faced, she tried to jerk away. "When were you going to tell me, Doriana?"

"Tell-tell you what?" She shivered under his touch.

"The game's up, Doriana. I know."

"I don't understand."

"The hell you don't."

She twisted, trying to free herself. At the fear in her brown eyes he loosened his grip but still held her. He'd rather suffer physical wounds on the battlefield than this ache at her deceit.

"Tell me," he said. "I want to hear it from you."

She licked her lips. He wanted to shake her. And God help him, he wanted to kiss her until all the years and all the hurt dissolved.

"Please," she said. "Let me handle Josh. He's my

son."

"And mine," he said quietly.

Her porcelain face turned ashen. Tears gathered in her eyes. Her silence shouted the proof he demanded. Pain, mingled with joy, took his breath. Josh. His son.

"Get your hands off my mom."

A teenage dynamo charged Logan, fists ready. Logan released Doriana and grabbed the boy by the shoulders, holding him at arm's length. Anger and determination tightened Josh's features, features so like his. The air in the room seemed to thicken.

Josh tried to kick, but Logan continued to hold him. He studied Josh's face, the high cheekbones and hazel eyes. His son. His flesh and blood. Pride ripped through him, threatening his control.

"Calm down, son. Calm down. I wasn't hurting your mother. I'd never hurt her. We were just having a discussion."

Josh looked toward Doriana.

She nodded. "It's okay, Josh. It really is."

Josh's shoulders sagged and Logan released him.

Doriana swiped at tears. She had to pull herself together. For Josh. She watched the two males as they faced off. Except for Josh's black hair, he was the mirror of Logan. Josh had the promise of Logan's muscled body on his lean frame.

She gasped at what she saw on Logan's face. Awe softened his hard features. Did he want Josh? Guilt ran through her, twisting her gut. Had she been wrong to deprive Logan of his son?

"Mom, who is this? What's going on?" Confusion marred Josh's perfect face. He looked close to tears.

Drawing a deep breath, she straightened, trying to hide her own fears. She touched Josh's arm. His muscles tightened under the soft fabric of his shirt. "I'll explain everything to you, Josh. Why don't we go home and we can talk."

Josh turned to Logan, studying him. Did he see the resemblance between himself and Logan? She hadn't meant Josh to find out this way.

"I think it's a good idea if you go home with your mom," Logan said softly.

"You can't tell me what to do," Josh said.

Josh's bravado shot Doriana with apprehension. Helping Josh through this would take all her parenting skills. Was she up to it? She had to be, for Josh's sake.

Logan turned to Doriana. Gold fire burned from his eyes. "I'll be at your place tonight." The tightness in his voice stopped any argument from her. He leaned closer. "We will talk."

"Mom, what does he mean?" The near panic in Josh's voice sliced through Doriana like a stonecutter's blade. She'd mishandled this whole affair. She'd only wanted to protect her son.

She pressed her hand around Josh's arm. "Everything will be okay. Please believe me."

Raising her chin, she swung her attention to Logan. "We'll talk, but you are not moving in."

"I will move in," Logan said, very calmly, too calmly. "I have even more reason now to protect you."

"Move in with us?" Josh said. "I don't want him there."

Logan flinched as if he'd been hit. "Go, Doriana. Take him home."

As if watching herself in a dream, Doriana grabbed her purse and coat and pulled Josh out of the room.

"What's going on, Mom? Who is he? Why does he look familiar?"

Doriana resisted the urge to pound the elevator to make it move faster. "Wait, Josh, please, till we get home."

"Why is he moving in with us?" Josh stayed close on her heels as they entered the garage. She nodded to several co-workers whose curious glances followed them.

"He's the guy you were kissing last night," Josh said as soon as he was in her car. "Is he your boyfriend? I don't want him to be your boyfriend."

Doriana put the key in the ignition with shaking fingers. "Please, Josh." She backed too quickly out of her parking spot, venting the frustration she couldn't voice.

"Is he my dad?"

Josh's softly spoken words sucked the air out of her lungs. She slammed on the brakes. Swallowing, she looked at Josh. He stared at her with angry eyes. How had he gotten so smart?

"You lied," he said. "You told me he left town before I was born."

The pain and accusation in his voice tore at her insides. She had two forceful males furious with her. Like father, like son. And when her own father found out, she'd have three angry males to handle.

"No one lied to you, Josh. I'll explain everything when we get home."

The blaring of a car horn behind her propelled her forward. She eased out of the garage. Tension rode with her and Josh on the long drive out of the city.

Doriana entered her house on leaden feet. She shrugged off her coat and threw it on the nearest chair and headed for the kitchen. She needed a drink, but she'd settle for a cup of tea.

Josh followed so closely she felt his breath on her neck, felt the anger and pain vibrating from him. Would Logan's presence in their lives drive a wedge between her and her son? Their relations were troubled enough.

"Mom, you have to tell me about this Logan guy. Now."

How could she tell Josh? If she only knew the right words things would be easier.

"Let's talk in the kitchen, Josh. I'll fix some tea."

"I don't want tea."

Doriana put on the kettle while a defiant Josh pulled a chair out from the high counter. The wooden legs of the chair scraped the tiled floor, grating her already tight nerves.

She lifted a mug from the cupboard, her movements slow and deliberate, as if she could force her anxiety away. Steaming cup of tea in hand, she took a seat facing her son. Part scared little boy and part rebellious teen, he glared at her with harsh features. Her insides quivered. She loved Josh so. And he was hurting.

She cradled her mug of hot tea and locked her gaze with her son's. She'd spent sixteen years hiding the truth. A strange kind of relief swept her. She drew deep, healing breaths and placed her hand over Josh's on the table.

"Logan is your father, Josh."

His face seemed to crumble.

"Oh, Josh, please. It will be okay. It really will."

Tears filled his eyes and he yanked his hand free. "He didn't really leave before I was born. He just didn't want me."

Her own tears spilled, hot on her cheeks. "No, you've got it wrong. I told you the truth about that. Logan left before I could tell him about you."

He shook his head. "I don't believe you."

"Josh, listen to me." She gripped her mug tighter to keep from grasping his shoulders and demand he believe her. She had to go easy with him.

He looked at her with hard, angry eyes. She stared down at the table, praying for strength, for the right words. The fragrant brew of the ginger peach tea touched her nostrils. Feeling nauseous, she pushed the mug away.

"Logan showed up about a month ago," she said, meeting his gaze. "Grandpop hired him to take Lisa's place. I didn't know anything about it. The day he walked into my office was the first I'd seen of him in sixteen years."

"I don't believe you," Josh said. The uncertainty that underscored his words gave her hope.

She reached out to grasp his hand. "If Logan had known about you he would have stayed. He would have wanted you." The lie cut through her. She had no idea if Logan would have stayed but she had to make Josh believe that.

Josh pulled his hand from hers and pushed away from the counter.

Doriana sat very still staring down at the white counter top. Josh opened the refrigerator and pulled out a can of soda.

Opening the tab on the can, he sat across from her again and took a long swig of soda. When he put the can down, he wrapped his white-knuckled hands around it.

"He's going to take you away." Anger and hurt showed in the tight muscles of his face. He looked away.

"God, no, Josh. I would never leave you. Not for anyone."

He turned his gaze to her. The defiant teen and confused little boy warred in his eyes, but hope was there too.

"Do Grandpop and Grandmom and Nonna know he's my dad?"

"Only Anita knows. She guessed." Doriana leaned closer, holding his gaze. "Please don't tell your grandparents or Nonna. I'll tell them when the time's right."

"Yeah, like you told me." The ache in his voice tempered his biting words.

"Josh, I know you're hurt and I'm sorry. But I did what I thought was best for you. I planned to tell you, but at the right time." She twisted her mouth in a wry grin. "So much for timing."

He chugged the rest of his drink and slammed the can onto the counter.

"Where's he been all this time?" he asked.

"I don't know," she said.

"Will he leave again?"

"He might."

Josh paled. Doriana squeezed his hand. "Do you want Logan to stay?" she asked.

"He's my dad. But he still doesn't want me." He crushed his empty drink can between his hands.

"Even if Logan leaves again, you can't think he doesn't want you. He moves around a lot. It's the way he is."

Did Logan want his son? The look on his face when he stared at Josh told her he did. Would Logan stay around, for Josh's sake? For her sake? Did she want him to stay? *Yes,* a small voice whispered. She closed her eyes against the fear wrapping her. She couldn't love Logan again.

"Why is he moving in with us, Mom? I don't want him here."

She drew a deep breath. "I've been getting some disturbing calls. Logan wants to protect us. And Grandpop thinks it's a good idea too."

"I can take care of you. We don't need him." Josh stood quickly, knocking over his chair.

Doriana pushed out of her seat and pulled Josh to her, hugging him tightly. "I know you want to take care of me. And I'm touched. I'm sure Logan will need your help. Whoever is calling is very nasty and I'm scared for both of us." She took his chin between her fingers. "We'll get through this together. The phone calls. And Logan back in our lives. It'll work out. Things always do."

"I don't want to talk anymore," Josh said. "I'm going to my room."

She started after him, then stopped and sank back into her chair. Josh needed space, needed time to absorb the turmoil that had become their life.

Doriana sipped her tea and stared at the wall. The tiny sprigs of green flowers on the wallpaper blurred. Like her life, she thought. Blurry, with no clear edges. How had things gotten so messed up?

****

The ringing of the doorbell set Doriana's heart to hammering. Logan. He had called an hour ago and said he'd be over soon, ready to move in.

She looked through the peephole to be sure it was Logan. She started to open for him, then stopped with her hand on the knob. She could keep the door firmly shut, closing Logan out. But Logan would always be part of their lives. She would guard her heart. Everything would be okay. The rapid beat of her pulse mocked the lie. Drawing a calming breath, she opened the door.

"It's about time," Logan said, an edge to his voice. His determined gaze locked with hers. He brushed past her, carrying two suitcases.

She stared at the expensive leather bags that he deposited on her living room carpet. How did a man without a permanent job afford such luxury? Something simmered just below the surface with Logan, something hidden and deep. Would she ever find the real Logan?

"My suitcases bother you?" he asked, arching an eyebrow.

She lifted her gaze to his and met the challenge in his eyes. "Yes. They and you don't belong here."

Folding her arms across her chest, she moved into the room. "You can't stay here, Logan. We'll talk and try to resolve our issues, but you have to leave afterwards."

"Issues?" His hard hazel eyes fixed on hers. "The only issue we have is that you hid my son from me for sixteen years."

She winced. "I did not hide him. You left me."

120

Pain flashed in his eyes. "I had my reasons."

"What reasons?"

"Where is Josh?" Logan scanned the room as if he expected Josh to jump out at any moment.

"My parents took him for the night," she said.

"Good," he said, moving closer. "We can talk."

She inhaled his citrus-outdoors scent. Gold sparked from his eyes. The hard planes of his face were shadowed. He looked like a very beautiful and avenging angel. She shivered.

"I need answers, Doriana. Honest answers."

"I've never lied to you," she said.

He gripped her upper arms. His fingers dug into her sensitized flesh through the thin wool of her sweater. She flinched but didn't pull away.

"You never told me." The smoothness of his voice and his clenched jaw hinted at his fury. "You had to know you were pregnant before I left town. Were you ashamed of me, Doriana? Ashamed the world would know you'd slept with a guy like me? A guy who didn't fit in with your Main Line friends?"

She forced herself to stand very still. Her tight muscles screamed their protest. "I was never ashamed of you. Never." But in her heart a small kernel of guilt and doubt opened. She'd hadn't introduced him to her prep school friends, hadn't even told them about Logan.

"Would you have stayed if you'd known?" she asked.

His mouth tightened into a thin line. He released her and moved away. "I had to leave. You don't understand."

Her throat thickened. "Why did you have to leave? What don't I understand?"

He shook his head. A mask slipped over his rigid features, shutting her out. He strode to the window and stared through the half-open blinds, his back to her.

She curved her fingers around the headrest of the nearest chair, swaying under the onslaught of old hurts. Tears welled. She stared at Logan's broad back. His muscles tensed under the leather of his jacket. Did he remember the past and all they'd meant to each other?

Her mind traveled sixteen years. She'd been so young. So afraid. She'd waited and waited for him at their special place. In all the time they'd snuck dates, he'd never missed a tryst. When he didn't show, she knew in her heart that he was gone. She'd sunk down on the muddy ground and cried until no more tears came. She didn't cry again until that lonely Christmas Eve when Josh was born.

"I was scared," she said. The words slid out, low and tremulous. She barely recognized her own voice. "Once I knew for sure, I went to meet you at our spot. But you never showed." A tear slipped down her cheek and she swiped it away.

"Nice story, Doriana," he said in an icy voice. He continued to stare out the window, his back ramrod straight.

She wanted to shout for him to look at her, to talk to her. Anger stiffened her spine. If he wanted a fight, she'd give it to him. He was the one who left her, damn him.

"You got my letter," he said. "You knew how to reach me."

"What letter?"

He whirled to face her. The darkness of his eyes, like clouds gathering for a storm, made her step back.

"Now you're going to tell me you never got my letter?"

She lifted her chin. "No, I didn't. Maybe my parents confiscated it."

"I sent it to your school so your parents wouldn't see it."

"All these years," she said. "They never gave it to me."

They stared at each other. Sixteen years of anger, hurt and frustration thickened the air around them.

"What did the letter say?" she asked.

He clenched his fists at his sides. She wasn't sure he would answer.

He blew his breath out and relaxed his stance slightly. "I told you that I'd joined the Army and where you could reach me."

His wrenching words sucked air from her lungs. She put a shaky hand to her mouth. Would things have been different if she'd gotten the letter? She'd never know. Every muscle in her body tightened with her effort to control the sorrow and longing she'd carried with her for sixteen years.

"You could have found me even without the letter," he said. "Your dad is a powerful man. But you never told him about me. A guy from the wrong neighborhood knocks you up. What if I'd been one of your private-school boyfriends? Would it have been okay then?"

She shook her head, fighting tears. "I didn't want Daddy to hurt you. I let my parents think my baby's father wanted to marry me, but I sent him away." She squared her shoulders. "I thought you'd used me for sex then left me for someone else, someone better in bed."

"Damn it, Doriana." He was next to her in two strides. He grabbed her shoulders. Her flesh burned where he touched. "You had so little faith in me." Hurt and anger twisted his features. "I loved you."

"You left me." She pulled free of him.

Lines of frustration bracketed his mouth. "Forget the past for now. You didn't tell me about Josh that first day in your office."

The accusation in his eyes slashed her with guilt. Hugging herself, she paced the room, trying to settle her roiling emotions. The cozy glow from the lamps did nothing to calm her churning stomach. Outside the wind rustled through the trees, promising a cold night. A cold and very long night.

Forcing calmness, Doriana turned to face Logan. "I never thought I'd see you again. I wasn't prepared."

His mouth curved in a bitter smile. "You've had sixteen years to prepare."

"You're leaving." The words slipped out. She bit her lip.

He tensed. "What do you mean?"

Tears filled her eyes. "Josh is at a vulnerable age. He needs a real father, not a temporary one."

His features hardened. He stared at her, a coiled, angry snake. She put her hand to her mouth. She'd gone too far.

"You think I wouldn't want my son?"

He walked slowly toward her. She dug her nails into her palms, quelling the urge to run away from him, from the ugliness and mess of her life.

When he reached her, he took her by the shoulders and pulled her close. "You've never thought much of me, have you, Doriana? It was okay to make love with me. But I wasn't good enough to be in your life, to help raise our son. That's the way it's always been."

"No, Logan. I was devastated when you left."

"No more lies." He made a chopping motion with his hand.

She shrugged, pretending indifference. "Believe what you want. Josh is my only concern. I will not have him get close to you only to have you leave."

He flinched. "I won't hurt him."

"You'll leave when your assignment is over," she said. "You never stay in one place long."

"Do you want me to stay?" His voice softened to a husky whisper.

She tensed, fighting her attraction to him. "I will not have you hurt my son."

"You mean our son, don't you? And you didn't answer my question. Do you want me to stay?"

She stared at him. He still held her tightly by the arms. Did she want him to stay? Her heart cried *yes* but her mind shouted *no*.

Awareness throbbed between them. Had he read her mind?

"God help me," he said with a groan. He pulled her against him. His mouth took hers, demanding and hard. She returned his kiss with all the frustration and yearning she'd kept inside her since the day he walked back into her life. He thrust his tongue into her mouth, brutal and unyielding. She moaned. She wanted him, wanted his body, his soul. But most of all she wanted him to hold her and cherish her with the love they'd once shared.

He set her away from him. His breathing was harsh. She put a trembling hand to her lips, swollen and warm from his kiss.

"Damn you, Doriana. Damn you."

She saw the anger and desire in his eyes. She'd kept his son from him. He wanted her.

He turned away and grabbed his suitcases. He strode to the stairs and started up, taking the steps two at a time.

"Where are you going?" She ran after him.

He stopped before the open door to her room. Her bed, covered in a pure white spread, seemed to mock her. Would things be different between them now if he'd taken what she offered that morning after Thanksgiving? Or would this anger still throb between them? .

She put her hand on his forearm. "You can't stay, Logan. You just can't."

He shrugged her off and continued down the hall. He hesitated at the doorway to Josh's room. "I didn't notice this room before." He gave a short, bitter laugh. "I must really be slipping."

She followed him into the last bedroom at the end of the hall. He stopped so suddenly she collided with him. He dropped his bags on the floor and scanned the room.

Doriana suppressed a smile at the horror in Logan's expression as he gazed at the overly feminine room with its ruffled curtains and pink and green flowers adorning the walls and repeated on the ruffled skirt of the small table. She heard his sharp intake of breath when he saw the large canopied bed, covered in a flowered spread.

"Still want to stay?" she asked.

He slipped off his jacket and threw it on the bed before turning to face her. She squared her shoulders and gave him a look of triumph. He took her chin between his fingers and tilted her face toward his. She widened her eyes.

"I've stayed in worse places," he said. "You can't get rid of me that easily."

"We'll see." She turned and marched out of the room, slamming the door behind her.

****

Logan sank onto the small, flower-covered chair and laid his head back, closing his eyes. He'd told her he'd stayed in worse places. He'd lied. He'd rather sleep outdoors on the cold ground than be smothered by this bastion of ruffles and flowers. But he was here for Doriana. And his son. He'd let Doriana think he was a wanderer with no permanent home or job. Would the truth calm her and make her agree to let him be part of Josh's life?

She'd never really had faith in him. They'd shared a wild passion, a passion that still burned between them.

But Doriana never forgot that they came from different worlds. He wanted to be in Josh's life. Wanted to be the kind of father he never had. Doriana thought him unstable, not a fit father. He would prove her wrong.

Would she think him father material if she knew about the thriving business he owned and his house in the exclusive Tucson suburb? He could provide well for Josh. His son.

He sat up and rubbed a hand over his eyes. He wasn't being fair to Doriana. She only wanted to protect her son. Their son.

He'd come clean with her, tell her the truth. His chest constricted. Was that what he wanted? For her to accept him because of what he owned, what he'd accomplished?

Hell, no. Logan jumped up from the chair and stalked to the window, hands fisted at his sides. He'd make her accept him for the man he'd become and not the successful businessman with all the outward trappings of success. He'd keep up the subterfuge. She'd take him for himself or not at all.

CHAPTER TWELVE

Doriana turned from her computer to stare out the window at the comforting sight of old Billy Penn perched on City Hall. She rubbed her tired eyes. Stress at work and at home took its toll in sleepless nights.

An uneasy truce had developed between her and Logan since he moved into her house three days ago. They spoke in guarded pleasantries at home. At work their conversations never veered from business. To her relief Logan didn't take meals with them. She had no idea where he ate and told herself she didn't care. But she wondered. And cared more than she wanted.

To her amazement, Josh didn't barricade himself in his room, as he usually did each evening. The last two nights he even finished his homework in record time and was seated on the sofa watching TV when Logan came back from dinner. Logan sat in one of the side chairs and watched with him. Tension hung heavy in the room and neither male spoke to the other but she caught Josh stealing curious glances at Logan.

Feeling twinges of jealousy that Josh seemed to tolerate Logan's company more than he did hers, Doriana retreated to her bedroom at night to work at her computer. She took work home now rather than stay at the office. She wanted to be around if things got too tense between Josh and Logan. But they seemed to handle each other's company just fine.

She was the one feeling left out. Father and son, looking so much alike, didn't appear to need her at all. They seemed content to gaze at the TV watching cars race around a speedway. All that testosterone threatened to overwhelm her. And the constant whirring of cars gave her a headache. What was it with men and fast cars?

The fax machine in her office came to life, signaling a transmittal and reminding her she had work to do. She jerked out of her reverie and glanced down at the papers strewn on her desk. She couldn't concentrate on her job. Even the weak December sunlight straining through the windows couldn't lift her spirits.

Doriana leaned on her desk and cupped her face between her hands. Try as he might to hide it, Josh seemed eager for a father. But what kind of father was Logan? Josh needed someone stable and steady. How long would Logan be around this time? She squeezed her eyes shut against the pain that stabbed her. How had Logan managed to twist his way into her life again? Her throat thickened. She tried to focus on old Billy but the statue blurred with her tears.

Logan's accusation that she'd been ashamed of him all those years ago punctured her with doubt. Would she have treated him and their relationship differently if Logan had been part of her elite crowd? Would she encourage a real relationship with Josh now if Logan had a steady job? She rubbed her forehead. She'd never thought of herself as a snob. But was she?

Doriana glanced at her watch. Noon. She wasn't hungry but she needed a break. Maybe a trip to the cafeteria and a light salad would clear the cobwebs from her mind. She grabbed her purse and headed out of her office. She froze in the doorway to the outer room.

Candi, legs crossed, short skirt hiked to her thighs, sat on Logan's desk. Doriana hadn't heard the woman come in. Candi turned towards Doriana. Triumph sparked in the blonde's blue eyes.

A look passed between the women, an understanding of something primal that made shivers run up Doriana's spine. She felt like a lioness in the jungle, preparing to fight another female for the alpha male's attention. She tore her gaze from Candi's. She wasn't an animal and she wouldn't behave like one, even with Logan as the prize.

"I'm heading to lunch," Doriana said to Logan.

He nodded. Had he felt the vibes between her and

Candi? His hazel eyes were shadowed, all emotion hidden.

Lifting her chin, Doriana walked out of the office.

****

When Doriana closed the door behind her, Candi let out a soft laugh.

"I guess the line's been drawn," she said.

Logan frowned. "What do you mean?"

Candi ran one of her red-tipped talons over Logan's lips. He rolled his chair back slightly, putting himself out of her reach. He'd thought he had Candi under control, that she understood they were just friends. His tastes ran to a different type of woman, a woman who hid a smoldering sexuality under a cover of respectability. Like Doriana.

"You saw what just happened between me and Boss Lady," Candi said. "She wants me to keep away from you. She wants you for herself."

Logan pushed away from the desk and stood. "You've got an overactive imagination, Candi. Doriana doesn't care what I do." Did Doriana care? Did he want her to? He tried to ignore the little voice that whispered, *yes*.

"You can't fool me," Candi said, laughing. "I've seen the way she looks at you." She slid off his desk and smoothed her hands down her skirt. "She's way out of your league, Logan." She gave him a sly smile. "Maybe she's just playing you."

Candi's words unleashed Logan's old insecurities. "Let's go to lunch." He headed out of the office with Candi close behind.

Hours later Logan unlocked Doriana's front door. A feeling of peace stole over him every time he entered her house. His son was here. So was Doriana, the woman he'd never forgotten, the woman who excited and tormented his dreams for the last sixteen years.

He closed the door and leaned against it, inhaling the scent of rosemary and oregano and other spices he couldn't identify. The odor of roasted chicken made the turkey sandwich he'd eaten at a diner seem paltry and dull.

Doriana never asked him to have dinner with her and Josh and he didn't want to push it. He wanted Josh and Doriana to accept him willingly. The softening of his son's attitude the last two nights gave Logan the hope that helped him get through the tense days and tortured nights. If only Doriana would soften right into his arms.

Josh came running down the stairs, wearing a jacket, his backpack slung over his shoulder. He stopped when he saw Logan.

"Going somewhere?" Logan asked.

Josh stiffened. Logan braced himself for "It's none of your business."

"I'm going to study with a friend," Josh said.

Josh's civil reply made Logan smile. In time he'd win over his son. He wasn't so sure about his son's mother.

A horn honked outside. "Mom, I'm going." Josh bounded the rest of the way down the stairs.

Logan moved aside, opening the door for him.

Doriana came into the hall. Dressed in jeans and a sweatshirt, her thick dark hair pulled back, she looked young, sweet, and sexy as hell. She looked like the Doriana he fell in love with all those years ago.

She hesitated when she saw Logan. Pink rode her cheeks and her chocolate eyes widened. Tension arced between them. Her beauty took Logan's breath and he fought the desire that gripped him. He wanted her. But on his terms.

The car horn blared again.

"Mom!" Josh's impatient voice cut through the thick air.

Doriana turned to her son. "I already talked to Steven's mother. She knows I want you home by ten."

"Yeah, yeah," Josh said.

Doriana leaned over and gave Josh a kiss on the cheek. "I love you."

"Love you too." Josh nodded at Logan before sliding through the door. He stopped and looked back, a mischievous grin on his face. "Behave yourselves." He shut the door.

Doriana and Logan stared at each other. Logan arched a brow. "Why do you think he said that?"

She shrugged. "I can't imagine."

Logan closed the few steps between them. He cupped her chin and tilted her face toward his. "I think you know."

Her pale smooth skin turned pink. Her breath hitched, but she didn't pull away.

"What do you mean?" she whispered.

He took her face between his hands and stared into her eyes. Apprehension and desire mixed in their caramel-laced depths. "We can't deny what's between us, Doriana. We share a son, but it goes much deeper than that."

"I have no idea what you're talking about." She shrugged free and walked into the living room.

He followed. When he placed his hands on her shoulders, she stiffened and stopped, her back to him. He bent to place a gentle kiss on her nape. She shuddered. The slight softening of her body urged him on. He pulled on the satin cord holding her hair and released the silky strands to slide over his fingers. She sighed.

"Beautiful," he whispered. Brushing aside her thick rope of hair, he trailed kisses along the soft skin of her neck. She leaned against him. Her scent of roses and woman enveloped him in a sensual heat.

"I've never forgotten you," he whispered.

She tensed. "I wasn't on your mind this afternoon when Candi was wrapped all over your desk."

He tightened his grip on her shoulders. "That's just Candi's way. There's nothing between us. Believe me."

She would have pulled away but he held her.

"You've been gone for sixteen years, Logan. Why should I believe you?"

"Can't we get past this?" he asked.

She turned in his arms. Her large liquid eyes searched his. "We can't go back . What we had was a long time ago. It's gone."

Logan ran his thumb along her quivering bottom lip. "Not gone."

He bent his head to take her lips. Desire darkened her eyes.

The ringing of the phone cut through the sensual haze around him. Years of military training made him jump back, on high alert.

Doriana swayed toward him. Logan grabbed her elbows, steadying her. He walked toward the phone and lifted the receiver, not speaking.

Cara Marsi

"I know you're there, prick. You think you can move in with her and keep me away. She's a sweet piece of ass. And I'll have her. I'll have them both."

Dial tone replaced the crude voice. Anger trembled through Logan. He gripped the receiver and forced himself to stand very still, calling on the coping skills he'd honed through countless dangerous missions. He had to be strong. For Josh. For Doriana. He slowly replaced the receiver.

"It was him, wasn't it?" Doriana asked.

Logan nodded. "The son of a bitch knows I'm here." He moved to her side and gathered her in his arms, holding her close. "It will be all right, Dorie," he said, kissing the top of her head. He pulled her tighter to stop her shaking.

"I'm afraid, Logan."

"He won't hurt you or Josh. I'll make sure of that."

"I know." She pulled away to look up at him. Tears glistened in her eyes.

Her trust filled him with longing for the life that had been denied him all those years ago. Denied him by the accident of his birth to a man who loved the bottle more than his only child. Logan forced his mind from the past. Despite his dad he'd made something of himself. And he'd be a good father to Josh if only he got the chance. He was nothing like his old man.

"What will we do now?" Doriana asked.

He held her at arm's length. "I've got a contact at police headquarters now, thanks to your father. Will you be okay for a few minutes?"

She smiled. "I'm no shrinking violet."

"I know you're not." He kissed her temple and released her. "Why don't you go in the other room while I make my call."

"I'll make tea." She turned to leave.

"Doriana."

She looked at him.

"Your caller said something strange. He said he'd have you and then he said 'I'll have them both.'"

She paled. "You don't think he means Josh?"

Logan shook his head. "No, it was clearly sexual and I had the definite sense he was talking about another woman."

"What other woman?" she asked, frowning.

"I haven't a clue," he said. "But we'll figure it out."

****

Doriana grabbed her meeting notes and rushed out of her office, glancing at Logan's empty desk as she hurried by. How long had he been gone on his break? She'd lost all track of time.

Shaking off a vague sense of unease, she punched the elevator button, her mind on Logan. Since he moved into her house she felt more secure than she had in years. She didn't want to acknowledge that, but she could no longer ignore her feelings. Even when Logan was a wild teen, she'd known he would protect her.

Despite the disturbing phone call last night, she'd felt safe, knowing Logan was by her side. Josh had come home early and the three of them watched TV together. Like a real family. Apprehenstion, mingled with hope, stirred a melancholy brew in her heart. Could they ever be a real family?

The soft whoosh of the elevator doors made her sigh with relief. She got in, feeling as if a benign monster had saved her from her own treacherous thoughts. She punched the number for the fifth floor. She needed to stop by the Sales Department to pick up some papers for the meeting.

She stepped off the elevator and froze. At the end of the long hallway, Logan and Candi stood talking. The intimacy of their expressions and the closeness of their bodies hit Doriana like a physical blow to her chest. Logan said there was nothing between him and Candi. Had he lied to her? Was she a fool all over again?

The elevator doors started to close. Doriana slid back in, wanting to put the heart-wrenching sight of Logan and Candi out of her mind. Before the doors closed completely, she hit the open button. Damn it, she would not act like a weak-spined teen. She had every right to confront Logan and Candi. This was her company. And Logan was her man. Her man? She must be under more stress than she realized to give voice to irrational thoughts like that.

Squaring her shoulders, Doriana left the elevator and marched toward the couple. They turned at her approach.

Candi looked down at the floor, but Logan's intense gaze held Doriana's.

"There you are, Logan," she said in her best professional voice when she reached them.

"I'll get back to the office in a few minutes," he said.

Doriana waved a hand. "It's okay."

Forcing a smile, she turned to Candi. Her smile froze and she sucked in her breath. An ugly purple bruise on Candi's jaw marred the woman's fair complexion.

"My God, what happened?" The sadness and humiliation in Candi's eyes told Doriana all she needed to know. Trembling, she reached out to touch Candi's arm, as if through mere touch she could release Candi from her personal hell.

Doriana had seen those kinds of bruises before. Her parent's former housekeeper Lila had had a husband who regularly beat her. Doriana's parents tried to help, but it was too late. Lila's husband killed her, then took his own life.

"Let me help you, Candi," she said. "The company has programs. I'll make some calls. We can get you to a shelter."

Candi pulled away and looked at Doriana with a mixture of resentment and embarrassment in her blue eyes. "Logan's helping me."

Jealousy slammed into Doriana again, but she forced it away and looked at Logan.

He slanted Doriana a grim look. "It's a tough situation."

His eyes challenged Doriana to trust him. The steel girders she'd erected around her heart began to slowly pull apart. Logan would help Candi, just as he helped her. But he had no other interest in the blonde. He'd told her that and she believed him. At Doriana's nod, relief softened Logan's harsh features.

"If you need me, I'll be here," Doriana said softly.

Awareness passed between Logan and Doriana. Everything else—Candi, the long hallway, the opening and closing of the elevator doors—receded until only she and Logan existed. The hint of a smile played around Logan's mouth. He reached out and touched a finger to Doriana's lips. Her pulse jumped in response.

Voices at the other end of the hall brought her back to reality. She glanced at her watch. "I'm late for my meeting."

She knew Logan watched her as she walked away. His gaze seared into her until she disappeared through the double doors of the Sales Department.

"That was interesting," Candi said.

Logan turned to her. "Doriana meant what she said. She'll help if you need it."

Candi threw him a knowing smile. "I wasn't talking about that."

"Don't go there, Candi. You called me down here because you're in trouble. What are we going to do about you?"

Tears watered her eyes. "What can I do? He loves me, Logan. Something ticked him off last night. That was all. He'll stop beating up on me once things work out for him. He's had a rough life."

Logan drew a deep breath, fighting frustration. "Lots of people have rough lives, but they don't abuse others. He's not going to stop, Candi. I know it and you know it."

He traced his fingers over her swollen jaw. "What do you tell your co-workers?"

"I don't say anything anymore. I used up all my excuses. They know, but they don't ask questions. They don't really care." Bitterness edged her voice.

"I know people who can help," Logan said.

Candi put her hand on his arm. "Only you can help me, Logan. You can save me."

Logan smiled and placed his hand over hers. "I'm no knight in shining armor. You give me too much credit."

"Meet me tonight, Logan. I need to talk to someone."

"I don't know, Candi." He couldn't leave Doriana and Josh alone.

She reached out a small hand to touch his face. "Please. I need help. I'm scared. I can tell you stuff. About work."

Doriana and Josh needed him. But Candi might have the information to crack this case. His suspicions grew stronger every day that Doriana's caller was connected to the problems at Callahan's. Would helping Candi also help Doriana?

He nodded to Candi. "You name the time and place and I'll be there."

****

Logan sat down to dinner with Doriana and Josh for the first time. But Doriana couldn't concentrate on the food. Tension lay heavier on her stomach than the pizza they shared. Candi's ravaged face and haunted eyes kept intruding, as they had all afternoon since she saw the blonde with Logan. With Candi's image came the doubts. Was she right to believe Logan when he said there was only friendship between him and Candi?

Doriana sliced a glance at Logan. He and Josh were debating the merits of one racecar driver over another. She studied Logan's strong profile, the straight nose and firm chin. She looked over at Josh, a mirror of Logan. The eagerness on Josh's face as he talked to Logan made Doriana's heart lurch. Had she really thought to keep the two apart?

Logan looked over at her, his gaze searching her face. Longing shadowed his eyes. Could he read her mind? They'd been denied a family all those years ago. Was it too late?

The scraping of a chair over the wood floor drew her back to the present. She looked at Josh. He pushed away from the table and stood up.

"Going somewhere?" Doriana asked.

Reddening slightly, Josh shrugged. "Steven's mom is picking me up. Steve and I are hanging out at his place tonight."

Doriana frowned.

"It's Friday, Mom."

"I'm aware of that," Doriana said. "But Mrs. Morelli usually calls me when you're going to spend time there."

"It's not a big deal." Josh slid his glance away. Alarm bells sounded in Doriana's head but she silenced them. Josh had never outright lied to her before. Had he?

Logan swung his gaze to Josh. "Maybe I could drive you over to your friend's, Josh."

Josh tensed. "No, it's okay. She'll be here any minute."

He left the room at a near-run.

Logan and Doriana stared at each other.

"Something's up with him," Logan said.

Doriana bristled. "You've only known him a few days and you think you can read him. I trust him. After all, I'm the one who raised him."

Logan flinched. "I guess I know where I stand."

Doriana's face burned. She had sounded like such a shrew. "Logan, I didn't mean..."

Logan put up a hand, stopping her. A muscle worked in his jaw. "Don't." He stood and dropped his napkin onto his plate. "I have to go out too,but I'll help you clean up first."

"I'll take care of it," she said. "Are you going to see Candi?" Jealousy threatened, but she tamped it down. The other woman was in trouble, serious trouble.

He nodded. "I don't want to leave you alone, but Candi wants to talk. Maybe I can convince her to get help before it's too late."

Doriana pushed out of her chair and stood facing him. "I'll go with you."

Logan placed his hands on her shoulders. "Thanks, I'd like you with me, but Candi won't talk with you there. You intimidate her."

Doriana arched an eyebrow. "I intimidate her?"

His crooked smile sent shivers of excitement skittering up her spine. "Hell, you intimidate me."

She returned his smile. "Now I know you're lying."

He took her chin between his fingers. His eyes softened. "You do intimidate me. Beauty and sweetness." He stroked her cheekbone. The feel of his calloused finger against her skin made heat pull low in her belly.

"Don't do that," she said in a husky whisper.

Logan looked at her for long seconds before he turned and strode away.

Doriana stared at the empty doorway. The sound of a horn blasting, followed by the front door slamming, pulled her from the room.

She was too late. Josh was gone. Minutes later Logan came down the stairs, his leather jacket flung casually over one shoulder. His masculinity made her heart do a crazy somersault. His gaze, tortured and dark, reached out to an answering need in her. She bit her lip, keeping back the words that would ask him to stay.

"Dorie, I don't want to go, but I have to. There are things I can't share with you now. All I ask is that you have a little faith in me."

Confusion jumbled through her head. Faith in him? In what? She sensed again the deep undercurrents in Logan. How could she have faith in what she didn't understand?

She swallowed. "You'd better go."

He brushed a hand over her arm. "Keep the door locked and the security alarm on. I've hired someone to watch the house, a retired detective. He's sitting outside in his car."

"I don't need a bodyguard," she said. "And how can you afford it?"

He stiffened. "Don't worry about it. And don't argue. Call me on my cell if you need me. I won't be long." He gently squeezed her arm. Then he was gone.

She set the dead bolt and leaned against the door. The silence in the house smothered her. Her arm tingled where Logan had touched, like a talisman protecting her. She lifted her head and looked toward the dining room, at the dirty dishes, open pizza box and wadded-up napkins. She headed toward the room and the clean-up that would keep her too busy to think.

Josh should arrive at Steven's shortly. She'd give Mrs. Morelli a call in a little while, just to be sure. She wanted to believe her son, but doubt chewed at her resolve.

Doriana picked up the plates belonging to Josh and Logan. Each had left a pizza slice with one identical bite taken out. In how many other ways were they alike? A chill clutched her chest. Had Josh lied? Could she believe Logan that he only wanted to help Candi?

No, she thought, shaking her head. She would trust them both. She froze in the kitchen doorway as a sense of foreboding worked its way up her spine. Was Logan walking into danger? Why would she think that?

Forcing her apprehension away, Doriana loaded the dishwasher, using the mindless task to calm her. A police siren in the distance set her nerves on edge. Feeling ready to scream, she switched on the radio and turned it off just as quickly. Darned Christmas tunes. They filled every airwave this time of year. As a child she'd loved Christmas, and especially loved the songs.

The lonely Christmas Eve when Josh was born changed everything. In the years since, she'd gone through the motions and the superficial trappings—the tree, the decorating, the shopping—for Josh's sake.

Could she keep up the pretense this year? Logan's return set her well-ordered life on its rear. Would she and Josh ever be the same? Did she want to go back to a life without Logan?

The truth that had been knocking at the edges of her heart burst free. She leaned against the kitchen sink. The plate she held fell onto the floor and shattered.

She loved Logan. Had never stopped loving him. She'd been in denial, but she could no longer ignore what her heart had always known. She wanted to believe in him again. The thought frightened her.

Doriana fisted her hand against her mouth and pressed against the cold, hard stainless of the sink. She welcomed the slight physical pain to ease the torture of her soul. Would Logan hurt her again? Would he hurt Josh? Logan had the power to hurt both of them deeply.

CHAPTER THIRTEEN

Cheap liquor and stale tobacco. Logan's stomach clenched at the memories that assaulted him. Memories of a scared, skinny kid standing in a seedy bar just like this one. A kid coming to drag his drunken father home while his mother lay dying of cancer. Logan blinked to clear his vision, clouded by smoke and pain.

He spotted Candi in a booth at the other end of the room and headed toward her, ignoring the belligerent looks thrown his way. In no mood for a bar fight, he avoided eye contact with the other patrons.

Logan slid into a seat opposite Candi and she threw him a nervous smile.

"I was afraid you wouldn't make it," she said.

"You're in trouble. I want to help." He gave her a reassuring smile and glanced at his watch. He wanted and needed to be with Doriana. But he had a job to do.

"Got a hot date later?" Candi arched an eyebrow.

Logan laughed. "Hardly."

A waitress whose time-worn face still held some remembrance of youthful beauty, came over to take his drink order.

"Ginger ale," he said.

Candi wrapped her hand around her glass of beer and watched the waitress walk away. She leaned toward Logan. "You don't drink? You really are too good to be true. The women at work get all hot and bothered whenever they see you. Are you an angel who looks like the devil?"

He waved a hand. "Don't, Candi."

"Modest too," she said.

He held her gaze. "Now tell me what's going on. And I want the truth."

She took a sip of beer, peering at him over the rim of the tall glass. Setting the glass on the table, she let out a deep sigh. "Some things are going down that scare me, Logan. I think I may have gotten in too deep." Her voice trembled.

"What have you gotten yourself into, Candi?"

Her face pinked and she slid her gaze to the large clock hanging on the wall.

The waitress came with his drink, distracting him. Candi chugged her beer and ordered another. They sat in silence, Candi looking out over the bar, anywhere except at him, until the waitress brought her new drink.

"Candi," he said softly. "Look at me."

She turned to him with eyes that had hardened to blue granite. What happened to the fear and vulnerability that had shadowed them a few minutes ago?

A chill passed over Logan. Candi was a survivor. They had that in common. She put on different faces, but he believed she was straight with him. Had he been wrong?

He shifted in his seat. Candi needed his help. And he needed her information.

"Is it Bryce James?" Logan asked.

Shock registered on Candi's pretty face. She coughed on the beer she just sipped. "How do you know about Bryce?" Her eyes glittered and her voice held a brittle, defiant tone.

"How I know is not important," he said. "I can help you, Candi. You don't owe him anything. Has he gotten you involved in something illegal?"

Sadness crossed her features for a fleeting instant before a calculating hardness took over. "Bryce buys me nice things." She fingered the diamond bracelet on her wrist and let out a short, bitter laugh. "I take real good care of him too."

"Is he the one beating up on you?" Logan asked.

"Bryce?" Her lips curled in a sneer. "Bryce wouldn't crush a bug. He's not man enough."

She flicked a nervous glance toward the clock, then

turned back to Logan. "He loves me, Logan." She wrapped her hands so tightly around her glass Logan thought it would shatter.

"Bryce?" he asked.

Candi wrinkled her nose. "God, no. Bryce will never leave that mousy wife of his."

"And you think this other guy loves you?" Logan asked. "He sure has a funny way of showing it. Open your eyes, Candi, before it's too late."

She pushed her glass aside. Her lips quirked in a flirtatious smile. "My eyes are wide open," she said in a husky voice. "And I like what I see." She reached out to glide one of her long, slender fingers over the back of his hand. "I know how to keep a man happy."

Pity coiled in Logan's stomach. How many drinks had she had before he got there? "Don't, Candi. You have a lot more to offer a man than just your body."

She threw back her head and laughed, a grating, bitter sound. Several of the bar patrons turned to stare at her. Despair clouded her eyes. "Try telling that to my uncles and all the other men from the old neighborhood who couldn't keep their sweaty paws off me. I learned real early what men want from me."

Logan took one of her hands in his. "Stop that, Candi. No matter what you did in the past, you deserve respect, not abuse."

Scowling, she pulled her hand away. "Get real, Logan."

Logan sipped his soda, buying time to control his anger and his frustration. Candi slid another glance toward the clock. The hairs on his nape prickled in warning. He quickly downed his ginger ale, but he couldn't wash away the feeling of unease that grew stronger every minute.

Pushing his empty glass aside, he leaned over the table, forcing Candi to look at him. "If you won't let me help you, why did you drag me here?"

She shrugged. "You got a date with Boss Lady later?"

"Leave Doriana out of this. Why did you ask me here?"

"I needed someone to talk to," she said. "I know things about work and I have no one else to trust."

Logan ignored the small voice in his brain that told him Candi wasn't being straight with him. He'd give her the benefit of the doubt this time. He sat back in his seat, trying to look relaxed. "What things?" He flicked at imaginary lint on his jacket. Clouds of cigarette smoke hung in the room, burning his throat. He signaled the waitress for another soda.

"I want to tell you, Logan," Candi said. "But I'm afraid."

He forced down his frustration. "Just say it, Candi."

She dropped her gaze to the table. "It's almost over so it doesn't matter."

Logan tightened his jaw. Candi's constant baiting, then pulling back, made him feel like a damn fish on a long line. "I'm tired of games." He stood and threw some bills on the table. "Let me know when you're ready to talk."

Candi licked her lips and looked over at the clock. She grabbed Logan's arm. "Don't go, Logan. Please."

The panic in her voice stirred pity in him. Despite the warning shivers that raced up his spine, Logan sat down and narrowed his gaze at her. "What is it you know about work? What kinds of things?"

"If I tell you, and he finds out, he'll hurt me real bad." Fear and defiance mingled in Candi's eyes.

Logan understood all too well the hold an abuser had on his victim. First his mother, then he, had lived through that particular hell. But he would not be Candi's enabler. He banged his fist on the table. Candi's glass rattled and beer spilled out.

"And if you stay with him, he'll kill you," Logan said. "Tell me what you know and I'll protect you. There are safe houses you can go to where he can't touch you." Some of Logan's anger drained away at the tears glistening in Candi's eyes. He placed one of his hands over hers on the table. "I promise I'll protect you."

The waitress set a fresh glass of ginger ale in front of him. He took a long chug, his gaze on Candi.

She pulled her hand free and swiped at a tear. "You know those bids being stolen at work?"

His pulse raced. "How do you know they were stolen?"

She paled. "It's all going to be over soon. And no one will get hurt."

"How do you know?" he asked.

She shrugged.

Logan bit back his anger. "That's all you can tell me?" he asked with as much calmness as he could muster.

Candi glanced toward the wall clock again. Logan followed her gaze.

"What crazy game are you playing, Candi?"

"I don't know what you're talking about." She refused to meet his gaze.

"I'm going," he said, standing up.

"You have to stay." She looked at him with desperation. "You can't leave."

The truth sucker-punched him and he cursed himself for ignoring the warnings. Doriana! He sprinted out of the bar. Candi's shouts followed him onto the street.

****

Doriana hung up the phone slowly. A bitter taste rose in her mouth and her stomach felt as if a clump of cement lodged there. Josh had lied. Her call surprised Mrs. Morelli. Josh wasn't at their house. Steven was in Wilmington, staying with his dad for the weekend.

Anger at herself and at Josh roiled her. Why hadn't she called Mrs. Morelli before she allowed Josh to leave? Because she was too intent on showing Logan she had control of her son. Their son.

The phone rang, insistent and shrill in the quiet. Josh! She raced to answer.

"I know you're alone, sexy."

The evil-sounding voice sent chills quivering down her spine.

"Your cheating pretty boy is gone," the smooth, cruel voice continued. "Let me in and I'll show you a real man."

Doriana slammed the phone down. She hugged herself to stop the trembling. He was watching her. How else would he know Logan was out? Fear formed a knot in her chest. But Logan had someone looking out for her. She'd be okay. Wouldn't she?

The security alarm. She'd forgotten to set it. Her feet wouldn't move. A knock sounded at the back door. The doorknob jangled and she stifled a scream. Like a frightened female in a horror movie, she stood paralyzed.

Anger shot through her, propelling her from her freezing fear. She wasn't some insipid character in a movie. She did a quick inventory of the room. She snatched the cordless phone and dialed nine-one-one, then grabbed a heavy crystal vase from a table. The back doorknob jangled louder. She emptied the vase, not caring about the flowers and water on the rug.

The nine-one-one operator answered just as the front door opened. Doriana let out a loud shriek and dropped the phone. Whirling to face the door, she held the vase high, ready to strike.

"What the hell?"

Logan strode into the room. Doriana's knees gave way. She dropped the vase and sank to the floor.

"Doriana." He ran to her. He knelt in front of her and hooked her chin with his fingers. "Sweetheart, what is it?"

"Back door."

As if on cue, the back doorknob jangled again, followed by a loud knock.

"Son of a bitch." Logan stood and clenched his fists. Rage flashed from his eyes. He headed for the kitchen at a run.

The sound of furniture scraping the hardwood floor, followed by Logan's loud cursing, told Doriana that he had bumped into one of the dining room chairs.

Fear pinned Doriana to the spot. She said a silent prayer for Logan. The back door opened and slammed shut and she knew Logan went outside. Long minutes passed. Where was Logan? Had someone been lying in wait for him? Was he hurt? She pushed up from the floor and reached for the vase, ready to go in pursuit. She froze at the sound of footsteps behind her and turned slowly.

Logan marched back into the room, fury darkening his face. He gathered her to him and cradled her in his arms. "The son of a bitch got away. If I hadn't tripped over the damn chair." He pulled her tighter. "I'm so sorry, sweetheart. I should have been here."

"It wasn't your fault, Logan. And you're here now."

"Everything will be okay." His soothing words stilled her trembling.

How easy it would be to let Logan take care of her.

Old fears reared up. She couldn't give Logan her heart again. He asked for her trust but he didn't trust her enough to tell her why he'd left all those years ago.

"I'm okay now, Logan," she said, pushing away from him. Her body missed his warmth but she fought her need to stay in the protective shelter of his arms.

"Are you sure?" he asked.

She hugged herself. "I'm fine. You arrived just in time."

His smile made her heart ache for what they once had. "You and that vase had everything under control." He rolled his eyes. "Unlike the useless guard I hired. Where the hell is he?"

Laughing softly, she bent to pick up the vase from the floor. She shook her head at the water soaking into her Oriental carpet.

The loud knock at the front door made her jump. She almost dropped the vase again.

"Police. Open up."

Doriana sucked in her breath. "The nine-one-one call. I forgot."

"I'll get the door," Logan said, striding across the room.

A half-hour later Doriana saw the police out. She turned to Logan, standing in the living room.

"Maybe they'll come up with something," she said.

He shook his head. "I know they'll try, but there's not much evidence."

She walked into the room and flopped down on the nearest chair.

Logan crossed his arms and leaned against the mantle, studying her. "You look tired. Go upstairs and get some rest. I'll wait for Josh."

Doriana's face burned and she averted her gaze. How could she tell him she didn't know where Josh was? Logan would think her a terrible mother. A knot twisted in her stomach. The responsibility of raising a child alone had always weighed heavy on her. Her parents helped, but they didn't live with Josh. And the way they spoiled him sometimes made her job harder. She lifted her gaze to Logan's. Maybe she wasn't so alone any more.

Doriana drew a deep breath and sat straighter. "I

don't know where Josh is."

"What?"

His face harsh with worry, Logan moved closer and leaned over her chair, bracing his hands on the sides. "He's only fifteen. What do you mean, you don't know where he is?"

"He's not at Steven's. He lied." Doriana stared at Logan's faint stubble of beard and inhaled his scent, citrus and male. Angry male. Angry at what? Her? Josh?

"Has he lied before?" Logan's gaze bore into hers and she pushed back in the chair.

"No, this is the first time. I think. I don't know."

Logan straightened. Concern and fear washed over his hard features.

Doriana relaxed her muscles as if a weight lifted off her chest. Logan wanted to help. She was no longer alone. Tears sprang to her eyes. "I've been having a little trouble with Josh lately. Just teenage rebellion."

Logan's intense stare made her shift uneasily. "It may be nothing," she said, sliding her gaze from his.

"Doriana, tell me what's been going on. He's my son. And I know a little about wild teenage boys."

She looked at him then and he shot her a wry smile. She saw a leather-clad Logan on his black motorcycle, exciting and sexy. "I guess you do know something about rebellious teens."

Logan took her by the shoulders and pulled her from the chair. Holding her at arm's length, he stared into her eyes. "Josh may be wild, but he's got a better chance than I ever did. He's got you for a mother."

Her throat thickened with unshed tears. "Thanks," she managed to whisper.

"I'm new at this parent stuff," Logan said. "Tell me what Josh has been up to and we'll get through this together."

She wanted to believe him, wanted his help. But her mind held her heart at bay. She had to be careful, to go slow. For her sake and Josh's.

She walked to the other side of the room. She couldn't think with Logan so close. Gathering thoughts and buying time, she ran her fingers over the clock on the mantle. The cool smoothness of the brass calmed her. "Josh has been breaking curfew," she said, turning to Logan. "He's secretive. He has friends I don't know. He won't tell me where he goes or what he does."

Logan's eyes narrowed and his forehead creased with worry. "Drugs?"

"I don't think so," she said. "I haven't seen any evidence, and I've been looking."

"Alcohol then?"

She shook her head. "I doubt it, but with kids you never know."

"Do you have any idea where he could be?" Logan's eyes hardened and his voice took on a professional tone. He reminded her of the two policemen who just left. Was Logan really what he seemed?

She swiped at a tear. "If I knew, would I be standing here?" She let her breath out. "Sorry. I didn't mean to snap at you. I know you're just trying to help."

His gaze softened. "You've been under a lot of stress."

She relaxed her stance. "Josh is a good kid. We're just going through a rough patch." Was that all it was? "My parents have been wonderful, always there for us. But they've spoiled Josh. They've tried to compensate for his lack of a father."

Hurt flicked in Logan's eyes. She wanted to bite the words back.

"Damn it, Doriana, if I'd known."

"What would you have done, Logan? Come running the minute you heard you had a child?"

He threw her a tortured look. "I wasn't always in places I could leave easily. But I would have gotten here as soon as I could."

She stiffened. "Were you in prison?"

"God, no."

The door opened and they both turned at the sound. Josh entered the hall. Surprise flitted across his face. His features tightened and the rebellious teen she'd come to dread took over.

"What's going on?" he asked.

"Where were you?" Doriana walked toward him.

"At Steven's."

"Don't lie, Josh. I called Mrs. Morelli."

Josh shrugged. "Then I wasn't at Steven's." His tone

dared her to argue.

Logan took a step forward. "You'll treat your mother with respect. She's been worried sick about you."

Josh narrowed his eyes. "You can't just show up out of nowhere and try to be my father."

Doriana heard Logan's sharp intake of breath and slid him a glance. Only the muscle clenching in his jaw revealed his inner turmoil. A mask had slipped over his face. How had Logan learned to hide his emotions like that? What secrets did he shield?

She turned back to her son and the painful job at hand. "Josh, go to your room. We're all too wound up right now. We'll talk in the morning. And you're grounded for the rest of the month."

"Whatever." He put his foot on the bottom step.

Logan grabbed the collar of Josh's coat, stopping him. Josh turned startled eyes to him.

"Apologize to your mother, Josh. Right now."

Josh reddened.

Logan pulled on his collar. "Do it."

Josh looked at Doriana. "Sorry," he muttered.

Logan sniffed and pulled him closer. "You smell like exhaust fumes." He examined the sleeve of Josh's jacket. "Grease. Where were you?"

"Where was I? Where have you been all these years?"

Logan flinched as if Josh had slapped him.

"That's enough, Josh," Doriana said. "Get to your room."

With a last defiant look at Doriana and Logan, Josh clumped up the stairs.

The slamming of his bedroom door released Doriana from her anger. Her knees buckled and she sat on the step, afraid she would fall.

Logan sat beside her and took her hand in his.

"I'm sorry, Logan." She leaned against his chest, too spent to move.

"It's going to be okay," he whispered, kissing her temple. He wrapped an arm around her and pulled her closer. "We'll get through this together."

She fought back tears. She wanted with all her heart to believe Logan meant what he said. Was she setting herself up for disappointment?

CHAPTER FOURTEEN

"Doriana."

The whispered word pulled Doriana from a wonderful, sensual dream, a dream filled with love and passion and Logan. She burrowed deeper into her covers. She refused to wake up.

"Doriana." The voice grew more insistent. A hand touched her shoulder and gently shook her.

"Go away."

"Doriana, for God's sake, wake up."

The deep, masculine voice penetrated her sleep-addled brain. She slowly opened her eyes to a bare-chested Logan standing by her bed. Pearly fingers of dawn squeezed through the blinds and stroked the chiseled muscles on his hard chest. Her gaze traveled to the waistband of his tight-fitting jeans. If she reached out, she could unbutton those jeans. Great dream.

"Doriana."

The urgency in Logan's voice woke her completely. A real flesh and blood Logan stared down at her. Much better than a fantasy.

She sat up and rubbed her eyes. "What is it?"

Logan's gaze swept her and he drew a shuddering breath. "You are so beautiful."

His husky voice covered her like satin. Her body responded with an answering heat.

A muscle worked in his jaw and he shifted his gaze to the windows. When he turned to her again his expression was guarded. "There's been an incident at one of the construction sites."

"Incident? What kind of incident?" She sat straighter. The covers slipped down to her waist.

Logan tensed. "Doriana, I can't think straight with you looking like that."

Her face burned. She glanced down at her sheer nightgown. It revealed more than it covered. She pulled the bedclothes up to her chin.

"As much as I want to stay," Logan said, "I have to leave."

"It's barely light," she said. "And how do you know about this incident?"

"Your father called."

She frowned. "I didn't hear the phone ring."

"He called my cell."

She clutched the sheet. "How does he even know your cell number? And why didn't he call me?"

"He didn't want to worry you." Logan knelt on the floor by her bed so that they were eye level. He reached out to touch her shoulder, his face grim. "There's been more vandalism. This time someone was hurt."

"No." She put her hand to her mouth. The covers slipped down but she didn't care. "Who's been hurt?"

"The night watchman. He's in the hospital. It's not serious."

"Thank God for that."

Logan stood. "Our culprit has taken things to a more dangerous level. I'm going out to meet your father at the site. I want you and Josh to stay in until I get back."

She jumped out of bed. "I'm going with you. It's my company."

He cupped her shoulders. "You're not making this any easier, Doriana. I want you safe. And Josh needs you. Stay here. Please."

Logan had played the Josh card. He knew she wouldn't leave Josh alone, especially after the stunt he pulled last night. Fear, and a draft of cool air made her shiver.

Logan's gaze raked her. Desire sparked in his eyes. "Get in bed and cover up. I'll be back as soon as I can."

"Do you have to go?" she asked, hugging herself.

He nodded. "I wish I didn't."

"Then stay."

151

His eyes looked tortured. "I can't." He bent to kiss her lightly on the lips. "I'll set the security alarm. And I've got someone new watching the house. He won't dare fall asleep like that other slacker I hired." Then he was gone.

"Be careful," she whispered to the empty room.

Doriana climbed back into bed, but sleep eluded her. She missed Logan already. Having him close filled her with a sense of belonging and security she hadn't felt in years. How had he managed to become part of her life again?

****

"Damn it, Tanner, I want this guy caught."

"So do I, Callahan. As much as you do. Maybe more," Logan added, his thoughts on Doriana and Josh.

Callahan paced his large office. Fear and anger creased his face.

Freezing December rain hit the windows like thousands of fragments of rock, making a dreary Monday worse. Logan remembered why he hated Philadelphia in winter. He missed the Arizona sunshine. But Doriana and Josh were here. No one waited for him in Tucson.

While Dan paced like an agitated bear, Logan studied his office, with its dark green walls and Wyeth and Picasso prints. The office reflected Callahan's wealth and power. But someone was determined to bring the great man down. And Logan had to stop that from happening.

"Dan, why don't you sit and let's go over what we know."

"I want results," Dan said, taking a seat across from Logan at the small table.

"And you'll get them." Logan slid some papers toward Callahan.

When Dan finished perusing the papers, he took off his glasses and looked at Logan. "Not much to go on. What's this about Candi Whiting? How is she involved and why haven't I heard this before?"

"I've always suspected Candi knew something about the thefts, but now I have reason to believe she's in this more deeply than I thought."

Dan rubbed his temples. "How so?"

Logan picked up his silver pen and twirled it between

his fingers, watching the overhead lighting play with the metal. He had to get his thoughts together. Doriana didn't want to tell her family about the near break-in Friday night, but Dan had to know.

The weekend had been a tense affair, with Josh holed up in his room and Doriana walking on eggshells whenever Logan was around. When he woke her Saturday morning, he saw the desire in her eyes. She wanted him as much as he wanted her. But for the rest of the weekend she seemed wary, afraid to meet his gaze. Why? He thought they were getting closer, but she still didn't trust him. Old hurts threw up blast-proof walls between them. Determination to punch those walls slammed into him.

Dan cleared his throat, drawing Logan back.

"Tell me about Candi," Dan said. "Why is she listed as a 'person of interest' in this report?"

Logan leaned forward. "Because Candi is having an affair with Bryce James. I thought he was stealing the bids to buy her things, but now I think it's much more dangerous than that. Especially after what happened Friday night."

Shock chased across Dan's features. "Candi and Bryce? She's the other woman?" He pounded a fist on the table. "Bryce may have a mistress but he sure as hell isn't roughing up my night watchman. He might be capable of stealing the bids, but physically hurting someone? Never."

Logan pushed some papers in front of Dan. "I'm with you about Bryce not harming anyone. I don't think he would. But he has no scruples about carrying on an illicit affair." He nodded his head toward the papers.

Dan skimmed the report. When he lifted his gaze, sadness shadowed his eyes. He shook his head. "Stupid bastard. To jeopardize his family for a tramp like Candi."

"Candi's had a rough life," Logan said. "Don't judge her too harshly."

Dan scrubbed a hand over his eyes. "You mentioned Friday night. What happened?"

"Someone tried to break into Doriana's house. We're almost certain it was her caller. She was alone at the time."

"What?" Dan jumped up. "Damn, it, man, I pay you to protect her. If anything happens to my daughter or grandson, Tanner, I hold you personally responsible."

"I don't intend to let anything happen to Josh or Doriana." Logan made a wry face. "I had someone watching the house, but he was useless."

"Where the hell were you?" Dan asked.

"Candi wanted to meet me," Logan said. "She told me she knew something about the problems at the company. I think she lured me out of the house so Doriana would be alone."

Dan's face reddened and a muscle throbbed in his neck. Logan feared for the older man's health.

"I'll fire Candi," Dan said. "I'll have her thrown in jail."

"Take it easy," Logan said. "I'm not sure yet just how involved Candi is in all of this. And we need her where we can watch her."

The energy drained from Callahan's face and he suddenly looked years older. He sat slowly down. "I didn't mean to come on so strong, Tanner. I worry about Doriana. But I'm glad you're there with her."

"Dan, you have my word that I'll protect her and Josh."

Callahan nodded and studied him. "You're a strong man, Tanner. Doriana needs someone like you. She's been alone too long."

Logan struggled to keep his expression blank. Callahan had warned him to keep his relationship with Doriana strictly professional. Was he playing matchmaker now? Logan wanted to confess to Dan about Josh. But the truth had to come from Doriana. When would she tell her family that he was Josh's father? Would she tell them? Or was she still ashamed of him?

Old insecurities tightened around him like a noose, constricting his chest. He'd come too far and worked too hard to let the old fears taunt him. The web of lies and deceit around this assignment had caused him too many restless nights. He wanted to come clean with Doriana too. Would her attitude toward him change if she knew the truth? He wanted her to accept him for the man he was, not for the success he'd become. But he hated the masquerade he played. Most of all, he didn't want to hurt her.

He looked at Dan. "Maybe we should bring Doriana into this. Tell her why I'm here."

Callahan shook his head. "Not yet. We've kept our secret pretty good. Let's not jeopardize things."

"You're the boss," Logan said, but he couldn't shake his guilt.

"Do you think the bastard threatening my daughter and my company are the same person?" Dan asked.

Logan nodded. "I suspect it is."

"What about our plan to give Bryce the false bid?" Dan asked. "I've worked hard on this and it's ready."

"Let's go with it," Logan said. "You never know what we might flush out." He picked up his pen and the report. "Let's go over some details. I've got my people working on a few leads. Candi's boyfriend, if we can find him, might be the key we need."

****

"Is Doriana in her office?"

Doriana jerked her head up at the sound of her mother's voice. This could not be happening. Her mother here. Seeing Logan.

The past six days since the attempted break-in had been calm. Josh sulked, but he didn't give them any more trouble. Was the dam about to break? Doriana braced herself for the storm known as Lena Callahan.

Lena, petite and stylish in a couture pantsuit, swept into Doriana's office. Slamming the door shut behind her, she turned to Doriana with fire sparking in her brown eyes.

Doriana gripped the pencil she held. "Mother, what a nice surprise."

Lena threw her coat and bag on the nearest chair and stalked toward Doriana. Tension tightened the lines of her slim body.

"How could you not tell me? Your own mother." Arms folded, Lena stood in front of Doriana's desk. Tears shimmered in her eyes despite the anger in her voice.

Doriana swallowed. "What, Mom?"

Lena flared her nostrils. "You're going to continue the lie? Even now?"

They stared at each other. Hurt softened Lena's eyes. Doriana sagged against her chair and dropped the pencil.

It pinged onto the wooden desk, the only sound in the unnaturally quiet room.

"You saw Logan," Doriana said. "You know."

"I wasn't completely sure until I saw the look on your face." A tear slid down Lena's smooth cheek and she sank into the chair by Doriana's desk.

"Mom, I'm sorry," Doriana whispered.

Lena jutted her chin out. "You're sorry? How do you think I feel? Coming face-to-face with my grandson's father. And with no warning."

Doriana gripped the edge of her desk and fought tears. "I didn't mean for it to be this way."

Her mother leaned closer. "How did you mean it to be, Doriana? Josh's father is here, working for you, and you kept him a secret."

Tears blurred Doriana's eyes. "Daddy hired Logan to take Lisa's place. I don't know where Logan's been for the past sixteen years. Please believe me."

Lena put a hand over her heart. "Your father knows and no one told me? I was in the delivery room with you."

"Mom, please settle down." Trembling, Doriana pushed up from her desk and walked to the small side table. She poured a glass of water from the pitcher on the desk. "Drink this," she said, handing the glass to her mother.

Lena gulped water quickly and slammed the glass on the desk. The half-full glass teetered for a minute before righting itself.

Doriana sat on the edge of the desk and faced Lena. "Daddy doesn't know that Logan is Josh's father." She drew a deep breath. "I wanted to tell you both, but I couldn't. Not yet."

"Josh," Lena breathed. "Does he know?"

Doriana nodded.

"Madone," Lena said. "My baby."

Doriana knelt in front of Lena and took her mother's hands between hers. "Josh is handling it. You know kids. And having Logan living with us helps."

As soon as the words were out, Doriana wanted to bite them back.

Lena widened her eyes and pulled her hands free. "Logan's living with you?" She jumped up, almost knocking Doriana over.

Doriana stood and faced Lena. She felt eight-years-old again. She took a calming breath. She wasn't a child anymore. "It's not what you think, Mom. And Daddy knows."

"Your father approves of your living with a man outside of marriage?" Lena's voice raised a few notches.

Doriana looked toward the closed office door. "Please keep your voice down. Logan and I aren't living together like that. It's complicated."

"Maybe I should call Logan in here," Lena said. "Maybe he'll tell me what's going on."

Panic skittled up Doriana's spine. "No, we can't do that. I'll work it out. I promise."

"Like you worked it out all these years?" Lena said, narrowing her eyes.

Doriana cupped her mother's shoulders. "Logan's showing up after all these years blindsided me too. Have some faith in me. I know what I'm doing." But did she know what she was doing? Not by a long shot.

"This will kill your grandmother," Lena said.

"Nonna's stronger than you think," Doriana said. "Nonna handled my pregnancy better than anyone. Dad wanted to kill someone and you took to your bed for three days."

Lena tensed. "Your father and I took it hard at first, but we supported you."

"I know, Mom. And I love you for it."

Lena pulled Doriana to her and hugged her in a fierce grip. Doriana inhaled the faint gardenia of Lena's perfume, the same perfume she'd worn since Doriana could remember. She was a little girl again, comforted in her mother's arms.

"Things will work out, Mom," Doriana whispered.

Lena pushed back to look at her. "You need to tell your father. After thirty-five years of marriage he and I keep no secrets. If you don't tell him, I will."

Doriana stroked her mother's cheek. "Give me time."

****

"We need to talk," Logan said. He and Doriana were in her kitchen, cleaning up the remnants of their usual Friday night pizza. A sullen Josh had escaped to his room.

157

He'd barely spoken to either of them since his grounding a week ago.

Avoiding Logan's gaze, Doriana sprayed the countertop with antiseptic and wiped. She wished she could wipe her problems away as easily. The pine scent of the cleaner mingled with the smell of pepperoni and sausage, making her eyes water.

"Talk about what?" she asked, not looking at him. Tension had hovered over them since her mother's visit to the office yesterday.

Logan shut the dishwasher door with a loud clunk. "You know what I mean."

She dropped her paper towel in the sink and turned slowly to face him. How did he manage to look so damn sexy dressed in jeans and a sweatshirt and holding a dirty plate?

He set the plate on the counter and folded his arms across his chest. The heavy ceramic dish thudding on the granite counter competed with the thudding of Doriana's heart.

"I saw the expression on your mother's face when she looked at me yesterday," Logan said. "She knew right away. To her credit, she tried to cover up her shock." Anger darkened his eyes. "Too bad you had to put her through that."

Doriana backed up to the counter, leaning against it for support. "I've already had a tongue-lashing from my mother."

Logan stiffened. Hurt chased across his features. "Not too happy to find that a transient fathered her grandson?"

"Oh, no, Logan. That's not it. She was upset that I didn't tell her or my dad about you. That was all."

Logan studied her. His features were harsh in the bright overhead light. He moved closer. She pressed against the counter edge.

"Did you ever intend to tell your parents or were you hoping I'd disappear again?"

The bitterness in his voice made her wince. "I planned to tell them. I was waiting for the right time."

Logan took her chin between his fingers. "You had sixteen years to figure out the right time. I think you didn't want to tell them for the same reason you never told your family or friends about us before."

"What reason?" she whispered.

"You were ashamed of me then and I think you still are. I never fit into your privileged life."

"Not true," she said in a shaky voice. But a small nugget of doubt opened in her mind. Was it true? She shook her head, dislodging the doubt. "You've got it wrong. I was never ashamed of you."

He gripped her shoulders. His touch burned. She tried to pull away, but he held her tighter. "Why didn't you tell them about us when we were kids? Why didn't you tell them that first day I walked into your office?"

Anger and hurt reflected in the gold-green of his eyes. And something else. Something that made her tremble. Could he love her?

"I was only sixteen, Logan. And I was afraid my father would hurt you."

His grip on her tightened. "What about now? You're not sixteen anymore."

Tears threatened and she blinked them back. "I didn't know how to tell them." She notched her chin. "And maybe I am a coward just as you think. You plan to leave again anyway. I didn't want them to know you'd walked out on me a second time."

"Doriana," he said in a tortured voice. "I never meant to hurt you." He pulled her to him.

She tensed, fighting her need for him. He'd walked out on her once and left her to raise a child alone. Could she forgive him? Could he forgive himself?

"I want to be angry with you," he rasped. "But when I look at you... Do you have any idea of what you do to me?"

Feminine power surged through her. "Tell me."

He drew a ragged breath. "I'll show you." He took her hands and kissed each palm, running his tongue over her sensitized skin.

She trembled and lifted her face for his kiss. Tonight she would pretend he still loved her. Tonight would belong to them.

Logan took her lips in a crushing kiss. He tasted of pizza and beer and male. She met his hunger and passion with an answering wildness. The demands of his lips peeled away the years. They were young and in love again. But she didn't want the past. She wanted Logan now.

With a small groan, she molded her body against his and opened her mouth, giving herself to him, body and soul. Twining her arms around his neck, she reveled in Logan's heat. His arousal pressed against her. Moaning, he softened his kiss and tangled his hands in her hair. Heat raced in her veins and pooled in her most private parts. She shuddered with her need for him.

"Doriana," he husked against her lips. He trailed searing kisses along her neck.

She drew away to cup his beautiful face between her hands and skim fingers over his high cheekbones, remembering the feel of him, the wildness and the tenderness. She looked deeply into his passion-filled eyes, the eyes of the man she'd never stopped loving.

"Logan," she whispered.

Heavy footsteps running down the stairs cut through the sensual fog of her brain. Doriana froze. "Josh," she said, pushing away from Logan.

Josh's footsteps grew closer. Logan put her gently aside and moved quickly to stare out the kitchen window, his back to the doorway. Doriana knew he needed time to compose himself.

She ran a shaky hand over her hair, mussed from Logan's touch.

When Josh entered the room he gave her a puzzled stare, then switched his gaze to Logan by the window. "What's wrong?" he asked.

Tension draped the room. Doriana smoothed her hands down the sides of her jeans, trying for calmness. "We're just cleaning the kitchen." Did Josh notice the false brightness of her voice?

"Your mother and I were discussing Christmas trees," Logan said, half turning from the window.

"Christmas trees?" Doriana choked the word out. Logan gave her a warning look. She nodded. "Yes, Christmas trees"

"What about Christmas trees?" Josh asked. The sullen look was back on his face.

"It's ten days until Christmas," Logan said with a

smile. "We need to get a tree."

Josh's expression hardened. "We have a tree. In the attic."

"A fake tree?" Logan said. "Nothing fake for this family. We get a real tree this year."

Doriana stared at Logan. Family? Her pulse raced.

She slid a glance at Josh. His attention was on Logan. Defiance hardened the planes of his face.

"We don't need a real tree," Josh said. He looked at Doriana with narrowed eyes. "He's never been here for Christmas before. Why should we listen to him?"

"Josh!" Doriana said.

"Josh, that's enough," Logan said in a quiet voice. He moved toward Josh and put a hand on the teen's shoulder. "You and I will finish cleaning the kitchen while your mother gets herself ready to go tree shopping."

The two men stared at each other like gunslingers facing off.

Josh's shoulders sagged and he shrugged away from Logan. Doriana caught Josh's gaze. Fear and uncertainty had replaced the defiance. She and Josh had been alone for so long. Now that Logan was back in their lives, what would happen to them, to their relationship?

She gave Josh a quick hug. "It will be okay, Josh. Everything will be okay. A real tree will be nice."

Doriana glanced at Logan. He watched her and Josh with hunger in his eyes. They were just shopping for a Christmas tree, but the yearning in Logan's gaze told her he wanted more. Happiness tugged at her heart, and smiling, she left the room.

CHAPTER FIFTEEN

Doriana hugged herself against the cold and inhaled the fresh, pungent scent of pine. The large Christmas tree lot was filled with clusters of people engaged in spirited discussions on the merits of various trees. Maybe she and Josh had missed out on something all these years.

She slid a glance at Logan standing next to her. Maybe she and Josh missed out on much more than Christmas trees. The cold air rustling through the pine needles seemed to whisper to her of all the lonely Christmases. She shivered.

"Cold?" Logan asked. He put an arm around her shoulders and drew her against him. His heat warmed her through the thickness of her coat.

Josh scowled at them. He wasn't used to seeing another man touch his mother. She hadn't dated much since he was born and she was always careful to shield him from her private life.

She met Josh's gaze but didn't move from Logan's embrace. Logan might walk out of their lives soon, but for a while she'd indulge in the fantasy that they were a real family. But was it a fantasy? Like the hundreds of trees scattered throughout the large lot, too many thoughts crowded her mind.

"Where do we begin?" she asked, looking up a Logan. "It's easier to put the same fake tree up every year."

Logan's laugh rang out in the crystal air. Several people smiled at them. Doriana smiled back. Being with Logan made her feel free and happy. He'd always had that effect on her.

162

"A fake tree's no fun," Logan said. "You miss spending time with all these fine people." He waved a hand to include the other customers. "You can't get this pine scent with a fake." He sniffed the air.

Doriana laughed. "A fake doesn't scatter pine needles all over my rug or coat our hands with sap."

"Spoilsport," Logan said with a teasing grin.

To her surprise, Josh, standing near Logan, laughed. Despite his attempts to look surly, Josh's eyes had lit with pleasure when they arrived at the huge lot filled with trees of all sizes. Josh watched her and Logan now with a mix of confusion and hope on his face.

Doriana separated herself from Logan. She didn't want to give Josh false hope. She didn't know how Logan felt about her or if he was capable of staying in one place for long.

Logan grabbed her hand. "Let's pick out a tree," he said, pulling her after him. "There are some Douglas firs over there. They have the best aroma of all the trees." He looked back at Josh. "Come on." The teen loped after them.

A frostbitten eternity later they still hadn't selected a tree. Cold seeped into every part of Doriana's body. She felt too cold to even shiver. But she knew the difference between a Douglas fir, a Fraser fir and a Scotch pine. And her head hurt.

"Notice this Balsam fir has a silvery cast," Logan said. An enraptured Josh hung on his every word.

"How do you know so much about trees?" Doriana couldn't quite hide the impatience in her voice.

Logan gave her a look. "I worked selling Christmas trees a couple of years when I was in high school."

"That explains it," she said. "Please, let's pick a tree. I've lost all feeling in my legs." She stamped her feet, trying to get her blood moving. Her breath spiraled into the night air, wispy testimony to the temperature.

"Mom, it's not that cold," Josh said. Both males stared indulgently at her. She glared at them, but hope soared in her heart. Josh and Logan had bonded in their quest for the perfect tree. Maybe Logan would stay, for Josh. But she wanted him to stay for her too.

"How about this one?" she said, pointing to a small,

full Scotch pine.

"Too common." Logan dismissed her choice with a wave of his hand. "We need something tall and majestic. Let's have another look at those Douglas firs."

"Yeah," Josh said. "They're cool."

Doriana groaned and Logan laughed. His eyes crinkled at the corners. He looked so gloriously masculine that she could listen to his mind-numbing tree lectures all night. A blast of cold air made her shiver. Maybe not *all* night.

She scanned Logan's muscular body. Tall and majestic he'd said. She'd take tall and majestic any time.

"Why don't you go back to the car and warm up, Dorie?" Logan said. "Josh and I will find the right tree."

She wanted to tell him that looking at him had warmed her, but she couldn't say that, not here, not with Josh watching them. "I'll tough it out."

"Good." Logan rubbed his gloved hands together. "We need a special tree for a special Christmas."

Doriana stared at him. A special Christmas?

A mask slipped over Logan's features, as if he'd revealed too much. Where had he learned to cover his feelings like that?

"There it is," Josh said, pointing to a full and very tall Douglas.

"Good choice," Logan said. He and Josh headed for the huge tree that stood apart from the others on the lot. Doriana hurried after them.

"That's too big," she said, craning her neck to see to the top of the fir. The lights surrounding the lot reflected on the tree's bluish-green needles.

"A Christmas tree can never be too big," Logan said.

"Right," Josh said.

Doriana rolled her eyes.

In no time they'd bartered the price with the lot's owner, had the tree bound with netting and were dragging it behind them to the Jeep. Josh and Logan wore self-satisfied grins. Despite feeling like a five-foot-two-inch Popsicle and smelling like pine cleaner, Doriana felt younger and happier than she had in years.

They bounced along in Logan's Jeep. He concentrated on driving, his hands gripping the wheel. The huge tree strapped to the roof slowed him down. Doriana studied his strong, chiseled profile. She squelched the urge to laugh out loud from sheer joy. She'd argued good-naturedly with both males over their choice of tree until they won her over. Or maybe she was so cold she would have agreed to anything.

Tonight Josh had looked more animated than he had in a very long time. What would life have been like had Logan not left all those years ago? She pushed the thought away. It did no good to dwell on 'what-ifs'. But she couldn't stop another thought from edging into her mind. Where had Logan been all these years and why didn't he trust her enough to tell her?

Logan turned on the radio, distracting her from her gloomy meanderings. Christmas tunes filled the car. For the first time in years, the songs didn't overwhelm her with sadness.

As if sensing her stare, Logan glanced at her. His smile heated her to her frozen toes. She settled into her seat. She would ignore her worries and enjoy this holiday season. If Logan left again, she would have these memories. But memories couldn't hug her, or kiss her, or share her bed. She wanted more than remembrances of Logan. She wanted Logan. But what did he want?

"How will we get this thing in the house?" Doriana asked when they pulled into her driveway. She jumped out of the Jeep and stared up at her townhouse, then back at the too-large tree Logan and Josh insisted they buy.

"Don't you worry your pretty head about that," Logan said, leaving the Jeep to stand beside her. He glanced at Josh. "We men will take care of getting this baby into the house. Your job, Doriana, is to make us some hot chocolate. Right, Josh?"

"Right," Josh said.

Doriana gave both males a quelling look. "Do I detect some sexism here?"

"Mom, we're just having fun with you, but you do make great hot chocolate." Josh's,grin, so like Logan's, and the happiness in his voice, made her heart do a crazy little dance.

"Flattery will get you a good cup of hot chocolate," she said laughing.

The tree up at last, the three of them sipped hot chocolate in the living room and stared at the huge fir that rose to the ceiling. Majestic it was. Doriana glanced at the pile of cut branches lying on the floor. She'd take care of them tomorrow.

"You were right, Logan," Doriana said. "Once the lights and decorations are on, it will look magnificent."

"Do I know trees, or do I know trees," Logan said, grinning.

Josh, next to her on the sofa, lifted his nose and sniffed. "Smells great."

"I told you that the Douglas fir has the best aroma of all the Christmas trees," Logan said.

Doriana groaned. "Lecture number one, repeated in lecture number twenty-five."

Logan, relaxing in the wingback chair next to the fireplace, faked a wounded look. Doriana stared at Logan's long, slender fingers wrapped around his mug of chocolate. Memories of the sensual magic his hands worked on her body made liquid warmth pool low in her belly, heating her more than the sweet, hot drink.

She tightened her grip on her mug. She really had to get a handle on her wayward thoughts. Her son sat next to her, for God's sake. And they were staring at a tree. The pungent aroma of pine perfumed the room. The hot chocolate tasted richer and smoother than usual. Being with Logan enhanced everything around her.

"Tree's cool," Josh said.

"I can't believe you actually got that thing in the house." Doriana shook her head.

Logan locked gazes with her. "A person can do anything he sets his mind to. And have anything he wants."

The room and tree receded into the sensual tension that sparked between her and Logan like short-circuited Christmas lights.

"Mom and I never had a real tree," Josh said.

His words diffused the spell Logan cast. Doriana took a quick sip of hot chocolate, burning her tongue. The slight pain mocked her foolish imagination. Setting the mug aside, Doriana turned to Josh and arched a brow. "You poor deprived kid."

Instead of the laugh she expected, Josh's face twisted with hurt. His unspoken words hung in the air between them. Josh had all the creature comforts growing up, but he'd never had a father.

"When should we decorate this beauty?" Logan asked.

Doriana shifted her attention to Logan. Had he noticed the interplay between her and Josh? Logan's eyes were unreadable, making her wonder again how he managed to hide his feelings.

"Maybe we can decorate Christmas Eve," Josh said.

"Josh, you know Grandmom and Grandpop have their party every Christmas Eve."

He shrugged. "I forgot." He turned to Logan. "Can we do it tomorrow?"

"Sure." Logan nodded at Doriana. "If it's okay with your mother."

"I have some Christmas shopping to do," Doriana said. She scanned the tree. "This is going to take a lot of ornaments. I don't have nearly enough."

"Not a problem," Logan said.

"No problem," Josh echoed. "We guys can trim this baby. And we'll buy new decorations. Right, Logan?"

The hope in Josh's voice made Doriana's heart thud. Her son had missed a father more than she guessed.

"Fine with me," she said.

"It's a deal," Logan said, smiling. "Josh and I decorate while you're shopping."

"Cool." Josh let out a loud yawn.

Logan glanced at his watch, then back to Josh. "It's late, son. Why don't you get to bed."

Doriana's head snapped up. Josh stared wide-eyed at Logan.

Logan's face held no expression. *Son.* Was it a meaningless slip, or something much deeper?

Josh stood slowly, his gaze riveted on Logan. Josh's eyes held a sheen, as if he fought tears. His mouth twitched in a small smile. Without a word, he set his mug on the table and slouched out of the room.

Words dried in Doriana's mouth. She turned to Logan.

A challenge stirred in the depths of Logan's gold-flecked eyes. A challenge that said she might have raised Josh but he belonged to Logan too.

Not ready to deal with the implications of this night, Doriana jumped from her seat and began gathering the empty mugs. She headed for the kitchen. She needed to keep busy.

She stood at the sink rinsing cups when she heard Logan's footsteps behind her. She stilled, her senses on alert. Logan stood so close. The warmth of his body reached out to her. She stopped breathing.

He wrapped one arm around her waist and pulled her against him. She dropped the cup she held. It clattered onto the counter. But she didn't care. Not with Logan's body pressed so close.

With his free hand, he pushed aside her hair, exposing her nape to him. His warm breath caressed and his lips brushed against the back of her neck. He smelled like pine and outdoors. The searing heat of desire spiked through her.

"Tonight was nice," he said. He nibbled on her earlobe.

"Um-mm," she said. "Very nice."

He slipped his hands under her sweater and massaged her ribcage. Sighing softly, she melted against him. He trailed long, slender fingers up her ribcage to unhook her bra. She gasped when his hands closed around her swollen breasts.

"I never knew buying a tree could be so sexy," Logan said in a husky whisper. He pulled her tight against him until she felt his hard arousal. He caressed her breasts slowly, gently. She thought she would die from the exquisite torture.

"Very sexy." She molded her body to the muscled contours of his and rubbed against him. She felt weightless, floating in a sensual bubble where only she and Logan existed.

"Do you know how much I want you?" he husked. "Do you know how difficult it is working with you every day? Sleeping down the hall from you every night?"

Joy and bittersweet sadness twined around her heart. He wanted her. No argument there. But he never said he loved her.

"That morning after Thanksgiving," she said. "You refused." Humiliation stung her at the memory.

Logan drew a deep breath. "I wanted you badly then. But you were scared. And reaching out for security. Reaching out for the past. We're not kids anymore. We can't go back."

She turned in his arms and cupped his face between her hands. "I know that. I don't want the past."

He grasped her wrists. "What do you want?"

"I'm not sure," she whispered.

His eyes darkened. "I want your body, Dorie. But I want something else. Something you never gave me before."

She swallowed. "What's that?"

He took her chin between his fingers and tilted her face toward his. "Your trust."

She jerked free of him and scooted to the other end of the counter, putting distance between them. She hooked her bra and smoothed her sweater, her gaze never leaving his. "The past won't go away, will it? You talk about trust. Tell me why you left me."

He stiffened. "I had my reasons. Don't ask. Not now."

Hurt settled around her heart, closing out the heat and love. "You don't trust me enough to tell me, but you demand my trust."

Logan was beside her in two strides. He gripped her shoulders. "I can't talk about it. Give me time. Trust me."

A tear slipped down her face. "You ask too much."

Their gazes locked. She wanted to tell him she loved him, but she couldn't give him that weapon. "Will you leave again?"

His haunted eyes and his silence spoke louder than words.

She turned away, hiding her hurt.

"Doriana." He grabbed her arm, turning her to face him. "Do you want me to stay?"

His penetrating gaze demanded the truth. She wanted to shout, "Yes, yes." But she couldn't. He had to want her enough to stay. He had to love her.

"You have to decide," she said.

The pain that flashed in his eyes made her want to throw herself in his arms and beg him to stay. She held herself rigid. Outside a dog barked and a horn blared. But inside, the house itself seemed to hold its breath, waiting.

A loud crash came from the living room. They jumped.

"What the hell." Logan dashed for the other room, Doriana close behind. She heard Josh's heavy footsteps on the stairs.

Logan stopped suddenly when he reached the living room. Doriana collided into his back.

"What a mess," Logan said.

They gaped at the large fir lying across the coffee table and sofa. The top of the tree pressed against the wall. The crystal bowl that had rested on the table lay shattered.

Was the downed tree a metaphor for her life? Doriana wondered. Get too happy and everything comes crashing down. Was the tenuous connection she and Logan made tonight as fragile as the shattered bowl?

Logan ran a hand through his hair. "How the hell did this happen?"

Josh stood on the other side of the fallen tree. His features were tight with worry. "Maybe I didn't secure it enough to the stand." Doriana wanted to console him, but the tree blocked her way.

Logan inspected the bottom of the tree trunk. "It's not your fault, Josh. I didn't cut it evenly. I usually do a better job. Hand me the saw."

At Josh's look of relief, Doriana wanted to hug Logan in gratitude.

Josh fetched the saw and handed it to Logan.

Once Logan sawed a perfect cut, Doriana and Josh helped him to right the tree and held it while he attached it to the stand. Doriana's arms shook from the effort and her hands were sticky with sap.

A phone chirped somewhere and she started. The tree swayed and she held on tighter.

"Damn it all to hell," Logan said.

"Is that your phone?" Doriana asked, nodding to Logan.

"Yes," he rasped. "It's in my pocket and I can't do anything about it. Wish the damn thing would shut up." The chirping stopped and they secured the tree. Logan backed away to stare up at it. "I think it'll stay this time."

"You think?" Doriana said. "You don't know?"

"It's okay, Dorie," Logan said. "Trust me."

His words brought their earlier conversation rushing back to her. "Another thing to trust you on?" she said softly.

"Yes."

"I'm going to bed," Josh said.

They both looked at him. Doriana had forgotten he was there. Her face warmed. A tired-looking Josh walked out of the room.

"I'd better get to bed too," Doriana said. She headed for the stairs.

Logan grabbed her arm. His fingers stuck to her sweater. "Damn sap."

"Told you about that sap," Doriana said.

He pulled his arm free. "We need to talk. Soon."

She bit down on her lip. "I know."

Doriana felt Logan's hot gaze on her as she walked away. She knew he wanted her. His searing looks and hard arousal told her how much. She wanted him too. But for what? One night? Or a future together? She couldn't ask him to stay. He had to want to stay for her. Heart heavy and steps slow, she headed up the stairs.

CHAPTER SIXTEEN

Logan paced the kitchen, nervous energy making sleep impossible. He'd returned the call from his second in command, Jo, but she wasn't in and he had to leave a message. He plopped his cell phone on the center counter, pulled out one of the high stools and sat down. Unable to remain still, he jumped up and resumed pacing.

Jo must have found something important. And leave it to the tough little redhead to call at the worst time. She sure as hell would have gotten a good chuckle if she could have seen him hoisting a huge fir tree with sap all over his hands. And seeing him shop for a Christmas tree would have sent her into an uncontrollable laughing fit.

Christmas trees. Doriana and Josh. His family? He leaned against the hard edge of the counter, letting the evening play out in his mind. Tonight had opened his eyes to the life he could have had. He'd fathered Josh but he wasn't a dad. Logan's gut twisted with regret. He'd always vowed to be a better father than the one he'd been saddled with, but he never got a chance with Josh.

It wasn't too late, he thought, rubbing his eyes. He would be a good father. But Doriana was part of the package. And he wanted the whole package. Could Doriana finally give him the acceptance he craved? Logan needed her acceptance as much as he needed her love. Love? Where had that come from? His phone chirped and he grabbed it, glad of the distraction from his crazy thoughts.

"Talk," he said into the phone.

"That's a nice hello." Jo gave a throaty laugh.

"It's been a long day, Jo. What have you got?"

"How are things working out with Doriana?" she asked.

Damn redhead could read his mind. He could almost see Jo's teasing grin. "You didn't call to talk about Doriana. Tell me what you have, Josephine."

"Oh, ho," she said with a laugh. "I hit a nerve with that one. You only call me Josephine when you're trying to hide something. Doriana's different. I can tell by your voice whenever you say her name."

"Cut it out, Jo or I'll demote you." He wasn't in a teasing mood when it came to Doriana.

"You couldn't run this company without me," she said. "But let's get back to business." Her voice turned serious.

"I'm listening," Logan said.

"I overnighted a package," she said. "You should have it on your desk Monday morning."

Adrenaline rushed through Logan and he gripped the phone. "What's in the package?"

"We found that guy, the son of Callahan's former partner." A note of triumph tinged her words.

"And ...." Logan said.

"He goes by the last name of Grove instead of Rove, which made him harder to find, but our crack team smoked him out."

"Where is he?" Logan asked.

"Philadelphia, we think. The police lost him."

Logan stiffened. "What do you mean, the police lost him?"

Jo sighed. "He's got a sheet, Logan. He's bad news. He was released from prison about nine months ago. Six months ago he stopped meeting with his parole officer. They've been trying to find him ever since."

"What was he in for?" Logan asked.

"Brutal assault with a deadly weapon, armed robbery, dealing drugs. I could go on."

"I get the picture." Logan walked to the kitchen window and peered out to the pitch-blackness. Black like the anger that covered his soul. Was this Grove guy the bastard who threatened Doriana? He had to stop the son of a bitch. And he knew just where to start.

"Logan? You still there?"

"I'm here." He drew a deep breath. "I think I know who might lead us to this scum."

"Take care of yourself, Logan. He's a rough one. Do you want me to come out there?"

"I can handle things," he said. "Thanks, Jo."

"Try to get some sleep," she said before hanging up.

Sleep, he thought with a wry grin. That was something he'd not had too much of lately. He raised his eyes to the ceiling, imagining Doriana all alone in her bed. He could think of something else he hadn't had in a very long time. His groin tightened. That particular line of thought did him no good.

Logan stared out at the dark night, forcing himself to reflect on what Jo relayed. This assignment was the most frustrating he'd ever had, for more reasons than one. He needed to put pressure on Candi. She'd been avoiding him since she'd lured him to that bar. She wouldn't answer his calls and she stopped going to the cafeteria for lunch. The rumor mill at work had it that she'd taken a few sick days because someone had beaten up on her. He clenched his hands at his sides. He could take bets on who that someone was.

****

Doriana struggled with her shopping bags. One of the smaller bags fell from her hands. She bent to retrieve it, dropping another one. "Damn it." Her words dissolved into the crisp night air.

Her arms ached from the strain and her feet burned from hours of shopping. The crushing crowds at the King of Prussia Mall had made her feel like a crazed rat in an overcrowded cage. She needed to take off her shoes and relax with a glass of wine. Maybe several glasses of wine. Hangover be damned. She leaned against the doorbell. The door opened to a worried-looking Logan.

"I just called your cell," he said, grabbing packages from her. He scanned the street. "It's getting late. You know I wanted you home before dark."

"I'm not a child." She gave him a look. "Are you going to let me in?"

He stepped aside and she followed him into the house.

174

"Don't take these phone calls lightly, Doriana. This guy's dangerous. I don't want you out alone at night."

Doriana dropped her bags on the living room floor and rubbed her arms. "Really, Logan...." The twinkle of bright lights stopped her.

She turned slowly to a grinning Josh and a Christmas tree that rivaled the one in Rockefeller Center in New York. "Oh. My. God." Holding her breath, she walked slowly toward the magical tree.

"Isn't it great, Mom? We found these cool decorations and Logan bought them all."

The towering tree sparkled with a rainbow of colored lights and ornaments in all shapes and sizes. A swath of dark green velvet covered the tree stand. A ceramic Manger scene nestled on the velvet folds.

The extravagant decorations must have cost Logan a full month's salary. Apparently he had no problem spending what little money he had. Was it lack of responsibility or Logan's generosity of spirit? She looked at Josh's smiling face. What did it matter?

The pine scent that enveloped the room triggered warm memories. Wonderful fun-filled Christmases with her parents and Franco and Nonna. What had happened to that happy girl?

She turned to Logan. His eyes glittered like a little boy waiting her approval. But his lean, hard body clad in tight jeans and black T-shirt was all man. Just looking at Logan made her forget the disturbing questions that swirled around him.

Her hungry gaze skimmed his body. "It's magnificent, Logan," she said in a breathy whisper. When her gaze locked with his again, the heat in his eyes scorched.

"It's for you," he said softly. "All of it."

Face burning, she turned to study the brightly lit tree. She recognized some of the ornaments she and Josh had collected over the years and smiled. Even those simple items looked elegant the way Logan had placed them.

"Are you a secret interior decorator, Logan?" she asked with a small laugh, trying to cool the sensual tension that covered the room like the velvet tree skirt.

"Do I look like an interior decorator?" He stared at

her mouth.

She flicked her tongue over her dry lips. "No."

Logan's husky laugh wrapped around her heart. She backed into the nearest chair and sat down, not sure her legs would hold her.

"This tree's the coolest," Josh said.

Doriana started. Josh! How much had he noticed between her and Logan? They had to be more careful.

"Mom, I know I'm grounded, but can Steven come over? I want him to meet Logan and see the tree."

Doriana put a hand to her stomach. She wasn't ready yet to introduce Logan as Josh's father. She and Logan had too much unresolved between them.

Josh looked hopefully at her. She glanced at Logan. He held himself rigid. Waiting for her answer?

She shifted in her seat. "Okay, Josh. But let's keep Logan's secret a little longer until I tell Grandpop."

"When are you going to tell Grandpop?" Josh asked with an accusatory look.

"Soon."

Josh stared at her, then shrugged. "I'll call Steve from my cell." With a smile at Logan, he bounded out of the room and up the stairs, taking the steps two at a time.

"I'm glad you're letting his friend come over," Logan said. "Josh has been a big help to me the last two days. He's a great kid. You've done a good job with him."

Doriana sighed. "Thanks. He is a good kid. Most of the time."

Logan closed the distance between them. He braced his arms on the sides of her chair and leaned over. "Hold off for a while telling your father about me."

"You surprise me," she said. "One minute you're railing at me because I didn't tell my parents and now you tell me to wait."

Logan straightened. "I know what I'm doing."

"I wish I knew what you were doing," she said.

The phone rang, jarring the silence.

"Damn things," Logan said. "I'm beginning to wish Alexander Graham Bell had never been born."

Laughing, Doriana reached for the phone on the table next to her. "Hello," she said into the receiver.

"Been shopping, I see."

The evil voice sucked her breath. She gripped the receiver until her knuckles whitened.

Logan pried the instrument from her hand.

"Are you too much of a coward to talk to me?" Logan said into the phone.

Logan held the phone close. His face paled. Doriana began to tremble. What was the scum on the other end saying?

"You bastard." Logan dropped the receiver into the base like a piece of vermin. When he looked at Doriana, his eyes were hollow.

She jumped up from her chair and ran to him. He pulled her into his arms and held her tight. "What did he say, Logan?"

"More of the say. Don't worry about it."

She pulled away and looked at him. "He said something. Tell me. I need to know."

He drew a deep breath and pulled her against him. "He said he hopes you enjoy this Christmas because it might be your last."

"No." Her breath seemed to stop and quivers shook her body.

Logan stroked her hair. "From now on, I won't let you out of my sight."

****

Monday morning Logan insisted on driving Josh to school before driving himself and Doriana to work. She'd argued that she could drop Josh off as usual and head into work by herself, but Logan was adamant. Since the phone call Saturday, Logan hadn't allowed her to go anywhere unless he went along. To her surprise he even accompanied her and Josh to church Sunday.

Doriana spotted the large envelope on Logan's desk the minute she entered the office. "What's this?" She grabbed the envelope. "I wasn't expecting a priority package."

"It's for me," Logan said, taking it from her.

Shrugging, she went into her office. She threw her briefcase on her desk and slipped out of her coat, then started the coffee. But the routine tasks couldn't stop her mind from going round and round like one of her father's concrete mixers.

Why was Logan getting priority mail? She'd had a quick glance at the return address. Someone named Jo in Arizona. A woman? Had Logan lied? Was there another woman in his life? Dread washed over her.

Her office phone rang. Logan picked it up. A few minutes later her intercom buzzed.

"Russell Meecham on line one," Logan said.

Doriana groaned. Just what she needed this morning—the head of HR whining about some employee problem.

"I'll take it," she said.

****

When Logan was sure Doriana was deep in conversation with Meecham, he slit open the packet from Jo and quickly scanned the contents. Grove had a rap sheet longer than Logan's leg.

He stared at the grainy picture enclosed. The guy looked familiar. Where had he seen him before? The photo on Candi's desk? Maybe. The hair on his nape stood on end. He could swear this was the guy who was watching Doriana the day they'd gone to the small deli for lunch.

Logan fisted his hand around the picture, squeezing it into a ball. The stiff paper crinkled in protest. He set it down and smoothed a hand over it. He couldn't let his anger take over. He had to remain cool. He wanted to strangle the guy with his bare hands.

He flipped open his cell phone and punched in numbers. Candi didn't know his cell number. She wouldn't ignore this call.

"Hello." Candi's voice came through loud and clear.

"Candi, we need to talk."

"Oh, Logan. Oh. I'm really busy now."

"Do you want me to come to your office? I'm sure your co-workers would like to hear what I have to say."

Silence.

"Meet me in the cafeteria," she said at last.

Logan was waiting for her when she walked into the nearly empty cafeteria. A few employees lingering over breakfast gave them curious glances. Logan ignored them.

Candi took a seat across from Logan at the small table.

"You look like hell," he said. "Is this why you've been

178

avoiding me? You didn't want me to see you?"

Her face, bearing the yellowed bruises of her most recent beating, paled. "You sure know how to make a girl feel good." Defiance showed in the rigid set of her body and the tightness of her features.

"I'm not here to make you feel good," he said.

"Then why are you here?"

Her eyes were the saddest blue he'd ever seen. He placed a hand over hers where it rested on the table. She tried to pull away but he held onto her. He wanted to help her, but she'd used him the night she tricked him into that seedy bar.

He swallowed the words that demanded she hand over Grove. He needed to go easy or he'd scare her away. His gut told him that the guy beating up on Candi was the same one stalking Doriana. Was he also responsible for the vandalism and bid thefts? All Logan's instincts screamed *yes*.

"Candi, he's going to kill you. You need to get away."

Tears sprang to her eyes. "I can't. I'm in too deep. He'll kill me for sure if I leave."

"Damn it, Candi. We've had this conversation before. I can help you escape."

She pulled her hand from his. "You would still help me? After what I did?" Desperation shadowed her eyes. "He promised no one would get hurt. And you weren't hurt, were you?"

"I wasn't hurt," Logan said. "But someone was."

She put a hand to her throat. "Who?"

"A night watchman at one of Callahan's sites was injured earlier. And Doriana's been threatened."

"No," Candi said, shaking her head. "He promised."

Logan leaned closer. "What do you know about all that?"

She stiffened. "Nothing. I swear it."

"You know a lot more than you let on," he said.

The tears in her eyes turned to ice chips.

"Are you still seeing Bryce James?" Logan asked.

"What if I am?" Her lower lip trembled.

"Do you love him?"

"Are you crazy?" Her mirthless laugh rang through the room, causing the few remaining employees to look over. She leaned toward him. Her cloying perfume, sweet and musky, assaulted Logan. He stifled a sneeze. "Love Bryce? Why would I love a man who thinks I'm no better than a whore?"

The raw pain in Candi's eyes tore at Logan's gut. But he couldn't allow himself to feel sorry for her. "What does Bryce say about your beatings?"

She shrugged. "Bryce doesn't really care."

"Damn bastard," Logan said. "And Bryce doesn't mind sharing you with the other guy?"

Her features hardened. "No. As long as I do the things he likes, the things his wife won't do, I can screw anybody I want. And Bryce buys me expensive jewelry."

"Does the guy beating up on you know about Bryce?"

She shook her head.

"You're playing a dangerous game, Candi. And you're the only loser."

She let out a bitter laugh. "Aren't I always?"

"It doesn't have to be this way," he said. "Help me and I'll help you."

"How, Logan? How can I help you?" She narrowed her eyes and studied him. "You're just a temp. Why are you so interested in what goes on around here?"

Logan smiled and pretended to relax. Candi was clever. He'd have to be more careful not to tip his hand.

"I want to help, Candi. Tell me where to find the guy who's beating up on you. I promise he won't bother you again."

"Are you going to kill him?" she asked.

He shook his head. "Nothing like that."

"Too bad." She leaned back in her chair and thrust out her large, high breasts. The gesture was natural. Logan suspected she'd learned early on to show off her assets to the highest bidder. He tamped down pity. She didn't need his pity, but she needed more help than he could give. Maybe once this whole sordid assignment was over, he'd talk her into seeking professional help. But right now he needed her trust and her information.

"If I tell you certain things," she said, "my life isn't worth much more than these chairs we're sitting in."

"There are people who can hide you where he won't find you," Logan said.

She shook her head, making her long blonde hair swirl around her face. "They'll find me. You don't know these people he's involved with."

"What people?"

She stood up. "I have to get back to work. I may be the boss's whore, but I still have to work for a living."

Logan grabbed her arm. "Will you at least consider what I said?"

Candi nodded and walked away. Her rounded hips swayed suggestively under her tight skirt. Several of the male cafeteria workers watched her and snickered.

Could anyone ever get past the shell Candi built around herself? He followed her out.

He'd call his contact at police headquarters. Get someone to watch Candi's house. Grove would have to show up sooner or later. The most he could hope for was that they would arrest the thug for parole violation. It wasn't enough but it would get the scumbag off the street for a while. He'd do whatever it took to get the bastard off the street for a long time.

He got back to his office to find a smiling Doriana waiting for him. Her bright eyes reminded him of the young girl who'd stolen his heart so many years ago. Was that vivacious girl still inside the gorgeous woman who stood before him now? He hoped so.

"Get your jacket, Logan. You and I are going out."

He arched an eyebrow and glanced at his watch. "A little early for lunch, isn't it?"

She grinned. "But not too early for a surprise."

"What are we doing here?" Logan asked thirty minutes later. He and Doriana sat at a red light in one of the city's worst districts.

Memories crushed Logan, making his chest tighten. He'd grown up two blocks away. The harsh, unyielding neighborhood had gotten worse in the years since he'd left. Despair and hopelessness reeked from every corner like the garbage piled up in the streets. Even the city seemed to have forgotten the miserable wretches who lived here.

Doriana pulled up in front of a sorry-looking building with a crooked sign proclaiming it a nursing home for the old and sick.

"What is this?" he asked.

She cut the engine and turned to him. "This is your Christmas present, Logan." Excitement colored her voice. "I hired a private eye to find him."

"Find who?"

Doriana grabbed his hand where it lay on the console between them. "Your father, Logan. He's here. In this place. It's my gift to you."

He struggled to breathe over the roaring in his ears. His father. The sorry bastard who made his life hell. He was alive. He could rot for all he cared. "Oh, God, Doriana. You don't know what you've done."

CHAPTER SEVENTEEN

"What's wrong, Logan?"

"You found my father. That's what's wrong."

"But he's your father," Doriana said. "You told me you didn't know where he was."

"I told you I didn't care if he was dead or alive. I didn't ask you to find him."

Doriana paled. Logan took a calming breath, hating himself for hurting her. Hating himself for the trembling that roiled his stomach at the thought of seeing his father again.

"I'm sorry, Doriana." He cupped her face between his hands, needing her touch and her spirit to chase the ghosts that damned his soul.

His head pounded with ugly memories. The beatings that left him bruised and worse. The verbal abuse heaped on him day after day for years.

"Logan?" Doriana grasped his wrist. Her huge chocolate eyes glistened with unshed tears.

He kissed her then, taking her full lips with a savagery he couldn't control. Only Doriana could exorcise the demons that plagued him. She resisted at first. Then her body softened against his and her mouth opened to him, giving him her trust.

And he was using her. He pulled away. Their heavy breathing mingled with the traffic noises on the busy street.

"What was that all about?" she asked in a shaky voice.

"I didn't mean to take it out on you."

"Take what out on me? What's wrong, Logan?" Her lower lip trembled. "I wanted to give you something for Christmas that would make you happy. But I've hurt you instead."

"Sweet Doriana. You didn't know." He gathered her into his arms. The wood console dug into his thighs. He welcomed the pain as atonement for the shame and guilt he'd carried for so many years.

She hugged him close, then pushed away to stroke a slim finger along his cheekbone. "You need to see him. He's dying, Logan. Cancer."

Her dark eyes seemed to dig into his very heart. He couldn't let her down. And he couldn't ignore the perverted curiosity that made him want to see what had become of the old man. Maybe it was time to banish the devil from his soul.

"I'll go see him," he said. "For you."

"No, Logan, do this for you."

He released a breath he didn't know he was holding and looked around at the menacing surroundings. "You can't stay alone in the car. Wait for me inside."

They got out of the car and Doriana locked it, making sure to set the car's alarm. Logan held onto her elbow, guiding her up the steep steps into the dreary-looking nursing home. The odor of urine and disinfectant and death assaulted them. Logan wanted to retch. Bored-looking staff milled around the reception desk. Even the workers' uniforms were yellowed and grungy.

"Stay here," he said, motioning Doriana to a cracked leather chair.

A middle-aged woman who reeked of cigarette smoke watched him approach the desk.

"Jerry Tanner's room," he said.

Giving him an annoyed look, she pulled out a small file box and thumbed through it. "Room 207. Elevators are down the hall on your left."

The odor of human waste stung Logan's eyes when he stepped out of the elevator on the second floor. He put a hand over his mouth. He'd been in worse conditions. He could handle it. But he'd rather face a desperate enemy than the man in room 207.

Logan trudged down the hall. His rubber-soled shoes

squeaked on the linoleum like perverted music to his own execution. When he reached the room where his father waited, he held onto the doorframe until the wave of nausea passed. Squaring his shoulders, he marched in.

A skeletal figure on the rumpled bed turned at the sound of Logan's footsteps. Father and son stared at each other. The old man's once-handsome face was shrunken and ravaged. The eyes that had glowed dark green were glassy with crusty deposits at the corners.

"You came," the old man said in a raspy voice. "I prayed you would."

"You prayed?" Logan said with a bitter laugh. "Why?"

"I drove you away," his father said.

"You did." Logan fisted his hands at his sides and moved farther into the room.

The old man's watery gaze locked with Logan's. Logan resisted the impulse to look away.

"When I lost your mother I lost everything," Jerry Tanner said.

"I lost both my parents when she died," Logan said.

His father clutched the yellowed bed sheets with a bony hand. "I made a mess of things. Wish I could change it."

"It's too late now." Incredible sadness welled up in Logan. He wanted to hate this man, but a part of him cried for what might have been.

His father's gaze raked over Logan. "You've done well. I can tell."

"No thanks to you," Logan said.

Tears wet the old man's cheeks. "I deserved that."

Some of the anger and pain that plagued Logan since he fled the city all those years ago seeped out. "What happened to you?"

His father's thin lips twisted. "Bad liquor and even badder women. Did you come to cheer my death?" Dry, hacking coughs racked his fragile body. He motioned toward the glass of water that rested on the table next to his bed.

Logan grabbed the glass and stopped. The last time he'd touched his father he wanted to kill him. Had almost killed him. That night set off a chain of events that had come full circle today in this place with the stench of

185

death all around them.

Shrugging off the painful memories, Logan bent to help his father sit up. Fighting the urge to recoil from the old man's wretched body that smelled of decay, Logan held the glass while his father sipped. His father waved the glass away and slid back onto the pillow, turning a sly gaze on Logan.

"Got your revenge now, huh? Seeing me die. You should have killed me that night."

"I thought I had," Logan said.

"Would have been better if you did, boy. Can't blame you for hating me. I made your mother suffer."

"I don't hate you. Not any more." The words slipped out, but Logan couldn't deny the truth. Some of his rage and need to strike back had dissipated into the choking atmosphere. He felt freer than he had in a long time. And all because of the woman who waited downstairs.

"Why did you come back?" his father asked.

"Work," Logan said. "And a woman."

"There's always a woman." The old man's eyelids drooped.

"You have a grandson," Logan said.

His father opened his eyes. His face lit up and Logan saw a shadow of the man Jerry Tanner had once been. "Where?" His father tried to pull himself up before falling back onto the dirty pillow.

"Here, in the city."

"You do right by him." His father's eyes began to drift shut. "Want to meet him." He closed his eyes. His shallow breathing and the whirr of the machines hooked up to his body were the only sounds in the room.

Logan stared down at his father. Hard to believe he'd spent most of his life consumed by hatred for the pathetic man lying before him. But he hadn't turned out like his old man, or had he? Despite his success, Logan had no one, just like his father. It was too late for Jerry Tanner, but not for him. With one last glance at the bed, Logan walked out of the room.

An attendant directed Logan to the manager's office. Despite the living hell his father put him through, he couldn't let his own flesh and blood die in this rat's nest. He'd make sure his father's last weeks were comfortable.

It was the least he could do.

Doriana stood when Logan entered the reception area. Anxiety clouded her eyes. He touched her elbow and led her out.

"Are you okay, Logan?"

The concern in her voice made his heart trip. Maybe Doriana cared for him after all.

"Let's get out of here," he said, anxious to be free of the despair that clung to the building like mud. He'd arranged to have his father moved to the best nursing home in the city. He could afford it. And maybe the guilt he'd carried all these years would finally leave.

Doriana eased the car out of the parking spot. Logan stared at her profile, the firm chin and proud Patrician nose. Her black hair swung free and loose around her face, as if begging for him to tangle his hands in the silken strands and bury his face in the smooth skin of her neck. Inviting him to taste the salvation she offered.

"Doriana, it's okay."

"I wasn't sure." She kept her attention on the narrow street as she maneuvered the car, but she couldn't hide the slight shaking in her voice.

"Thank you," he said. "I have a lot to think about."

"Did your father have something to do with your leaving?" Her hands tightened on the steering wheel and she kept her gaze straight ahead.

"Yes."

They'd come to a red light. She looked at him. "Do you want to talk about it?"

His gaze locked with hers. "I need to talk about it."

"Let's go home," she said.

"What about work?" he asked.

"Don't worry about it."

****

The afternoon quiet of the house helped settle Doriana's pounding heart. "I'll make tea." She headed for the kitchen. Some instinct propelled her to keep busy, to keep her fears and insecurities at bay. Did she want the truth? What if Logan admitted he never loved her, that her memories of their time together were a myth?

"I don't want anything," he said, grabbing her arm. "Sit down before I lose my nerve."

187

Doriana shrugged off her coat and sat on the living room sofa. She clasped her hands on her lap to stop their shaking.

Still wearing his leather jacket, Logan paced the room. "I never knew a time when my father didn't drink. I think my father loved my mother, but he was never happy. I don't know why." Bitterness and hurt colored his voice.

"Oh, Logan," Doriana said. "I'm so sorry."

He turned tortured eyes on her. "I don't want your pity, Doriana. I didn't want it then and I don't want it now."

She nodded.

Logan leaned against the mantle and stuffed his hands into his jacket pockets. His harsh, unyielding gaze bore into hers. "In his drunken stupors my dad threw things. Sometimes he put his fist through the wall. Once he broke all of my mom's best china. I never saw him hit her, but she'd have bruises on her face and arms. She always denied that he'd put them there." Logan's face twisted with grief. "I should have protected her."

Doriana fought tears. She wanted to go to Logan, to comfort and hold him until the pain went away, but he needed to talk. "You were just a child, Logan."

"I've told myself that a thousand times," he said. "But it doesn't help. I don't know why my mother put up with him. Maybe she hoped he'd change."

Doriana dug her fingers into her palms. "Maybe she loved him and didn't want to give up on him. And I'm sure she loved you very much."

He nodded. "My mom shielded me as best she could. But I hated being home. School was a refuge to me. Until I was old enough to hang out on the streets."

He took deep breaths. Doriana suspected he was working to hold his emotions under control. A door slammed outside. The mantle clock ticked softly in the quiet room.

Logan's intense gaze lasered hers. "When my mother died, my dad started on me. At first it was just verbal abuse. Then it turned physical. I stayed away from home as much as possible. I drank. I joined a gang, did some street fighting." He gave a short bitter laugh. "I was becoming my father."

"I had no idea," she said softly.

"You saved me from myself," he said with a small smile. "I remember the day we met. You were so sweet and innocent. And sexy. You were from a better world. I began to hope again."

"Oh, Logan." Her throat thickened with unshed tears.

A muscle worked in his jaw. "But you can't escape who you are. One night after we were together, I went home feeling good about myself. You did that to me. I should have known it couldn't last."

"What happened?" she asked.

"Dad was drunker than I'd seen him in a long time. I tried to ignore him, but he was itching for a fight. He hit me hard."

Logan's features tightened and he glanced away. "This time I hit back. A lot. We had a drag out fight. Things got broken. But we didn't let up until he was on the floor bleeding."

He looked at her then. She put a hand to her mouth to keep from crying out at the raw pain in his eyes.

"I thought I'd killed him," he said. "And I was glad."

Doriana's stomach quivered. "You ran away, didn't you?"

He nodded. "I threw some things in a bag and took all the money I could find. I didn't stop until the money ran out, in Tucson, Arizona."

She gulped deep breaths. Her muscles ached from holding herself so stiffly. "And later when I went to our meeting place to tell you I was pregnant, you weren't there." Tears for all the wasted years threatened.

She had to stay calm, for Logan. "What happened when you got to Tucson?"

Some of the tension left his features. "I stayed at a shelter where I met a priest, a good man. I told him my story. He made a few phone calls. Found out my father wasn't dead." Logan looked deeply into her eyes. "I should have stayed here and owned up to what I did, but I got scared and ran. I'm not proud of that." He raked fingers through his hair. "Once I knew he was okay, I couldn't come back, Doriana. I may not have killed him that time, but I would have eventually. I couldn't chance that."

"So you joined the Army?"

He nodded. "If I'd known you were pregnant, I would have come back. But I thought you were better off without me."

Joy tempered with sadness mingled in Doriana. Logan would have come back for her. Could she believe him? She wanted to. She went to him then. He opened his arms and gathered her close. They clung to each other.

Logan stroked her hair. "I didn't want to leave you, Dorie, but I had no choice."

"Logan, I'm so sorry." Tears slipped down her face and dampened the front of his shirt. "So sorry for everything."

"It's over, Doriana. It's in the past."

Swiping at tears, she pulled away to look up at him. "It's not over, Logan. Not yet. No matter what he's done, he's your father. You need to forgive him. For your sake."

"I'm working on it, Doriana. Let it go."

She knew not to press him. She suspected he hadn't told her everything, that he held part of himself back. But it was a start.

"Logan, why didn't you tell me about your father then? Maybe I could have helped. My father would have helped."

"Come on, Doriana. You and I were in different worlds. You wouldn't have understood."

She turned, hiding the hurt in her eyes.

"Doriana, I'm sorry. I didn't mean it like that." He cupped her chin, turning her toward him. "I never meant to hurt you. You were the best thing that ever happened to me."

Longing shimmered in the depths of Logan's eyes. He'd loved her once. Could he love her again?

She'd been safe for too long. The past and the future didn't matter. There was only now, this moment and this man. She brushed her hands over his arms, her gaze never leaving his. His muscles flexed under the smooth leather of his jacket. Did her eyes tell him what was in her heart?

He pulled her to him and kissed her, slow and deep. She snaked her arm around his waist and smoothed her hand along the firm muscles of his back. His soft groan fueled her heady sense of power.

"I never stopped wanting you," he whispered against her mouth.

He lowered his head to rain light kisses along her neck. She trembled with need and with the knowledge of what he could do to her. At nineteen Logan had been an incredible lover, taking her to dazzling heights of passion that fulfilled her every fantasy. He satisfied her like no other man ever could.

"I've waited a long time for you," he whispered. He skimmed his fingers over her breast. She shuddered and arched against him, lost in his heat.

She clutched at his waist, afraid her legs wouldn't hold her. He tangled his hands in her hair and kissed her with an urgency that matched hers. She moaned into his mouth.

His breathing ragged, he pulled away to stare down at her. "Doriana?" His eyes held the question she'd longed for.

Molten desire surged through her. She took his hand and led him out of the room. The bright Christmas decorations swirled by in a blur of color as they headed for the stairs.

She began undressing him before they hit her room. She pulled his jacket off and flung it onto the hall floor. Logan half carried her into her bedroom, kissing her with a hunger that set her on fire. Wild with wanting him, she unbuttoned his shirt and yanked it from the waistband of his pants.

Logan set her aside and stripped off the rest of his clothes. He stood before her, proud and beautiful. His tanned skin glowed golden in the sunlight streaming through the blinds.

Her ravenous gaze devoured him. The lean, handsome boy who stole her heart all those years ago had matured into a magnificent man with broad, muscled chest, slim hips and long legs. His erection, large and hard, rocked her with the promise of unbridled passion. She held out her arms in invitation. He moved toward her, slow and languorous, like a lion stalking willing prey. Desire pulled low in her belly.

He cupped her face between his hands and took her

Cara Marsi

lips in a smoldering kiss that set her on fire. Whimpering sounds came from deep in her throat. "Please," she whispered.

"Soon," he husked.

Logan slipped her suit jacket off her shoulders, letting the soft wool slide down her arms like a caress. With maddening slowness, he unbuttoned her blouse, kissing each section of skin that he exposed. Trembling, she shrugged out of the delicate silk. The rest of her clothes followed.

She straightened and met Logan's burning gaze. Was her body still desirable to him? His sharp intake of breath and the worship in his eyes told her the answer. The afternoon sunlight paled against the desire that sparked between them.

"I've dreamed of you like this," he whispered. He skimmed calloused hands reverently over her shoulders and down her sides to her waist. She gave herself up to his careful exploration of her body. He pulled her close. His hardness throbbed against her. She thought she would die from wanting him. When he cupped her sensitive breasts in his hands, she gasped and clutched his shoulders.

Her nipples pebbled in response. He bent to suckle one breast, then the other. Moaning softly, she wound her fingers through his hair. When he raised his head, the longing in his eyes made her tremble. "You're even more beautiful than I remember," he whispered.

He took her lips in a kiss that shattered her control. She twined her arms around his neck and opened her mouth to him, savoring his heat and his hardness. His scent, musky and citrus and all male, filled her.

Memories stirred of the time they were young and wild for each other. But she was no innocent girl now. She loved Logan with a woman's love, deep and full. And she needed him the way a woman needed a man. With a moan, she pressed closer.

Holding her, he walked to the bed and released her to slide down the length of him. Her intimate brush against his hot flesh burned. She sank onto the bed, bringing him with her. The softness of the cotton spread and the scent of lilac linen spray cocooned them in a sensual cloud.

He leaned over her, his eyes fathomless and dark. She flattened her hands over his chest. The golden hairs sprang to life under her touch. She teased his nipples with her fingers, reveling in his maleness, remembering the pleasure he could give.

"You drive me crazy," he rasped. "You always have."

She imprinted his chiseled features on her mind. No matter what happened in the future, today belonged to them. She would savor this moment for the rest of her life.

She traced her hands down his chest to his flat stomach. His gaze swallowed her. When she wrapped her hand around his swollen penis, he shuddered. She stroked the hard length of him. Moisture pooled between her thighs and she bit back a groan.

He put his hands on both sides of her head and kissed her, plunging his tongue in and out of her mouth, promising the fulfillment that only he could give. She kissed him back with an intensity that scared her. Logan was her drug. The more she had of him, the more she wanted him.

She was where she belonged, in Logan's arms. Only he could ease the aching torment of her body and the loneliness of her soul. She would not lose him again.

He grazed kisses along her neck to her swollen breasts. With his hands and mouth, he stroked and kissed and suckled her breasts until she cried out his name. Raising himself on his elbows, he stared down at her. "Dorie," he whispered. "My beautiful Dorie."

"Love me, Logan."

He covered her body with his and slanted his mouth over hers in a bruising kiss that sealed his possession. She moved her hips in a sensual circle against his. Groaning, he pressed her into the soft mattress.

"Need you," she rasped.

With a fluid motion, he grabbed his pants where they lay on the floor and reached into the pocket. He pulled out a foil-wrapped packet and drew on protection. Her heart felt ready to burst with love for him.

She took his maleness and guided him into her. He filled her completely. She'd waited half her life to feel Logan inside her again, to be part of him again. She closed her eyes against her tears.

Cara Marsi

"Look at me," Logan whispered. "I want to see you when I love you."

She opened her eyes to meet his darkened gaze. Desire shone from the depths of his eyes, but something more, something that made hope soar in her. She clung to him. He groaned and drove hard into her like a man possessed, telling her with his body that she belonged to him. She arched her hips to meet his thrusts. She never wanted to let him go.

His low groans powered her with feminine pride. No other man could ever make her feel this way. He'd been her first. She wanted him to be her last.

Crazy with his feel and touch and taste, she dug her nails into his back and moved her head from side to side. He thrust deeper and harder, making her cry out . She watched the ecstasy and the torment play across his beautiful face and knew she had always belonged to him.

"Dorie," he said in a tortured whisper.

"Logan. So good." Her moans filled the room Wildness overtook her and all rational thought fled.

He plundered her mouth with his tongue. She scraped her nails along his back and met every thrust of his tongue and his hard penis. Her female heat, moist and slick, wrapped around him. Logan plunged deeper and deeper inside her, taking her, claiming her.

Doriana clutched his shoulders. Logan took her higher and higher. Spasms trembled through her and her screams reverberated through the room. Then he took her higher. His body shuddered and he cried out his release. The fire and the fury of their passion spiraled them into a private paradise that she never wanted to end.

Logan collapsed against her. Doriana welcomed the crush of his body. She couldn't move. Her body ached in places she'd forgotten.

Logan's breathing finally slowed. He rolled off her, pulling her into the protective curve of his arms. She rested her head against his chin. She wanted to stay locked in his embrace forever.

They lay in blissful silence until sounds from the outside world intruded. Children shouted and cars raced by on the street. Wishing the world would go away, Doriana snuggled closer to Logan. "Afternoon delight."

"What?" He kissed her temple.

"Like the song," she said. "Afternoon delight."

He laughed softly. "You delight me any time of the day or night."

"Do I?" She propped herself on her elbow to study him. "You're beautiful, Logan. There's never been anyone like you in all these years."

Pain flashed in his eyes and he put a finger to her lips. "Don't. I don't want to think about you with other men. That's in the past."

"What's in the future?" The words slipped out.

He gave her a long look. "I don't know."

The mask had slipped over his eyes again. Logan hid something. Could they have a future if he wouldn't trust her with the truth?

She shivered. He pulled her next to him and wrapped the covers around them. Her body felt satiated and spent. But her heart felt ready to break. She'd lied to herself. This one moment wasn't enough. A lifetime with Logan wouldn't be enough. What would she do if he walked away again?

****

Pale shadows of late afternoon fingered the room. Doriana slept next to him, breathing softly. Logan held her tightly and stared at the ceiling. Soon he would have to wake her. They needed to dress before Josh got home from school. Josh couldn't find them like this. He tamped down the anger that threatened. He was Josh's father. He shouldn't have to hide his relationship with Doriana. For these next peaceful minutes he'd hold her and pretend that the hurt and lies of the last sixteen years didn't stand between them. Doriana filled the emptiness in his soul and excited him like no other woman ever could. Fear vined around his heart. He'd loved her once. He'd hurt her. She'd hurt him too. In subtle ways she'd always shut him out of her world.

Did she care about him now? Or was he still the rough kid from the bad neighborhood, exciting, but not someone she wanted in her life permanently? If he told her the truth, would she ask him to stay? To be a father to Josh? But he'd never know if she accepted him for what he was or because his wealth made him part of her world.

He pulled her closer. He wasn't being fair to her. But he had to know that she wanted him for himself. Logan closed his eyes against the old pain. He'd walked away from her once. The next time would destroy his soul.

CHAPTER EIGHTEEN

"Logan, did you hear what I said?"

Logan turned from the window in the penthouse office to face a perplexed-looking Callahan.

"I heard you, Dan. You and James worked on the final bid for Devlin. You submitted the bid and then you promptly replaced it with one that only you know. If another outfit submits a bid close to your original, you'll know James sold it to them."

Dan smiled, looking relieved. "Damn, you are good. I was worried there for a while. You spent so much time staring out that window I wasn't sure you were still with me."

"Don't worry," Logan said. "I'm with you."

"You sure everything's okay?" Dan gave him a searching look.

Callahan would probably throw him through the window if he knew about him and Doriana. Logan's body tightened thinking about their passionate lovemaking yesterday. Doriana had trusted him enough to give her body to him. Would she give her heart? Did he and Doriana have a future or would all the lies, past and present, forever haunt them?

"You look distracted," Dan said.

"I'm fine," Logan said. "Just a little tired." *And distracted by your daughter.*

Dan gestured to a chair. "Sit down. We need to discuss our plan."

Forcing himself to concentrate on the assignment, Logan sat across from Dan at the large conference table.

Dan adjusted his glasses and pulled papers out of the folder in front of him. He slid some papers to Logan. "That first sheet is the bid Bryce submitted, with my okay. The next piece is the replacement bid."

Logan studied them. "Not much difference between the two," he said, looking at Dan.

Dan nodded. "But just enough. Most bids are close for these types of jobs."

"Let's hope this flushes out the culprit," Logan said.

Callahan steepled his fingers and stared toward the window. When he looked back at Logan, sadness shadowed his eyes. "I want to catch who's doing this to me. But I don't want it to be Bryce."

"I know," Logan said. "I can't quite figure Bryce out. He might steal the bids if he needs money, but I can't see him vandalizing the sites."

"That bothers me too." Dan leaned closer. "Any luck on finding Rove's kid?"

"Not yet," Logan said. "The police promised to stake out Candi's house. Let's hope they are and let's hope no one gets hurt before we get him." Logan fisted his hands on the table. If that scum laid a hand on Doriana....

Dan took off his glasses and rubbed his eyes. Lines of fatigue feathered his eyes and mouth. Too much stress for a man his age, Logan thought. Compassion for the older man washed over Logan.

Callahan met Logan's gaze. "You really think Rove might be Candi's boyfriend and Doriana's caller?"

Logan nodded. "My instincts are usually right. The theft of your bids resulted in losses of millions of dollars for your company. If we can get Rove on grand larceny, assault on your watchman, malicious threats to Doriana and destruction of your property, we can put him away for a very long time."

"How do you think Candi figures in all this?" Callahan made a wry face. "I know she's sleeping with Bryce. But does she know what's going on?"

"I suspect Candi is up to her pretty neck in all of it," Logan said.

Dan slipped on his glasses and leaned back in his chair, folding his hands across his stomach. He studied Logan. "I'm putting my trust in you, Tanner. Don't disappoint me."

Uncomfortable under Dan's close scrutiny, Logan held himself still, his gaze never wavering from the older man. "I won't let you down, Callahan."

"Doriana tells me she invited you to our Christmas Eve party," Dan said.

"Is that a problem?" Logan asked. Old insecurities spiked him like knife points. Maybe he wasn't welcome in the Callahan house.

"No problem at all," Dan said. "If she hadn't invited you, I would have." He gave Logan a sly look from behind his glasses. "My daughter likes you."

Logan struggled to keep a bland expression. Dan would definitely throw him through the window if he knew in just what way Doriana liked him. But he and Doriana were no longer teens and their affair was their business. Their affair. Was it as temporary as this job?

Pushing the gut wrenching thought aside, Logan stood and began gathering his papers. "I'd better get back to the office before Doriana wonders what's taking me so long." He missed Doriana and needed to hold her, needed to reassure himself that yesterday was real.

"When will you hear about the winning bid?" Logan asked.

"A few days after Christmas."

"Hopefully things will stay quiet till then," Logan said.

Logan entered his office and locked the door. He wanted to take Doriana in his arms and kiss her until she begged him to stay with her forever. He threw his briefcase on the desk and headed for her office. She looked up from her computer, a question in her wide-eyed gaze.

He quickly closed the distance between them and took her hand to pull her gently from her chair. Her eyes darkened and she parted her full lips, waiting for him.

He gathered her to him and kissed her, telling her with his body how much he needed her. She opened to him, giving herself. He tasted the softness of her mouth with his tongue. She moaned and swayed into him. He slid his hands under her sweater to cup her breasts. She was fire in his arms, hot and sweet and all woman. His woman.

He unhooked her bra and massaged her swollen breasts. The nipples pebbled under his touch. Desperate to possess her again, he licked and nibbled his way down her neck, inhaling her heady scent of roses. Her pulse beat a staccato under his lips.

"Logan," she whispered in a shaky voice. She raked fingers through his hair.

He cupped her buttocks and pulled her against his hard erection. "I missed you."

"I can tell," she said with a husky laugh.

He stroked her hair, letting the silky strands slip through his fingers. "You made me sleep alone last night. Do you know what hell that was?"

She snuggled closer. "We can't make love with Josh in the house. You know the rules." Her voice was muffled against his chest.

"You're going to break that rule," he said.

"I've never let anyone ...." She pulled away to look up at him. "You know what I mean. Josh has never seen any man..."

Logan put a finger against her lips. "You're with me now. And Josh is my son. And I'm not just any man."

"You certainly aren't just any man," she said, running a slender finger down his cheek.

He turned his head and took her finger in his mouth, sucking it.

She let out a small groan. "The things you do to me." She pressed her breasts against his chest. His blood heated.

She gave him a seductive smile. "Josh isn't here now."

"What?" Logan stopped breathing.

"We need to have a private business meeting," she said.

He swallowed. "A business meeting?"

She nodded. "Here and now."

She kissed him lightly on the lips, then pushed gently away to kick off her shoes. Her gaze, sensual and dark as velvet, never left his. She pulled off her sweater and bra and reached under her skirt to slowly peel off her pantyhose and white lace panties, dropping them on the floor. Her full breasts thrust out, enticing and seductive.

An invitation in her eyes, she skimmed her hands over her breasts and down her body to her hips.

Logan released a breath. "You never fail to surprise me. Or excite me."

Laughing, she turned to sweep a hand over her desk, knocking everything to the floor, and hoisted herself onto the cleared surface. Her skirt slid up her thighs, exposing the ivory smoothness of her skin. Logan's heartbeat drummed in his ears.

"Lock the door and join me," she said in a sultry voice.

"It's locked."

"A man who thinks ahead. I like that."

"I've got lots more you're going to like," he rasped. He quickly shed his slacks and underwear and drew on protection.

Her smoky gaze swept him. "You have remarkable business assets," she whispered. She ran her tongue over her lips and held her arms out to him.

With a growl, he went to her. She laughed softly. He pulled her toward him until she sat on the edge of the desk. Her skirt slid higher. He kissed her waiting lips with a need that shook him and ran his hands over her satiny thighs to her hot center. He slipped his fingers into her slick folds. She was wet and so ready for him.

With a small cry, she wrapped her legs around his waist and slid her tongue into his mouth.

He moved his fingers in and out of her velvety softness. Her tongue slid in and out of his mouth, matching his thrusts. He plunged deeper and watched the passion on her beautiful face. She belonged to him and always would. Her body shook and she cried out her release. He held her until she stilled.

"More, Logan," she whispered. "Please."

He entered her, hard and fast. She arched her hips against his. Her moans filled the room. He drove harder and faster. He couldn't get enough of her. Her fingers dug into his shoulders. She met his every thrust, wild and passionate, and all his. Spasms quivered through her. He covered her screams with his mouth. His body shook with the force of his climax.

Doriana trembled in his arms. They clung to each

other. Finally, she let out a long, contented sigh and he released her. She slid off the desk and smoothed her skirt over her nakedness. They dressed quickly and he took her in his arms again.

Doriana rested her head against his shoulder. He rubbed his hands up the smooth line of her back and kissed her lips and the tip of her nose.

With a throaty laugh, she looked up at him. Her flushed face and swollen lips filled him with a possessiveness he'd never known. From now on only he would make her look like that, satisfied and thoroughly loved.

"I'll have to call more of those business meetings," she said with a smile.

"I'm ready any time, Boss," he said with an answering grin.

****

"Happy Birthday, Josh," Logan said, handing the teen a brightly wrapped package. Doriana, Josh and Logan sat around the Christmas tree drinking hot apple cider. Logan insisted Josh open the birthday and Christmas gifts from him before going to Doriana's parents' house for their annual Christmas Eve party tonight.

Josh ripped the paper off and pulled out a framed photo. He studied it, a look of pure joy on his face. "Wow! Cal Steward. And it's autographed to me. Look, Mom." He turned the photo toward Doriana.

"Who is Cal Steward?" she asked.

Josh rolled his eyes. "Only the best Formula One racer in the world." He looked at Logan. "Thanks, Logan. How did you get this? Do you know Cal Steward?"

Logan shook his head. "A friend knows him and got the picture for me." Logan's gut twisted at the lie. Someday soon he would tell his son about his friendship with the racing legend.

"Here's your Christmas gift, Josh." Logan handed him a large white envelope.

Josh tore the envelope open and jumped up, waving the contents in the air. "Tickets to the Montreal Grand Prix. And passes to the pits. Cool." He turned a smiling face to Logan. "Thanks. You give the best gifts. Look,

Mom. Three tickets and passes. One for each of us."

Logan heard Doriana's sharp intake of breath.

"When is it, Josh?" she asked.

The teen glanced down at the tickets. "June."

Logan felt Doriana's stare and turned to meet her gaze. He couldn't answer the question in her eyes. He'd be around in six months if she asked him, but she wasn't asking.

Her features tensed and she glanced down. He had the feeling he'd disappointed her in some way.

"You can take your grandfather and Uncle Franco, Josh," she said.

"I want you, me and Logan to go," Josh said.

At least his son wanted him around. Logan shrugged off his hurt. This was Christmas Eve. And Logan hadn't had a real Christmas since before his mother died. He determined to enjoy this holiday with Doriana and Josh. His family. Would this be his first and last Christmas with them?

Josh pulled a sloppily wrapped package from under the tree. Cellophane tape held the paper together. A shiny red bow slipped off as Josh, beaming proudly, handed the gift to Logan.

"This is for you," Josh said.

Logan stared at the package. His eyes watered. He blinked to clear his vision.

"Open it," Josh said.

With hands that shook slightly, Logan unwrapped the gift. "A black Lamborghini." He held up the small plastic model, a scaled-back version of the real one parked in his garage in Tucson.

Josh grinned. "You told me once that if you could buy any car you wanted, you would buy a black Lamborghini."

His son remembered. "Thanks, Josh." Logan averted his gaze, hiding his guilt. He hadn't exactly lied to Josh. He just didn't tell him that he already had the car.

"I've got to call Steven," Josh said, standing. "Wait till he hears about the tickets." He raced out of the room and up the stairs.

"Are you okay?" Doriana asked Logan.

Logan turned to her. "I didn't expect a gift from Josh."

"Why wouldn't he give you something? It's Christmas. I've got a gift for you too. Maybe you can wear it tonight."

He smiled. "You gave me a gift already, Doriana. Because of you I made peace with my father."

Her face pinked.

He reached under the tree and pulled out a large package. The colorful tree lights reflected on the metallic silver wrapping. "Merry Christmas, Doriana."

She stared at it for long seconds before taking the gift from him. She unwrapped it carefully, as if afraid of the contents.

She pulled the heavy book from the wrapping and ran her fingers slowly over the glossy cover. "An architectural book," she whispered and looked at him with glistening eyes. "It's beautiful. Thank you."

"You'll make a great architect," Logan said.

Shadows darkened her gaze. "It's too late for that."

He took her chin between his fingers and tilted her face toward his. "It's never too late to fight for what you want. And to ask for what you want."

"Isn't it?" she whispered.

The bright lights of the tree and the soft Christmas tunes on the radio faded as their gazes held. She stared at him, her eyes like melted chocolate and caramel. Would she fight for him, for them?

Josh's heavy footsteps on the stairs shattered the mood. Logan reluctantly pulled away.

Josh entered the room carrying a large duffel bag. He would spend the night at his grandparents, as he did every Christmas Eve. "I can't wait to get to Grandmom and Grandpop's. Grandpop promised me a car for my birthday."

Doriana gasped and stood quickly. "No, Josh. They will not get you a car. I told them I forbid it."

Josh shrugged and grinned at her. "I forgot my cell." He dropped the bag and ran up the stairs.

"What was that about?" Logan asked. "He can't be serious that your parents will get him a car."

Doriana rubbed her forehead. "They wouldn't dare. Josh isn't ready for a car."

"Josh is a good kid," Logan said. "I've seen both sides

of him. He can be spoiled and willful, but he can also be polite and respectful like he was when we visited my father this morning at the home. Josh made my father happy and proud, something the old man hasn't been for a lot of years. Josh made me proud too."

Doriana touched Logan's arm. "It meant a lot to Josh to meet his grandfather."

Logan put his hand over Doriana's. "Josh will be fine. He just needs a strong hand to guide him."

She pulled away. "Don't you think I know that? He gets guidance from me."

"But not from your parents," Logan said. "They indulge him."

Doriana bristled. "He is my son. My parents will not go against my wishes on this car thing."

****

Her parents' annual Christmas gala looked like another raging success. Doriana glanced around the crowded rooms. Laughing and talking, guests shouldered each other to get to the huge tables filled with copious amounts of food. The sweet scents of cinnamon and apples mingled with the luscious odors of turkey and ham and succulent vegetables prepared by the city's best caterer. The tinkling of sterling flatware on delicate china competed with the soft Christmas tunes played by a three-piece string ensemble in the large living room.

"Logan sure is a sight for starving females," Anita said, coming up to her.

Doriana's face heated and she glanced toward the dining room where Logan stood deep in conversation with her tiny grandmother. Her gaze swept his sexy body dressed in crisp khakis and the black cashmere sweater she'd given him for Christmas. The way he listened intently to Nonna made Doriana's heart swell with pride and love.

"Nonna likes Logan," Anita said. "And you're in love with him."

Doriana choked on the eggplant parmesan she just put in her mouth. Anita thumped her on the back.

"I'm okay," Doriana rasped, refusing to meet Anita's gaze.

Did her love for Logan shine from her eyes like the

crystal lights on her parents' tree? Her body tingled with the memory of making love with Logan on her desk. Had it really been two days since she held him close and felt his body on hers?

"I'm right, aren't I?" Anita asked.

"Stop that, Anita."

Anita took a sip of champagne from the glass she held and studied Doriana. "Nonna and the aunties and cousins will figure it out about Logan and Josh. You need to tell your dad."

"I know," Doriana said.

"What are you afraid of Doriana? You're a grown woman."

Doriana set her plate on a nearby table and grabbed a flute of champagne from a passing waiter. Averting her gaze from Anita's, she sipped the cool drink. Why hadn't she told her family about Logan? A small kernel of guilt blossomed in her chest. Would she feel differently if Logan had a stable job? Or was she afraid that if Logan left again, others would know the humiliation she couldn't hide this time?

She wanted Logan in her life. How would she survive if he left again? What would his leaving do to Josh? The urge to touch Logan, to reassure herself that he was still here, overwhelmed her.

"Talk to you later, Anita." She hurried to the dining room and Logan.

Logan's gaze met hers as she approached. Something passed between them. Love? Need? Her pulse quickened.

Doriana slipped her arm through Logan's when she reached him. He smiled down at her and pulled her closer.

Nonna gave Doriana a knowing grin and patted her cheek. "Logan is a good man," Nonna said. She looked at Logan. "Treat my Doriana well."

"I will," Logan said.

Love surged through Doriana. With a smile, Nonna moved away.

Doriana looked up at Logan. He bent and kissed her lightly on the lips. Several guests watched them. Did they see the resemblance between Josh and Logan? She loved Logan. But could he love her?

She shook her head against the thoughts that

jumbled through her mind like New Year's confetti. She'd worry later. She handed her empty glass to one of the servers.

"Let's find Josh," she said to Logan. "It's getting late. Dad usually makes a big deal about giving Josh his birthday gift."

Logan placed his hand over hers where it rested in the crook of his arm. "Do you know what your dad is giving Josh for his birthday?"

"No," she said. "And I don't care, as long as it's not a car."

"Attention." Her father's voice boomed through the rooms. Doriana turned to see her father standing by the hall staircase, a smiling Josh next to him. Lena stood on Josh's other side.

"Tonight is a very special night." Dan put his arm around Josh's shoulders. "My favorite grandson is sixteen today."

The other guests laughed and applauded. Josh beamed.

"You know what sixteen means," Dan said. Josh looked at him expectantly.

Doriana held her breath. No, please, don't let it be.

"Sixteen means a driver's license," Dan said. "If you have a license you need something to drive."

A gasp went up from the crowd. Doriana's heart stopped.

"What is he talking about?" Logan asked.

She couldn't look at Logan, didn't want to see the accusation in his eyes. Didn't want him to see the fear in hers. Josh was her son and her responsibility. Would her parents go against her wishes?

"Everybody outside," Dan said. An excited Josh followed his grandparents outside.

Doriana moved slowly on leaden feet. She crowded with the other guests on the marble steps leading down to the driveway. She shivered and Logan put his arm around her. She wanted to lean into his rock-hard body, but tension kept her immobile.

A sleek black sports car, driven by one of the parking attendants hired for the evening, pulled up the circular driveway. The attendant jumped out and held the door open, dangling the keys in his hands.

"There it is, Josh," Dan said. "It's all yours."

"Wow, Grandpop, Grandmom, thanks. You're the best." Josh gave each of them a quick hug and scanned the crowd.

"Look, Mom, Logan. Isn't it cool!"

Doriana chewed her lip to stifle her cries of protest. She couldn't make a scene in front of the guests.

Logan stiffened beside her. "Who are Josh's parents? Lena and Dan? Or you and me?" Anger heated his voice.

"Not now, Logan," she said, pulling away from him.

"He can't keep the car," Logan said. "He's too young and irresponsible."

Doriana lifted her chin. "You're telling me how to raise my son?"

"He's my son too."

Doriana didn't care if anyone overheard them. The tension that throbbed between her and Logan overwhelmed everything else.

Laughing, Josh and his grandfather ran down the steps and jumped into the car. The other guests clapped. Doriana couldn't breathe.

"We need to talk," Logan said. "Tonight."

208

CHAPTER NINETEEN

The click of the front door locking behind them echoed the tension that rode in the car with Doriana and Logan on the long trip home from her parents' party. Doriana walked slowly into her house and removed her coat and hung it in the hall closet. She would remain calm despite Logan's pointed silence and her own fury at her parents.

She marched into the living room and switched on the Christmas tree lights. Might as well make the place comfortable for the storm smoldering between her and Logan. The last hour at the party had been torture. Logan simmered with his censure of her and her parents. Some of her nosier relatives voiced their opinions that Josh was too young for such an expensive car. The not-so-subtle message in their looks and words was that she had lost control of her son, if she ever had it.

"Sit down," Logan said, coming into the room. "We're going to talk."

"I prefer to stand," she said, whirling to face him. She stiffened her spine. He would not intimidate her. How could he look so damn sexy, even glowering at her?

"Suit yourself." He slipped off his jacket and threw it on the nearest chair. Tension showed in every line of his muscled body. "I've been trying to figure out for a while how to say this." His voice was tight. "After what happened tonight, I can't put it off."

Foreboding formed a knot in her chest. Was it time for him to move on? But why was he so upset over her parents' giving Josh a car?

209

Logan paced the room, a sleek lion ready to spring. When he turned to face her, a vein throbbed in his temple. "I knew Josh was spoiled, but I didn't realize how much. Giving him that expensive car was irresponsible of your parents, especially when they went against you. You're his parent, not them."

She bristled. "I know that. But you have no right to say anything against my parents. I couldn't have raised Josh without them."

Pain flashed in Logan's eyes. "I wasn't around. I understand that. And your parents are good people. But they're blind where Josh is concerned. They knew how you felt and they got him a car anyway. What kind of message does that send Josh?"

She raised her chin. "I'll have a talk with my parents. I'll make them send the car back."

"Why do you think they'll listen to you this time? Josh needs a firm hand. And he doesn't get it with them or you."

Anger propelled her to his side. They faced each other, like fighters squaring off. "You've been his father less than a month," she said. "And you're telling me how to handle Josh?"

He gripped her upper arms. "That's not quite fair is it, Doriana? You tried to hide the truth from me. If I hadn't confronted Josh that day in your office, would you have told me at all?"

"I was protecting my son the only way I knew"

He tensed. "Protecting him from his own father? And how much of an effort did you make to find me all these years?"

Doriana jerked free of his grip. "Even if I found you, would you have come back?"

He flinched. She wanted to reach out to him, to touch him and tell him she was sorry for her harsh words, but he'd hurt her too. Would they ever make peace?

"You've never changed your opinion of me, have you?" he asked in a hard voice. "I'm still the boy from the bad neighborhood, not fit to be a father to your son." With a contemptuous glance, he turned away and strode to the fireplace. He leaned on the mantle, his profile to her. His chest rose and fell with his shallow breathing.

Doriana studied him. His jaw set in a tight line. His entire body looked coiled and ready to fight. Or maybe flee. Tears sprang to her eyes. They'd come so far in the last weeks. How had it all gone so terribly wrong?

"What do you want, Logan?" She tangled her fingers through the long strand of pearls she wore, trying to rein in the anxiety that churned her stomach.

Logan's hazel gaze impaled her. "I want to be in Josh's life."

"What?" She yanked on the pearl necklace. The strand came apart in her hands. She watched helplessly as beads rolled all over the floor. *My life is coming apart the same way*, she thought. She raised her gaze to find a stony-faced Logan staring at her with unyielding eyes.

"What's your answer?" He spit the words out.

"How long will you be in his life, Logan? You'll leave again and what will happen to Josh? I will not see him hurt."

Logan was at her side in an instant. He grasped her shoulders. She winced at the anger in his eyes. The twinkling lights of the tree reflected on the golden stubble of his beard, mocking the tension that arced between them like an electrical current. "I'm Josh's father," he rasped. "I'm not some stranger, here one day and gone the next."

"Aren't you?" She bit down on her lip. Hurt shattered the chiseled planes of Logan's face. She glimpsed the vulnerable young boy he'd once been, the boy she fell in love with. He released her as if he couldn't bear to touch her. Her throat thickened with tears.

"So that's it." The quiet calmness of his voice damned her more than shouts. "I've never been more than a temporary diversion to you."

"That's not true," she whispered. "I loved you. I ...." She stopped herself before she blurted that she loved him now.

"Do you really know what love is?" His gaze raked her. "You have no problem giving your body to me, but I'm not worth bothering with on any other level."

Fury and pain pierced her like a carpenter's awl. "How dare you talk to me like that?"

He released a breath. "I'm sorry, Doriana. I was out

of line." Sadness creased his features. "I just want to be in my son's life."

"How do I know you'll be around for him?" she asked.

"Trust me, Doriana. Damn it, just trust me."

Could she trust him? Maybe she should ask him to stay. What if he said no? Could she take that chance? Her insides quivered. "I can't."

"You can't trust me?" Steel hardened his voice.

She shook her head. "No, that's not it."

"Then what is it, Dorie?"

Words dried in her throat. He had to want her enough to never leave again. She wouldn't beg.

"Damn you," he said in a thick whisper.

He pulled her to him and took her lips in a bruising kiss. She held herself tight, resisting his pull. His relentless lips demanded her surrender. She could no more fight him than she could stop breathing. And she loved him. She twisted her arms around his neck and urged his lips apart with her tongue.

He let out a low groan. His lips softened against hers and he opened his mouth for her. He tasted like cinnamon coffee and mint. She pressed closer. He might leave and break her heart. But he belonged to her now.

They slid to the floor together. He leaned over her, his eyes dark and mysterious in the soft Christmas lights. His unique scent of male and citrus mingled with the pine of the tree. Those scents would forever remind her of Logan.

She wrapped her arms around him and pulled him down. Molding her body to his, she kissed him with all the love and hope she couldn't voice. His taut frame covered her. The urgency of his mouth and tongue excited her to a new wildness. She would love him tonight with all she had to give.

His mouth plundered hers while his hands wandered down her body, massaging, stroking, driving her crazy with want. Her soft cries filled the quiet room.

He leaned on his elbows and looked down at her. Desire darkened his eyes, but something else stirred deep in the gold-flecked depths, something that reached out to the longings in her soul. Could he possibly love her? "Love me tonight, Logan," she whispered.

"God help me, but I need you," he husked.

He undressed her quickly and flung her clothes aside. His own quickly followed.

She lay down again and held her arms out to him. He lowered himself on top of her. His flesh burned her heated skin. The wool of the Oriental rug pressed into her bare back. The slight pain intensified her passion for him.

"Now," she whispered. She wrapped her hand around his hard penis and guided him to her. He entered her, taking her with a possessiveness that inflamed her. She arched her hips against his, welding her body to his. She belonged to Logan. She would not think beyond this moment. She met his every hard thrust, urging him with her body to make her his forever. She barely recognized the sound of her voice crying out his name.

He cupped her bottom, lifting her to meet him, driving deeper and deeper into her.

Her climax erupted, fast and furious, like a shower of dazzling stars, shooting her into the sky. The lights from the tree overhead blurred and danced before her eyes.

Logan shuddered with his own climax. She clung to him, running her hands over his muscled back, reveling in his heat and masculinity.

He collapsed on top of her. The fragrance of pine joined with the musk of their lovemaking.

Doriana wound her arms around Logan's neck and closed her eyes. She would sear this moment onto her brain.

****

Doriana stood at the kitchen window and sipped coffee, inhaling the sweet vanilla almond scent. The first rays of sunlight teased through the curtains and danced on the stainless steel appliances. It promised to be a perfect Christmas day.

Her body thrummed with a new awareness. After their frenzied lovemaking under the tree, Logan carried her to bed and made love to her slowly. Several times. She gripped the mug, remembering just how thoroughly he'd loved her.

For the first time ever she spent the night in the arms of the man she loved. She smiled, picturing Logan asleep in her bed, eyes closed and long lashes fanned against high cheekbones. He looked young and untouched by life's cares. And very virile, even in sleep.

Their lovemaking had a bittersweet quality. Was Logan trying to tell her that he would leave soon? Tears threatened and she brushed them away. She couldn't lose him again. Maybe she should forget her pride and her fear and ask Logan to stay.

How did Josh feel about Logan? Did he want Logan in his life? Despite her love for Logan and her despair at the thought of his leaving, Josh's welfare came first.

The sound of bare feet on tile pulled her from her confused thoughts. Her pulse quickened. Logan's heat reached out to her before he touched her.

He wrapped his arms around her waist and pulled her against him. "Come back to bed," he whispered in her ear.

She leaned into him. Her perfume scented him, evidence of their lovemaking. Desire pulled low in her stomach.

"Do you want coffee?" she asked. "Or don't you have that addiction?"

"I want you," he rasped. "You're my addiction." He slipped his hands inside her robe and massaged her breasts. Her nipples pebbled in response. The silk of her robe brushed against her body like a sensual whisper. The coffee mug slid out of her hand to land on the floor. Her body felt as liquid and hot as the coffee that splashed onto the tile.

"We have to go to my parents for breakfast," she said.

His hands trailed a path down her stomach. He caressed her mound. She felt the wet rush of arousal between her thighs and moaned.

"It's early," he said. "I haven't finished giving you your Christmas gift." Pressing her close, he slid fingers inside her.

Her body quivered at his touch and the promise of sensual pleasure. "I like your gifts."

****

Late afternoon shadows pearled the room and wrapped around Logan and Doriana as they reclined in her bed watching a classic Christmas movie. Logan wished their sensual isolation could last forever, but the outside world would soon intrude. They had to deal with her parents' giving Josh a car. But not now.

He and Doriana had spent most of Christmas at her parents' and came home late last night, too tired to do more than fall asleep in each other's arms. He smiled. They'd made up for that today. Lucky for them, Josh had begged to stay at his grandparents a few more days.

Doriana snuggled closer. Her soft skin, smooth and hot, stirred desire in him. He kissed the top of her head. "We've spent all day making love and I want you again."

She laughed, a low throaty sound, and wiggled her naked body against his.

He groaned. "Don't do that."

She looked up at him with a seductive smile. "This is our time, Logan. We never had this before. And Josh will be home tomorrow."

He kissed her lightly on the lips and trailed fingers slowly over her breast. "You are one insatiable woman."

"I'm making up for lost time," she whispered.

The look in her eyes provoked a craving deep inside him. He needed so much more than her body. What did she want from him? "Let's not waste time talking," he rasped.

Much later, Logan lay in bed and stared at the ceiling. The dim light from the bedside lamp lent a rosy glow to the room. Doriana dozed beside him, her warm body curled against his.

Thoughts tripped all over his mind like green Army recruits on maneuvers. He and Doriana had laughed and talked and made hot, sweet love over the last two days. But neither of them mentioned a future together or his need to be part of Josh's life. The unresolved issues hung over them like a vengeful enemy ready to snatch their happiness.

Logan looked down at her. Silky black hair spread over the pillow. Her full lips were swollen from his kisses. Could he give her up again? Hell no! Sadness and frustration stabbed him like a bayonet. If Doriana loved him, she wouldn't hesitate to ask him to share her life and Josh's. But she hadn't asked.

Time was running out. This assignment would be over soon. He'd promised Dan secrecy, but he wanted

Doriana to know the truth. He couldn't wait any longer, hoping she would accept him for himself and not for the success he'd become.

He'd take her on whatever terms he could get her. Doriana and Josh were his family. He'd do right by them. And if she didn't want him, at least he'd have his son. Damn it! He wanted her too. How had he spent the last sixteen years without her? He'd tell her the truth tomorrow, in the light of day when he could think clearly.

The shrill sound of the phone disrupted the quiet. Doriana stirred. Stomach tightening, Logan reached across her and grabbed the cordless on the bedside table. Was it the nursing home calling to say that his father's death was imminent? He'd been expecting that call for days now.

"Tanner here," he said.

"Oh, thank God you're home." Lena Callahan's near-hysterical voice hit him like ice water in his eyes.

He sat straighter. "What's wrong?"

"He's gone," she said. "It's been hours."

"Calm down, Lena. Who's gone?" The lump in his throat told him that he already knew the answer.

Doriana jerked awake. She sat up and clutched the sheets to her chest, staring at him with wide, frightened eyes.

"Josh is missing," Lena said. "For hours. He won't answer his cell."

Fear punched Logan in the gut. "Josh is missing?"

Doriana's face drained of color. "Josh? Gone?" She grabbed for the phone.

Logan shook his head and put his hand out, stopping her.

"Lena, tell me everything," he said. He listened intently to Lena's nervous voice. Doriana stared at him, chewing her lip and twisting the bed sheets between her fingers.

According to Lena, Josh had been acting secretive all day, spending most of his time on his phone. A few hours ago they heard him go out. When they checked the garage they found that his new car was missing. His grandfather was out now looking for him. Lena ended her story on a strangled sob.

"Josh probably wanted to take his new car out for a spin," Logan said. "He'll be back soon and everything will be okay."

He kept his voice low and smooth, trying to settle Lena. The quiver in his stomach belied the calmness of his words. "Call us as soon as you hear something. Doriana and I will start phoning his friends." He replaced the receiver and looked at Doriana.

She grabbed his arm. "What happened? Where's Josh?"

He gathered her close and stroked her hair. "Josh left your parents' house a few hours ago. Your father is out looking for him."

Doriana pushed away from him. "He's driving that car. He has only a learner's permit."

"Dorie, he's sixteen years old. And he has a hot car."

Tears glistened in her eyes. "That damn car. Things were going too well with Josh. He was just waiting for the right time."

Logan took her chin between his fingers. "We'll find him, Dorie. I promise."

****

Doriana clutched the mug of chamomile tea that Logan insisted she drink. She took small sips. Anxiety clenched her stomach muscles until they hurt. Hours had passed since the phone call from her mother. And still no Josh. Lena reported that Dan had come home, defeated.

Logan paced the kitchen, running his fingers through his hair. Lines of tension bracketed his mouth. They'd called all of Josh's friends. If any of them knew where Josh was, they weren't talking. Logan's contact at the police department promised to help.

Logan stopped in front of her. "I'm phoning Steven again. He's hiding something."

Doriana shook her head. "We've spoken to him twice."

Determination tightened Logan's features. "I'm calling again."

He reached for the phone. It rang before he touched it. Doriana and Logan stared at each other. Her heart thudded and her hand shook so hard she couldn't hold the ceramic mug. She set it on the counter.

Logan grabbed the phone. "Yes?" The word, clipped and hard, shot into the mouthpiece. He stiffened. "This is Josh's father."

Doriana stopped breathing.

"How serious?" Logan asked at last. "Which hospital?"

Doriana clutched the counter edge. "Hospital?"

He hung up the phone and looked at her with raw fear.

"Josh is dead, isn't he?" She sank to the floor.

"No, Dorie, no." He knelt beside her and cradled her in his arms. "Josh is hurt. He had a car accident. That was the police on the phone."

Tears spilled from her eyes. "That damn car. I told my parents. If Josh dies, I'll never forgive them."

"There's no time for that," he said, pulling her up. "Let's get to the hospital."

****

Doriana and Logan ran through the double doors of the hospital emergency room. Doriana's head throbbed. Every nerve in her body seemed to scream out her anguish.

"Josh Callahan," Logan shouted to the desk clerk.

The clerk barely glanced at them and typed a few keys on her computer.

"Hurry up," Doriana said, pounding her fist on the desk. "I want my son."

A nurse wearing green hospital scrubs walked up to them. "I know where he is. Follow me."

They hurried after the woman. Doriana clung to Logan and ran with him through the halls. Her heels clicked on the hard floor, echoing the rat-a-tat of her heart. The strong odors of antiseptic and blood made her gag. The beds lined up in the hallways and the other people milling about passed by in a colorful collage.

The nurse stopped in front of a small curtained room and pulled aside the drapes, motioning them in. Josh lay on a bed, eyes closed. Blood and dirt clung to his face and his skin glowed deathly white. Tubes were hooked up to his arm and one pale foot peeked out from the sheet. His other leg was bloodied and bent at an unnatural angle. The jeans on the bloodied leg were ripped open.

218

Doriana burst into tears and sagged against Logan. He grabbed her, breaking her fall. Holding onto each other, they approached the bed.

Doriana looked down at her son, his beautiful face marred by scratches and cuts. One eye was swollen shut. "My baby," she choked out. Sobbing, she touched his face. His fevered heat burned her fingers. Her tears spilled onto the bed.

Josh opened his good eye slowly. He blinked and turned toward them.

"Mom," he whispered.

He looked over at Logan and managed a thin smile. "Dad."

CHAPTER TWENTY

Doriana jerked upright. The hard back of a chair pressed against aching muscles. She blinked, trying to focus sleep-filled eyes. The glare of sunlight on stark white walls and the harsh odor of industrial cleaner made her eyes water. A faint beeping sound came from somewhere, bringing her fully awake. Panic seized her, tightening her chest. Her gaze swung to the still body on the bed.

Josh! Her baby! She jumped up, almost knocking over the chair where she'd spent the night. It teetered on the wood floor before righting itself.

Rubbing her eyes, she walked toward the bed. Josh slept, his breathing even. Thank God. She took one of his pale hands in hers and stroked the soft, dry skin. Bags sending fluid through his body were hooked up to one arm and machines monitored his vital signs.

She brushed hair back from his face. He felt hot. The doctors had warned that Josh might have a slight temperature for a few days. At least they'd cleaned the blood and dirt from his face. Despite his cuts and bruises and a black eye, Josh looked so like Logan with long lashes shadowing high, chiseled cheekbones. Her heart lurched. Why had she ever thought to keep father and son apart?

She glanced at Josh's leg, wrapped in a cast. The doctors had operated on his broken leg late last night. Because of the severity of the break and a concussion, they'd kept Josh overnight.

She shifted her attention to the other chair in the

room. Empty now. She and Logan had kept vigil at their son's bedside. She smiled, remembering the new closeness that bound them. Sleep had been next to impossible. Only total exhaustion had allowed her to drift off just as dawn broke. Had Logan gotten any sleep at all?

Leaning over, she kissed Josh's forehead. "What were you thinking?" she whispered. "Drag racing and driving without a license?" His soft breathing was her only response. Thank God he would be okay. She'd worry about punishing him later. She rubbed a hand over Josh's shoulder. Not getting his driver's license for a long time might be punishment enough.

"You're awake." Logan's low voice touched her like a caress. She turned and smiled at him. Lines of fatigue creased his eyes and mouth. He looked as tired as she felt.

"I brought you coffee." He handed her a Styrofoam cup.

"Thanks." She sipped the strong, hot brew. The liquid coursed through her body, making her feel more alert.

Logan put an arm around her shoulders and drew her close. "I know coffee is one of your addictions."

She laughed softly. "I've found a new addiction." She leaned against his strong body, drawing his energy and comfort.

Logan kissed the top of her head. "How's our boy?"

"Sleeping," she said.

"No, I'm not."

Doriana jumped at the sound of Josh's weak voice. Coffee splashed out of the cup, burning her hand. She didn't mind the pain. Josh would be all right and Logan was at her side. Nothing else mattered.

Josh blinked his good eye and tried to smile. "You're both here."

Logan reached over and gently ruffled Josh's hair. "We'll always be here for you, son."

Did she imagine the catch in Logan's voice? She glanced at him. His eyes shone. Tears? Love filled her. She and Josh needed this man in their lives.

She stroked Josh's forehead. "You have to rest, baby."

"I will." Josh slid his gaze between the two of them. "Mom, Dad, I'm sorry."

Doriana's throat thickened with tears. "We'll get

through this together," she said. Logan pulled her tighter against him.

"How's my car?" Josh asked.

"Totaled," Logan said.

Josh grimaced. "Bet Grandpop is mad."

Doriana lifted an eyebrow. "You've got more problems than an angry grandfather. Now, no more talking."

****

"Josh is napping," Doriana said, coming into her kitchen and taking the mug of steaming coffee her mother held out to her. "He's got a long road ahead of him, but at least he's home." Doriana inhaled the cinnamon-laced liquid. "Smells delicious, Mom. Thanks."

"I made soup," Lena said. "I'll fix you a bowl."

"Soup's good," Logan said, smiling at Doriana. He sat at the center counter, a bowl of thick soup and a slice of crusty bread in front of him.

Lena swung her gaze to Logan, then back to Doriana. "You both look tired. Your dad and I wanted to stay at the hospital last night, but at our age, we just couldn't."

She fixed Doriana with a pointed stare. "Your father was up half the night ranting that no one told him about Josh and Logan. He shouldn't have had to find out something like that in a hospital."

Doriana set her mug on the counter. "I know, Mom. And I'm sorry about that. I should have told you." She let out a breath. "But,Mom, you and Dad knew I didn't want Josh to have a car and you bought him one anyway. I tried to tell you that he's not responsible enough yet." She stared at her mother, leaving unsaid the accusation that hung in the air between them.

Lena reddened. "We owe you an apology, too, Doriana. If we hadn't bought him that car, none of this would have happened." Her eyes glistened with tears. "What if Josh had been killed?"

Doriana gave Lena a quick hug. "Josh is going to be okay, thank God, and we've all learned something from this."

Lena swiped at a tear. "Sit, Doriana, and have some soup."

Doriana sat at the counter and Lena ladled soup into a bowl and placed it in front of her. "It did Josh good to have both his parents there," Lena said.

Doriana's face heated. She dipped her spoon into the bowl of soup and stirred, not looking at her mother.

"You and Logan need sleep," Lena said. "In separate beds."

Doriana dropped her spoon. It clattered onto the tiled surface of the counter. "Mom!"

Logan chuckled and Doriana narrowed her eyes at him. He tried, but failed, to squelch his smile. "I could use some sleep," he said, scrubbing a hand across his face. "But I have to check with the police first. I want to see what charges they're filing against Josh."

"Drag racing," Lena said, shaking her head. "How could he do that? And what kind of friends was he hanging around with?"

Doriana bristled at the recrimination in her mother's voice. "Josh has been rebelling for a long time. I knew he was up to something, but I couldn't get it out of him. I would have stopped him if I'd known he was involved with drag racing."

Lena relaxed her stance. "You did the best you could, Doriana. You always have. The stress has been hard on us all." She grabbed a towel and began wiping the counters.

Doriana smiled. Just like her mom to clean to relieve her worries.

The phone rang. "Maybe that's Dad," Doriana said, reaching for the phone hanging on the wall.

"You played dirty, bitch. Now I'm going to hurt you."

The evil voice on the other end of the line made Doriana freeze.

Logan jumped up from the table. He moved Lena out of the way and grabbed for the phone.

Shaking, Doriana sank back into her chair.

"Scum hung up," Logan said, replacing the receiver.

"Who was that?" Lena asked.

Doriana swallowed. She couldn't look at her mother.

Logan crouched in front of Doriana until they were eye level. "What did he say, sweetheart?" he asked, brushing hair back from her face.

Doriana knew her mother was watching them, but she didn't care. She took Logan's hand and kissed the palm, needing his comfort.

"He said I'd played dirty and he'd have to hurt me."

"What?" Lena shrieked the word. She leaned toward Doriana. "What's going on?"

"That son-of-a ...." Logan glanced at Lena and stopped. He stood slowly. "Don't worry, Dorie. I won't let anyone hurt you. I promise."

"Who was on the phone?" Lena asked.

Doriana released a shaky breath and met her mother's worried gaze. "I've been getting some calls. Daddy and Logan are taking care of it."

"Madone," Lena said, crossing herself. "And no one told me?"

"Mom, I'm sorry. We didn't want to worry you."

Lena sank into the chair opposite Doriana.

Another phone rang somewhere, a low, trilling sound. Doriana jumped.

"It's mine." Logan reached into his jeans pocket and pulled his cell phone out and flipped it open. "Tanner here."

He listened for a few minutes. His features tightened. Doriana watched him, her senses on alert.

"I can't leave now," Logan said into the phone. "Doriana just had another call." He listened some more, then nodded. "Okay. I'll be over once Franco gets here."

He closed the phone and slipped it into his pocket.

Doriana stood and touched Logan's arm. "What is it?"

He glanced at Lena. "Let's go into the other room, Dorie."

Lena twisted the dishtowel in her hand. "What's wrong?"

Logan smiled at her. "There's nothing to worry about. That was your husband on the phone. I need to go into work. Franco's on his way over. You'll be fine."

Lena jumped up from her chair. "What do you mean we'll be fine? Are we in danger?"

"Mom, sit and relax," Doriana said. "If Logan says everything is okay, it is."

Doriana slipped her arm through Logan's. "We can talk in the living room."

With a glance at her anxious mother, Doriana left the kitchen with Logan. When they reached the living room, he turned to her and took her by the shoulders. His gaze was soft and lit by something that made Doriana's pulse trip with hope.

"Thanks," he said.

She frowned. "For what?"

"For that vote of confidence in front of your mother."

"I meant it, Logan. I know you'll protect us."

He pulled her close and held her against him. "I'll protect you with all I've got. I don't want to leave you now, Dorie, but I have to. It's important. If things go the way I hope, we'll get rid of your caller."

"I don't understand," she said, pulling away to look up at him. "What's going on?"

He kissed her lightly on the lips. "I'll explain everything soon. Just keep trusting me."

Her gaze searched his. "Okay."

His smile made her breath catch.

She stroked a finger down his cheek. "Go now. The sooner you leave, the sooner you'll be back. I'll set the security alarm and Franco will be here shortly."

"I won't leave you until Franco gets here."

Despite the love that washed over her, a frisson of foreboding tingled up her spine, making her shiver. "I have a funny feeling, Logan. Be careful."

He hugged her close. "I'm always careful."

He set her gently from him and looked at his watch. "I need to get some things from my room."

Doriana paced, waiting for him. She chewed her lip. Something was very wrong.

A knock at the door made her jump. "Who is it?"

"Franco."

She let in a puzzled-looking Franco. "What's going on?" he asked. "Dad told me to high-tail it over here."

"I don't know," she said. "Mom's in the kitchen with homemade soup."

He grinned. "That makes up for the speeding ticket I got on the way over." He loped off to the kitchen.

Logan ran down the stairs, car keys in hand. "Was that Franco?"

She nodded.

Their gazes locked. "I'd better go," he said, turning.

"Logan, stop."

"What, sweetheart?"

225

Cara Marsi

She ran into his arms and gave him a fierce hug.

"What's that all about?" he asked.

"I'm afraid."

"I can take care of myself, Doriana."

She looked deeply into the eyes of the man she loved. "Logan, I can't let you leave until I tell you something I should have said a long time ago."

His eyes darkened. "Go on."

Doriana clasped her hands together to stop their trembling. "I want you to be part of Josh's life. He needs you, Logan."

His eyes softened to molten gold and he cupped her shoulders. "And what about you, Dorie? What do you need?"

She licked her lips. "I need you too, Logan."

He closed his eyes for a second and exhaled as if he'd been holding his breath for a long time. When he looked at her again, joy lit his face. "I've waited so long to hear you say that, sweetheart."

He touched her chin and tilted her face toward his. He kissed her with a tenderness that spoke his feelings louder than words. "I have something to tell you too. We'll have a long talk when I get back."

****

"Sit down," Dan said, ushering Logan into the small conference room next to his office.

Logan took a seat in one of the upholstered chairs.

Dan paced the small room, agitation evident in the rigid set of his shoulders. He whirled to face Logan. "If I'd known about you when my Doriana was scared and pregnant, I would have found you. And I would have hurt you."

Logan stiffened. He stood slowly to face Dan. "We made mistakes in the past. Some things can't be changed. But Doriana and I should have told you the truth before you had to find out at the hospital last night."

"Damn straight," Dan said. "My grandson is injured, his car totaled, and I find out that the man who's worked for me for almost two months is his father." Dan ran fingers through his close-cropped graying hair. "That was a hell of a way to find out what I should have known sixteen years ago."

Dan's eyes darkened to thunderclouds. Logan expected lightning bolts to shoot from them. Dan Callahan could teach some Colombian drug lords a thing or two.

"I don't blame you for being upset," Logan said. "Doriana and I may have mis-handled things in the past. But I intend to do right by her and Josh now." Pride surged through Logan and he squared his shoulders. "They're my family," he said softly.

"You hurt my daughter again," Dan said in a tight voice, "and you'll answer to me."

"I won't hurt her, Dan. I never meant to hurt her before. If I'd known she was pregnant, I would never have left."

Logan straightened under Dan's unflinching gaze.

"I believe you," Dan said at last. His shoulders sagged. "I should have listened to Doriana and not bought Josh that car." Regret creased his face and he turned and walked to the window, his back to Logan.

Logan kept quiet, letting Dan deal with his private pain. He slid his gaze to a Picasso print hanging on the opposite wall. His insides felt like the jumbled colors and shapes in the painting. He meant what he told Dan. He would never hurt Doriana again. She hadn't said she loved him, but she told him she needed him in her life. Wasn't that the same thing? He wanted to get back to her as soon as possible, to hold her and never let her go.

"Let's get to work," Dan said, turning from the window. "I'm paying you to do a job so let's finish it."

Logan exhaled. He could easily deal with the powerful mogul Dan Callahan. The wronged father was another matter.

Dan sat at the table and gestured to Logan to take a seat opposite. He handed Logan a paper from the stack in front of him.

Logan scanned the paper and set it down. "This is your bid," he said, raising his gaze to Dan's.

Dan nodded. "The winning bid, I might add."

"Congratulations," Logan said.

Dan pushed another piece of paper across the table. "This is the nearest competitor's bid. I told you I had ways to get the information." A shadow passed over Dan's face.

He pushed another sheet forward. "This is what Bryce James submitted."

Logan did a quick calculation in his head. He blew a silent whistle and looked at Dan. "The competing bid is just enough under James's figure to get the contract. If you hadn't submitted a second one, the other company would have gotten the job."

Dan nodded. "You were right about Bryce. He's involved in the thefts. I got that out of him earlier. But let's hear the whole story from him."

Dan got up from the table and walked to the door separating the conference room from his office. He opened the door and gestured to someone. "Get in here."

A cowed-looking Bryce James walked slowly into the room. His eyes behind his black frames were huge and frightened.

"Sit," Dan barked.

Bryce sank into one of the chairs surrounding the table.

"Tell Logan what you told me earlier." Dan settled into a seat next to Bryce.

Sweat beaded Bryce's forehead and his gaze darted from Dan to Logan. "What are you doing here, Tanner?"

"He's my security expert," Dan said.

Bryce sneered. "I knew there was something funny about you, Tanner."

Logan tamped down his impatience. He wanted to jump across the table and demand Bryce start talking, to tell what he knew about the scum threatening Doriana. But they'd get more information by careful questioning.

"Damn it, man," Dan shouted. "We don't have all day."

Bryce jerked as if he'd been electrocuted. Logan feared he'd bolt for the door.

"Take it easy, Dan," Logan said. He leveled his gaze at Bryce. "Tell us what you know. All of it."

Bryce cleared his throat. "I sold the bids."

"Were you the only one involved?" Logan asked.

Bryce shook his head.

Logan imagined his hands around the man's neck. Pulling information from James was harder than running a cable down thirty floors in one of Callahan's buildings.

228

"Who else was working with you?" Logan asked as calmly as he could.

"Candi Whiting."

He spoke in such low tones Logan had to strain to hear.

"Candi? You sold the bids to her?"

Bryce nodded.

Disgust and sadness arced through Logan. He'd hoped Candi wasn't involved. Under her blatant sexuality and coarseness, he sensed a decent person trying to get out. She'd sure played him for the fool. Straightening, Logan forced himself to focus on Bryce. "How did all this come about?"

Bryce fidgeted in his seat and ran his finger around his collar. "Candi approached me about nine months ago and said she had a way to make us both some money." Bryce's thin lips twisted in a leer. "Candi's hot. I'd been trying to get into her pants for a long time. She promised to put out for me as part of the deal. And I had some gambling debts to pay." He slid a frightened glance to Callahan.

"You're dumping the whole thing on Candi?" Dan said. "And you're gambling again?" Disgust dripped from his voice.

"Spare us the slimy details, James," Logan said. "You gave Candi the bids and she gave them to someone else. Right?"

Bryce nodded. "She gave them to that no-good boyfriend of hers. As long as she put out for me, I didn't care."

Logan fisted his hands, fighting the urge to throw Bryce across the room. Candi may have used Bryce but he used her too.

"You sicken me," Dan said, throwing Bryce a look of contempt. "You sold me out for a piece of ass."

Bryce's face reddened. He swallowed and his Adam's apple bobbed up and down.

Logan narrowed his eyes at Bryce. "Who paid Candi's boyfriend for the bids? Was it the other companies?"

"I'm not sure," Bryce said. "The boyfriend has mob connections. I assume he sold the bids to them and they gave them to the other companies for a cut. The mob is

Cara Marsi

involved in tons of construction jobs around the city."

Dan pounded his fist on the table. Bryce jumped. "My God, man. The mob? Are you out of your mind?"

Logan held a hand up, silencing Dan. He pulled his attention back to Bryce. "You know we faked the bid this time."

Bryce's features tightened. "I got a frantic call from Candi this morning. She didn't come to work. She said the boyfriend's in big trouble over the wrong bid. He'd been beating on her. She sounded scared."

Apprehension skittered up Logan's spine. "Where's Candi now?"

Bryce shrugged. "Home, I guess."

Logan leaned over the table until his face was inches from Bryce's. The other man moved back. "The scum beat Candi up," Logan said. "And he's likely not finished with her. And you did nothing?"

Bryce curled his lip. "Why do you care about Candi? You want a little piece of the action too? If you're not already getting it."

Logan grabbed the man by his tie and dragged him across the desk. "You pathetic piece of shit." He threw Bryce away from him. Bryce hit the wall and slid to the floor. Logan yanked him up by his shirt. The stench of fear covered Bryce like poured concrete.

"What do you know about Doriana getting threatening calls and about the vandalism?" Logan asked. "I want the truth."

The other man's eyes bugged out and sweat poured from him. "I wasn't involved with any of that, I swear." He looked at Dan. "Believe me, Dan. Candi alluded to the calls and the vandalism, but I didn't want to know. I had nothing to do with that. I don't know why the guy had it in for you."

Logan pushed Bryce away from him. The other man stumbled, then righted himself to lean, shaking, against the wall.

"I've got to get to Candi's," Logan said.

Dan nodded. "My secretary has the address."

Dan turned back to Bryce. "The police are on their way. I'm bringing charges against you for grand theft, among others."

230

Bryce's entire body quivered. "But, Dan, my family. What will I tell them?"

"Tell them you're a worthless piece of ... I don't care what you tell them."

Dan turned sad eyes on Logan. "I thought he was my friend."

"I'm sorry, Dan." Logan slipped on his jacket and reached into the pocket for his cell phone and turned it on. He'd kept it off during the interrogation. The message indicator flashed.

He punched in his password and listened. "Logan." Doriana's voice. He stiffened. "I got a call from Candi," she said. "Her boyfriend beat her bad. He went out but he's coming back. He took her car. She's afraid he'll kill her. I'm going to her house to get her out of there. Franco will stay here with Mom and Josh. I'll be okay."

Dread washed over Logan. "Damn Franco. He was supposed to protect her." He snapped his phone shut and jammed it into his pocket.

He looked at Dan. "Send the police to Candi's house and tell them we need an ambulance." He rushed out the door.

CHAPTER TWENTY-ONE

Damn red light. Doriana gripped the steering wheel until her fingers hurt. She must have hit every red light between her house and the Fishtown section of the city where Candi lived.

Apprehension churned her stomach. Maybe she should have called the police. But Candi was adamant. If the police came she'd deny everything and send them away. She begged Doriana to come quickly and take her to a shelter.

The light changed and Doriana inched the car forward in heavy traffic. Memories of her parents' maid Lila propelled her to rush to Candi's aid. They'd not been able to save Lila. Maybe she could save Candi. She wished Logan were here.

She sighed. Logan. He said they would talk. Did he love her? Would he stay for her? For Josh? She shook her head. She'd save those thoughts for later when she knew Candi was safe.

She found Candi's street at last and eased her car into the nearest parking space. She turned off the engine and exited quickly, making sure to lock the car. Hurrying up the debris-strewn street, she checked the house numbers as she walked. The suspicious glares she drew from some of the residents made her clutch her purse tighter. She reached Candi's house and lifted her hand to the dull brass knocker. Before she could touch it, the door creaked open.

"Candi?" Silence. She stood in the doorway. Should she stay or run? "Candi?"

"In here," a small voice squeaked.

Doriana moved cautiously into the house. She blinked, adjusting to the dimness. The blinds were closed against the winter sunlight and the only light came from a small lamp in a corner of the living room. Furniture and knickknacks crowded every available space. The metallic odor of blood hung in the stale air. A chill raced through Doriana.

Candi rose slowly from the couch. She held a bloody rag to her face. One eye was swollen shut and her right arm hung limp by her side. Patches of skin showed on her scalp where the blonde hair had been pulled out.

Doriana screamed. She clamped a trembling hand over her mouth.

"He'll kill me for sure this time," Candi said in a quivering voice.

Doriana fought the urge to run as fast as she could from this place that reeked of death. "Let's get the hell out of here." Doriana grabbed the suitcase that rested on the floor next to Candi and headed at a trot for the door. Moaning softly, Candi shuffled close behind.

Footsteps pounded on the cement steps outside. Doriana's heart jerked. She stopped. Candi bumped against her and let out a small cry.

Doriana dropped the suitcase and reached an arm out to steady Candi. They backed away from the door. Whoever the guy was, he didn't have anything against Doriana. Maybe she could talk their way out.

The door opened, then closed with a bang, making both women jump. A man, muscular and wiry, with sharp features, stared at them. Shivers crawled up Doriana's spine. She'd seen him somewhere before.

He swaggered toward them. Candi began crying.

"Well, well, what do we have here?" He scanned Doriana with red-rimmed eyes.

His cunning, evil voice raised the hairs on Doriana's nape. She knew that voice. God, what had she gotten into?

He dropped the paper bag he held and walked closer. Candi ran to the other end of the room, leaving Doriana to face him.

He tossed Candi a malicious grin. "You did good, slut.

Saved me the trouble of killing Miss Rich Bitch in her house."

"Did you set me up, Candi?" Doriana kept her gaze on the man facing her and backed slowly away, scanning the room for a weapon, anything that would inflict enough harm to allow her and Candi to escape.

Candi sobbed. "I didn't set you up, Doriana, I swear. I helped him with the bids, but that was for us, so we could get out of this dump. I knew about the other things, the calls and the vandalism, but he promised no one would get hurt."

Doriana stared into the man's malevolent eyes. Icy fingers of fear gripped her like a vise. "You're the one who's been calling me."

His lips curled in a sneer. A gold tooth flashed in his mouth.

Doriana dug her nails into her palms to stop her trembling. "You were in the deli that day."

He licked his lips. "You and Pretty Boy were having lunch, all googly-eyed. Now it's my turn to have fun with you. I'll show you things Pretty Boy never thought of."

Doriana bit back a scream. She had to keep her wits. The small fireplace caught her eye. A poker lay on the floor in front of it. She inched away from the menacing figure staring at her with lust and hatred.

"Who are you?" she asked. "And why do you want to hurt me?" She had to keep him talking until she could get her hands around that poker.

His cackle-like laugh sent chills coursing through her.

He edged closer. "I'll make your father pay for what he did to my family."

Fear formed a lump in her throat. She had to be calm if she and Candi were to stay alive. "What are you talking about?"

"The last name's Rove," he said. "Mean anything to you?"

"My father had a partner by that name a long time ago." She moved sideways, taking small steps toward the fireplace and the life-saving poker.

He slitted his eyes. "The great Dan Callahan ruined my father, stealing his share of the company. Your family got filthy rich. My father drank himself to death. Hard work killed my mother. I did jail time while you and your pansy brother went to fancy schools." His face twisted with rage. "And Callahan's coward of a foreman fired me just because I got a little rough with him. You'll pay all right."

He moved closer. She gagged at his stench of alcohol.

She inched toward the poker. "Your father wanted out. He couldn't handle the stress. My dad bought his share." She lifted her chin. "Don't blame my father for your own weakness."

He slapped her across the face and sent her reeling against the wall. She licked her bottom lip, tasting blood, and fought the urge to retch.

"Don't hurt her, Charlie," Candi said. Clutching her bad arm, she ran to Rove. "Doriana is only trying to help me. She didn't do anything."

"Shut up, bitch." He hit Candi hard, knocking her down. She moaned, then lay still.

Doriana struggled to breathe. "You might have killed her, you bastard."

He looked at her with cold, cruel eyes. She would die in this place. Panic froze her to the spot.

He reached out and grabbed her hair, pulling her toward him. She winced in pain and flailed her arms out at him. He bent her arms behind her back.

"A regular tigress, aren't you? Bet you show Pretty Boy a good time. Now you'll find out how a real man treats a woman."

Doriana choked back bile. She tasted the coffee and soup her mother had given her. Her mother. Her dad. Logan. Josh. She would not die in this place. "Hurting me won't bring back your family.Let me go. My father will hire a good lawyer for you."

He twisted her arms. She stifled a scream.

"Don't try to sweet talk me," he growled. "Your dad played dirty, rigging the bid. Now I've got some very bad people after me. I had big plans for your riverfront site. Blow the whole thing up tonight. Then I was gonna be out of this hellhole."

"What do you mean about rigging the bid?" she asked. *Keep talking, Doriana. Buy yourself time.* "What

235

happened to all the money you got from selling the other bids?"

He laughed. "It went up my nose. The payout from this last job was better than the others. But your daddy ruined it."

"Why did you hurt Candi?" Doriana asked. "You were going away with her, weren't you?"

"That slut was two-timing me," he said with a snarl. "She wasn't going anywhere. And you talk too much, bitch."

He crushed her against him and lowered his head. Doriana jerked free. She ran toward the fireplace and dived for the poker. He tackled her and her head slammed on the hardwood floor. The blow made her ears ring and her head throb.

His vile body covered hers, pinning her. "Now, I've got you where I want you, bitch."

Doriana screamed and reached out, feeling for the poker.

From somewhere she heard a crash and the sound of wood splintering. Then the foul body was pulled off her.

Logan slammed Rove against the fireplace and threw a hard punch to his jaw. With a roar, Rove rushed Logan. The men went down together, locked in a death grip. They rolled on the floor, hitting each other and knocking against furniture. Vases and knickknacks flew off tables, scattering shards of glass on the floor.

Doriana grabbed the poker and stood on unsteady legs. She held the poker with both hands, ready to help Logan.

Blood trickled from Logan's mouth. He threw Rove on the floor and jumped on top of him, pummeling the man with his fists. She heard a bone-chilling crunch and guessed that Logan had broken Rove's nose.

Sirens sounded down the street. The police. Tears of relief streamed down Doriana's face and she relaxed her grip on the poker.

Logan straddled Rove. The anger and power in every thrust of Logan's fists into the other man's face made Doriana tremble. Rove reached into his pocket and slid out a knife.

"Logan, watch out!" Doriana yelled.

Rove jabbed the knife into Logan's arm. Blood spurted onto the floor. Swaying, Logan loosened his hold on Rove. The other man put his hands around Logan's neck, strangling him.

Screaming, Doriana held the poker high and rushed toward the men. She swung, slamming the poker against Rove's head. He released Logan and looked at her with shock in his dull eyes. She swung again. He reached up and grabbed the poker from her.

"Police!" The shouted word came from the doorway.

Then it was over. Blue-jacketed police swarmed the room. Doriana ran to Logan. She knelt beside him and clutched him to her chest. His blood seeped onto her coat. She didn't care.

Paramedics rushed in and pushed her aside. They began working on Logan, applying pressure to the wound on his arm. Other medics worked on Rove.

Strong arms lifted Doriana. A paramedic wrapped a blanket around her. When he tried to wipe the blood from her mouth, she pushed his hand away and went to Logan.

They lifted Logan onto a stretcher. Behind her, Candi moaned as medics wrapped her broken arm. Thank God Candi was alive.

Doriana took one of Logan's cold hands in hers. "Logan, if you die on me, I'll kill you."

He opened his eyes and smiled. "We make a good team." His eyes rolled back and he passed out.

****

"I'm not an invalid, Doriana. I can get up the steps on my own." Logan gently brushed her hand away and walked slowly up the steps leading to her townhouse.

Men! Doriana shook her head. Logan would be okay. And they were together. Despite the long hours in the emergency room, her lack of sleep, and the pain from the stitches on her lip, she felt gloriously free.

Rove was in the hospital under police guard. He would no longer hurt them. Candi wasn't under guard, but the authorities would arrest her when the hospital released her. Sorrow for Candi tugged at Doriana. She would persuade her father to pay Candi's bail. The woman deserved a break.

Her father and Franco had stayed at the hospital

237

most of the day. Police bustled in and out, taking statements from her and Logan and her dad. Her dad spent a lot of time alone with Logan. The gruff Dan Callahan cared about his employees, even the temps.

Doriana opened the door and stood aside to let Logan into the house. She followed him into the living room and shrugged out of her jacket, tossing it onto a chair. She slipped Logan's jacket off his shoulders and placed it over hers.

The still, quiet house felt like a welcoming shelter after a storm. Thankfully her mom had taken Josh home with her where she and Nonna could tend to him and spoil him.

Logan sank into the sofa and laid his head back. He looked pale and drawn with fine lines fingering his mouth. A pink-purple bruise rode one of his high cheekbones. Blood stained the front of his shirt and his arm was in a sling.

"You need to rest, Logan. Take the pain killers the doctor gave you and get to bed. I'll help you."

He sat up and shook his head. "I told you, no pain killers. I can handle it. I've been worse."

"Worse?" she said. "In the Army?"

A guarded look tightened his features. "The Army. And as part of my work."

"Today was rough," Doriana said. "But beating up bad guys isn't part of your normal job description." She let out a small laugh, trying to lighten the mood. When she didn't get the laugh she expected from him, a warning sounded in her head. "What's wrong, Logan?"

He let out a deep breath. "You might want to sit, Dorie. I have something to tell you."

Fear roiled her stomach. She sat in the chair opposite him and clasped her hands on her lap. Would he leave again? Resolve stiffened her spine and she sat straighter. Logan wouldn't leave without a fight from her.

"I never meant to hurt you, Doriana. Please believe that."

She clenched her hands tighter. "Go on."

He raked fingers through his hair. "I told you I joined the Army after I left Philly."

She nodded.

"I didn't tell you everything."

Give me strength, she prayed. "What didn't you tell me?"

"I was in the Special Forces. After my military stint, I started my own business, using the skills I'd learned in the Army."

"Business?" She couldn't be hearing right. "You're a temp worker."

"That was just my cover," he said. "I'm head of my own security firm based in Arizona. I've been working for your father."

"Working for my father?" Had she heard right? "He never told me." A sliver of hurt stabbed her.

Logan's gaze held hers. "Your father hired me to find who's been stealing the bids and vandalizing the sites."

Anger and confusion tumbled in her mind. She jumped up. "You lied to me."

He stood. Tension crackled between them.

"I promised your father secrecy. I had to keep my contract with him."

She stiffened. "What about me, Logan? Didn't I deserve the truth?" Apprehension, like a heavy mallet, punched her in the stomach. "Was everything between us a lie?"

"No, Dorie. Making love to you is the truest thing I've ever done," he said softly.

"How can I believe anything you tell me?" She turned away to hide the pain in her eyes. "Was I just a temporary diversion until you can go back to your real life?" Choking back tears, she slid her gaze to his. "What is your real life, Logan? A wife? Kids?" The cut on her lip throbbed, a painful reminder that her world was crashing around her with the speed of a demolition ball.

He was by her side in two strides. He gripped her shoulder with his good hand. "No wife, no kids. I have no one, Doriana. I told myself I was too busy building my business to settle down. But now I know the truth."

"What truth?" she whispered. His gaze fastened on her mouth. Her body ached to hold him, to never let him go. She couldn't, not now.

"Listen to me, Dorie. Please. It's not easy for me. I've spent a lifetime keeping my feelings hidden."

A tear slipped down her face. Logan gently brushed it away with his thumb. His touch ignited her with yearnings. She needed this man.

His eyes turned molten gold. She knew he wanted her. But did he love her? Not trusting herself with him so close, she jerked free and walked to the window. The partially opened blinds revealed dim streetlights and no traffic. She had nothing more to fear from Rove. But could she survive losing Logan?

"Talk, Logan."

She heard his sharp intake of breath.

"When I took this assignment," he said, "I convinced myself you were married to some hotshot lawyer and living on the Main Line. I knew you were a company vice president, but I figured that was an honorary title. I could have given the job to one of my subordinates. But I wanted to come here. I wouldn't admit it, but I came for you."

She kept her body rigid, not looking at him. "Don't toy with me, Logan."

He moved to stand behind her. His heat wrapped around her like a sensual blanket. He placed a hand on her shoulder. She drew a shuddering breath, fighting her need for him.

"I will never hurt you again, Dorie."

She turned slowly. Longing, hope, and fear chased across his rugged face. He touched her arm. She wanted to believe.

"You gave me something precious," he said. "You gave me my son. And you freed me from the past. I've made peace with my father. I'll always be grateful."

"Is that all you feel, Logan? Gratitude?" Afraid of his answer, she slid her gaze from his.

He took her chin between his fingers and tilted her face toward his. "No, Dorie. I love you. I always have."

Joy surged through her. And fear. She couldn't risk her heart again. She stepped back. The uncertainty in his eyes mirrored the uncertainty in her heart. She wanted to touch his face, to kiss his lips. She kept her hands at her sides.

"When we became...intimate, Logan, why didn't you tell me then? If you really cared about me, you would have been honest with me."

He let out a breath. "I wanted to tell you, but I was too damn stubborn and held hostage to the past."

"What do you mean?"

"I thought I'd put my demons behind me," he said. "Coming back to Philadelphia opened the old wounds. On some level I knew I came here to banish the nightmares for good. But that didn't stop them from taking one last shot at me."

"How?"

He skimmed fingers over her cheekbones. She swayed toward him. She stiffened. She had to be sure.

Sadness shaded his eyes. "I never really belonged in your world. A motherless boy with an alcoholic father. You were the one good thing in my life. I didn't deserve you."

Fighting tears, she put a hand over her mouth.

His lips drew into a thin line as if he struggled with strong emotion. "I needed you to want me for the man I am and not the success I'd become."

She touched his arm. "Maybe I was a little shallow when we were young. You left me without a word. And I was scared when you came into my life again. I didn't want Josh hurt. I didn't want my heart broken again."

"And now?" he asked.

"I was afraid Josh would get attached to you and you'd leave. But I know that Josh is lucky to have a man like you for his father." She gave him a tremulous smile. "It doesn't matter if you're a temp worker or own your own company. You're a good man, Logan Tanner."

A muscle worked in his jaw. His intense gaze lasered her. "What about you, Dorie? Can you ever love me?"

The ticking of the clock and the low rumble of a car outside competed with the racing of her pulse. She touched his hair and skimmed her finger down his face. "I have loved you all my life, Logan."

The fatigue and pain that lined his face melted away. He looked nineteen again, young and vulnerable. "I was afraid to hope," he whispered.

She went to him. He held her with his good arm. She rested her head against the firm muscles of his chest. The steady, sure beating of his heart told her that Logan would always be with her. She would never be alone again.

He stroked her hair. Shivers of awareness raced along her nerve endings.

"Will you forgive me?" he asked.

She leaned back to look up at him. "I forgive you. Will you forgive me for not having enough faith in you all those years ago? I should have told you about Josh then."

Logan slid a thumb down her cheek. "You were a young girl, Doriana. God, we were both so young. Let's forget the past and start over."

She forgot to breathe. "Start over, how?"

"You and Josh are my family and my life," he said. "Marry me, sweetheart."

Tears threatened. "Are you sure?" she whispered.

He touched fingers to her chin and stared into her eyes. "More sure than I've been about anything in my life."

She smiled. "Yes, Logan. A thousand times yes. I'll marry you."

"God, Dorie. I love you so much. And I'll make you happy." He kissed her gently on the lips. "What a pair. I've got one good arm and your lip is swollen."

She laughed. "But we beat the bad guy."

His eyes darkened. "We're a team forever. I'll never leave you again. I'll move my base to Philadelphia."

She smiled. "Arizona sounds very nice."

"You would come with me?" His smile lit her heart.

She nodded. "I don't care where we live as long as we're together. I'd already decided to give my Dad notice. I'm going back to school to study architecture. You gave me something very precious, too, Logan. You gave me back my dreams."

"Sweetheart, do anything you want," he said. "Just don't ever leave me."

She wrapped her arms around his neck. "A jackhammer couldn't pry me from your side." She kissed him lightly. "I think Josh needs a sibling or two."

He threw back his head and laughed. She laughed with him. All the pain and fear that she carried for so many years fell away.

His expression turned serious. The love shining from

his eyes stole her breath. He raised her hand to his lips and kissed her palm. "Maybe we should start on those babies now."

"But you're hurt," she said.

"Don't worry, love. I can handle it."

"I'm sure you can." She pressed against him and kissed him hard, ignoring the pain from her lip. He moaned and pulled her closer. His tongue found hers. Desire flamed through her.

The years peeled away. They were young and wildly in love. Only now their love was deeper and steadier. And fueled with a passion that would never end. Body and soul they belonged to each other. What had started all those years ago had come full circle, completing their lives.

A word about the author...

I credit my love of romance to the romantic comedies I watched on late night TV while growing up. I began writing love stories in my head as a teen.

After years in the corporate world, I decided to pursue my dream of becoming an author. I joined Romance Writers Of America and honed my craft by putting my stories on paper. I'm thrilled to be a part of The Wild Rose Press.

I have one book with Avalon, A Catered Affair, written under the name Carolyn Matkowsky. I live in Delaware with my husband, son, and a fat black cat named Killer.

Please visit me at www.caramarsi.com . I'd love to hear from you.

Printed in the United States
204776BV00004B/1-18/A